The Genesis Murders

William Coulombe

Copyright © 2019 William Coulombe

All rights reserved.

ISBN:9781099252211

To David Schorran
Best colleague, mentor and friend

ACKNOWLEDGMENTS

I would like to thank my wife Helen for all her support and nudging to keep me going.

Chapter 1

Lake Tahoe does not give up its dead.

The measurement tasks on Lake Tahoe should have been free of peril. Cherished for clarity that exceeds 65 feet, this alpine lake is unrivaled in scenic grandeur. Winter snow-covered mountains, resplendent against a 190 square mile azure surface, create a magnificent tableau when viewed from ashore or high mountain trails.

Marcus Kieslar, a Research Assistant for the Nevada Research Institute (NRI), is elated to be skimming along the lake's surface on a research vessel owned by the Institute. He is performing clarity measurements of the lake and is proceeding to the first monitoring station. At this time of the year, mid-winter, boat traffic is minimal. Lake clarity is assessed using several methods. Today Marcus is performing Secchi Disc transparency readings where a black and white disc is lowered over the side of the boat using a graduated cable. The weighted disc is allowed to sink until it just disappears and is then raised until it reappears. The distance from the water surface to the depth of the disc is recorded and represents the transparency at the given location. This process is repeated at predefined areas along the lake. Navigation to these open water monitoring sites is accomplished using the onboard GPS system.

Clarity measurements are outside Marcus's usual duties for the Institute, however, for this run, he is substituting for a colleague who is defending his Master's thesis. In addition to the personnel change, he also is violating Institute policy by being out on the lake alone. His roommate, scheduled to meet him on the dock this morning, is a no show due to the aftermath of a heavy night of drinking. He called earlier stating that he had just awakened. Not wanting to fail his colleague, nor wait at the dock for 90 minutes, Marcus decided to perform the measurements solo. He is a skilled yachtsman having spent every spare moment of his youth on his parent's 41 foot Hunter sailboat docked in Marina Del Rey, Los Angeles. In addition, he is familiar with the operation of the Institute's vessel from previous excursions with other scientists.

However, being alone, and on this type of boat, his father would have been disappointed that he is not wearing a flotation belt. Although the day is sunny, with little wind, the air temperature still is 25 degrees, requiring a heavy coat. Adding the belt would have increased the garment's bulkiness, slowing down his measurement duties.

Having reached the general area of the first monitoring

site, final adjustments are made in the boat's position to the correct latitude and longitude. At a depth of 1000 feet, an anchor is not used. A small amount of drift near the final location is acceptable. No other nearby boats are visible.

Marcus ties a Secchi Disc to a marked location on the starboard railway. Leaning over the rail, entirely focused on the disc as it just disappeared from sight, he senses movement behind him but dismisses it as impossible. This momentary distraction requires him to repeat the process by raising the disc to full view. His sensors again are placed on alert as an impossible yet faint footstep is detected on the boat's floor. Before he can turn around, a hand is on his left shoulder. Almost simultaneously, another hand grabs his crotch. With a quick force, he is lifted skyward, his feet thrown above his head into the air and over the side of the boat. Unable to process the confusion of being upside down in midair, he is greeted, shockingly so, with the frozen blue water of Tahoe.

The shoreline is visible, Marcus is an excellent swimmer and, with considerable effort could cover the distance. In good shape, he also is capable of treading water for hours. As Marcus's body rotates 180 degrees, with his head now rising to the surface, he watches the boat drifting away from him. Today, Marcus will not be swimming to shore, he will not be treading water. Having read accounts of others who had fallen into the 40-degree water during the winter, Marcus is in full panic mode, if only cerebrally. His diaphragm, the body's air delivery system, is quickly paralyzed, ceasing intake of all oxygen. Gasping for air, slipping below the surface, he can see the research vessel making way through the ultra-clear water.

The homicidal stow-a-way notes the current GPS reading and drives the research craft to a waiting boat tied to a mooring buoy. The mooring rope is retied behind the NRI vessel, set for towing. Returning to the original GPS location with both boats, he turns off the motor but leaves the key in the ignition. The Secchi Disc that had been pulled out of the water before traveling to the buoy is returned overboard. With no visible watercraft in the area, both boats are drawn together. After a last glance around to make sure that there is no trace of his presence, the assailant carefully steps onto the second vessel and unties the tow rope from the research craft. Getting underway, a cursory scan of the water for Marcus reveals no sign of a body or clothing. As his lungs filled with water, Marcus already had sunk to a depth invisible from the surface.

Chapter 2

Taking off my first Saturday in a month, I am carving tracks down blue, and some black diamond runs at a local ski resort 30 minutes from Reno. Admittedly, the difficulty of the black diamond terrain I choose, is just a step above the blue runs, no moguls or trees, but I ignore this thought. They are black diamonds, and that's all that counts. I need to bolster my confidence. Today is the day I will finally attempt 'The Chutes,' a ski area that was once backcountry, the domain of young hotshot skiers and boarders that ignored the 'out of bounds' markers and flew down the 200 acres of steep, narrow terrain with their hair on fire. As this area of the mountain is now open, the skilled, and nearly skilled in my case, can choose a gate to enter the ungroomed mountain. Also, the chairlift back to the top avoids the long walk back to the resort's parking lot. The highest levels include near-vertical drops, rock outcroppings and plenty of pine trees. Unfortunately, while getting dressed today, I apparently left my gonads on my dresser because this was my second peek at the gates without ever entering one.

From the drive up to the resort, the steepest area appeared to be at the top, east side. Other locations to enter come in from the west side of the mountain at progressively lower elevations. Intuitively they must be less demanding, I conclude. Standing near one of these gates, I'm subconsciously crunching my underwear as I study the narrowness of these runs. My briefs are starting to feel like a thong. As soon as skis are pointed downhill, gravity, sometimes a friend, sometimes a foe, accelerates them without mercy. When making a turn, at some point, even if only briefly, skis are facing directly downhill. On a steep incline, I prefer to keep the length of time in this position short. In other words, I endeavor to make my turns quickly to control my downward velocity. Others blithely fly straight down the hill at speed. In these narrow 'Chutes,' I'm concerned that I won't be able to make turns quickly enough before the terrain turns into bushes, rocks, and trees. Visions of sliding down the hill out of control, perhaps on my back, head first, result in my skis turning in the opposite direction. 'Pussy.'

On the next ride up the ski lift, I share a chair with a couple. After the requisite 'sup?' head nods the man asks,

"Don't you work at NRI?"

Donned in a helmet, goggles, and a neck gator, I can't image how he would know this.

"I do, how did you recognize me in this ensemble?"

"Haha right, we arrived in the parking lot just behind you, a couple cars over, and saw you mounting your gear. You looked familiar, but I couldn't place where I knew you. I'm Dr. Neil

Patrick down at UNR. We were in a meeting last week, you're Grant Selser?"

"Oh right. It's Stelzner."

I don't recognize him in his snow gear either but remember the name. He says,

"What a beautiful day. Have you been down the chutes yet? The snow is in excellent shape."

Fine, rub it in. Instead of lying and saying I'm heading over after a few warm-up runs or some other false bravado, for some reason I tell him the truth.

"No I haven't gotten up the nerve to try them yet, I'm worried they are too narrow."

"If that's your concern, the next to last gate on the east end, I can't remember the name, is the widest. If you are doing any of the groomed black diamond runs you probably could handle it."

Just before we exit the chair, I say,

"Thanks, I'll check it out."

Of course, it's going to require me to go grow a pair. From the lift, I navigate down a series of runs that will take me to the east side of the chute's bowl. I ski over to what I think is the next to last gate and learn instead that I've gone too far. This is the last gate. Three other skiers are considering entering the gate and descending the mountain, but one looks a little nervous. Looking over the edge, I can't see anything immediately below due to the steepness of the drop. Yeah, I'm out.

I see the gate that the couple recommended about 30 yards west, slightly downhill. It looks like I can ski down to it along the ridge, which will allow examination of the mountain to assess the likelihood of not dying. It is a hell of a drop, and unbeknownst to me, my autonomic nervous system begins a weight shift to my left side in an attempt to move to safer ground. You've got to love a subconscious that looks out for you.

As I'm moving at moderate speed along the ridge, two parallel skis jam into my left ski turning me toward the precipice. Having sufficient downhill momentum, the weight of the blow sends me hanging over the edge. Before I can turn and utter some colorful epithet at the jerk, the weight of my right ski is sliding over the edge, followed quickly by my left. An immediate panic surge flushes through my mind and body.

In an instant, I am in the air over a sheer rock wall. Absent of ground, I can feel the weight of my skis pulling on my legs. The rate of descent is ridiculously fast. After flashes of becoming rock spatter, pools of blood, and the like, one thought remains. I need to twist the lower half of my body to align the boards parallel to the fall of the mountain. I can't fail. There is too much I want to do. I want a wife, kids, family. This can't happen now, this can't be my last act.

With a serious ground rush problem, I lift my tips and pull my flailing pole ends behind me. My mind is running a mantra in the background, 'keep your ski tips up, 'keep your ski tips up.' My heart is pounding like the peak of a Led Zeppelin drum solo. I force my attention to the probable landing area. A big problem, a rock cropping directly below and a large tree down my fall line, should I not die on impact. If I catch these rocks, any rolling summersaults are going to result in severe tree bark trauma.

So first the landing and then a hard turn to the right to avoid the tree. I barely finish the thought when my skis slam into the snow, just missing the rock. Miraculously, the backs of the skis hit first, nearly simultaneously, then the tips. On impact, I manage to keep my weight slightly behind my center of gravity. Even though the snow is relatively deep, my ass slams onto the rear half of the skis, followed by my back and then my helmet. The force of the blow and steep incline causes me to bounce back to a near standing position and thankfully, with bent knees. This allows me to retain some control. No time for celebration as the aforementioned tree is now looking much larger in my field of view, dead ahead.

As I start cutting an edge, both skis are chattering

viciously as I race toward the tree. I begin to rotate both boots several degrees to the right while pushing hard with my left leg. Any overcorrection or incorrect weight shift will send me on an uncontrollable fall, ripping both skis from my boots.

Extremely relieved, I successfully complete the turn to the right, just missing the tree, but now see I'm overdue to turn left to avoid a stand of aspens. I push hard on my right ski, angling both boards to turn left and successfully enter one of the established runs. Finally, I'm traversing the hill under control. Time for the bunny slopes.

Having recovered some composure, a thought flashes through my mind, and I make a sharp stop by slamming my skis parallel to the hill so that I can face back up the mountain. At the top, directly where I went over, I can barely make out someone staring down in my direction. I remove a pole and glove and give him the middle finger salute, jabbing up and down maniacally trying to shove it up his ass. Not very classy on my part, but I was still burning off excess adrenaline. He slowly skis out of sight. Was this the person that looked nervously over the first entrance gate? Had he followed me down to the lower entrance and became out of control and accidentally ran into me? It's preposterous. If one considers skiing the chutes, there must be a minimal skill level that would prevent a collision with another on a relatively gradual slope. Perhaps he was a lost green run skier, but I doubt it. Wait, could it have been Dr. Patrick? I'm losing it, why would anyone want to push me off a cliff? Forget the bunny slopes, time to head to the bar.

Chapter 3

Sunday afternoon in his lab at NRI, Dr. David Piehl is trying to make up for lost time due to equipment problems. Piehl has a Ph.D. in physics but does not work as a physicist, in the classical sense. He is an atmospheric scientist, an expert in most components of the physical world. He is skilled in mechanics, electricity, basic chemistry, thermodynamics, instrumentation, etc. Piehl is an invaluable person to have on any scientific experiment. Lately, he has been collaborating with Grant Stelzner on multiple projects. They met 15 years ago while Piehl was a Post Doc at the Institute, and Stelzner was working for a local consulting firm. The firm engaged NRI to perform some specialized measurements for which Stelzner was the Principle Investigator. Later, Piehl received a full appointment to the Institute and Stelzner was hired as an Associate Research Scientist after strong urging by Piehl. They now work at the same rank in the institute, but for each project, one or the other takes the lead as Principle Investigator.

The Nevada Research Institute is part of the University of Nevada system. Although some staff are advisors and mentors to university graduate students, there is no classroom-type teaching that occurs. Scientists must support themselves by obtaining grants and contracts from both private and governmental funding sources. Areas of interest include atmospheric sciences, biological sciences, archeology, geology, and hydrology. Numerous laboratories support each field.

Currently lying on his back, Piehl is working on a faulty nitrogen valve in a 9-foot square recessed area, 6-feet below the floor, referred to as the pit. The pit houses gas supply lines and an air compressor. It is reached by a door in the floor. Having identified the problem with the valve, he scrambles to his feet and climbs the ladder out of the pit. He continues out of the lab, heading to his office to retrieve replacement parts.

Seeing Piehl heading to his office, a person, lying in wait, quietly but quickly slips into the lab. On a workbench near the pit, a small length of Tygon tubing is connected to a gas valve built into the bench. The other end is connected to a calibration mass flow meter. Attached to the exit end of the calibrator is a long coil of similar tubing, camouflaged by pumps and instruments. Finally, the opposite end of the tubing is connected to digital flow meter in the off position. The intruder disconnects the long line of tubing at the digital flow meter and opens the gas valve.

By placing a finger over the open end, it is confirmed there is gas quietly exiting the tube. The line of tubing is moved over to the edge of the bench and positioned on the floor near the far corner of the pit door. It is adjusted to within a few inches into the pit opening. The tubing is hidden by the open door to the pit. The intruder heads to the exit while the heavier-than-air gas sinks into the enclosed area.

A 6-ton tank of pure CO_2, located in a back lot of the campus, supplies several laboratories and a research greenhouse with large quantities of the gas used in various experiments. The pressurized gas is piped through to several locations in the building. CO_2 is colorless and at low concentrations is odorless and harmless. However, large quantities of pure CO_2 can be a problem if the gas displaces all the oxygen from an enclosed area. This was now becoming the case in the subfloor of the lab, as the heavier-than-air gas sinks into the pit. Breathing a pure CO_2 atmosphere is lethal, as the CO_2 molecules occupy all the sites in the lungs, resulting in asphyxiation due to lack of oxygen.

Piehl returns to the pit with the needed parts. He steps down carrying a solenoid and a couple of gaskets. Progressing down the steps, Piehl stops near the halfway point when the lab phone starts ringing. He ignores the audible plea and takes another step down, but remembers that the lab is a cellular dead zone and the caller probably is his wife. As he reverses direction and climbs back up the stairs to answer the phone, a wandering sense of danger is registered in the back of his brain.

"Atmospheric Sciences lab."

"Hey, how's it going?"

"Fine, I should be able to get out of here on time."

The conversation with his wife continues, covering activities of their kids and a problem with the garage. A few minutes later, they end the call. Throughout their discussion, Piehl's nagging feeling that something was wrong intrudes, but he cannot identify its source.

Retrieving the parts from the bench, he heads back to the pit to resume his decent to the valve. Walking down the steps, he slows and stops at the point where the phone call was received. Unaware that he is standing in pure CO_2 at a level up to his neck, he descends another step.

Now it is clear to him, that there is a tinny iron taste that seems to have wrapped around his tongue making it feel thick. Perhaps there is an acid odor present. Most scientists know that CO_2 is odorless at the concentrations in which they usually work, but often forget that it has a pungent acid odor in concentrated form. There is a battery charging on the bench. Concerned it may be overheating and might explode, he starts back up the ladder to inspect it.

Cursory examination of the battery reveals no problem or acid odor. However, having walked around the back of the bench, he sees the tubing on the floor, a pet peeve of his due to the potential for contamination. Piehl pulls the tubing up off the floor and detects gas flowing out the end.

"What the hell?" He whispers to himself.

He traces the line back through the meters and finds it connected to the bench valve and quickly closes the valve. This makes no sense to Piehl as he walks around studying the equipment. He recognizes the flow rate calibration setup remembers that Marcus was calibrating several flow meters last Thursday. Piehl mentally hypothesizes that although the rule is to close the main valve at the end of a calibration, Marcus must have inadvertently left it open. There would have been no flow as the meter was off. Because Marcus used a friction fitting rather than a compression fitting, which is tightened with a wrench, the continuous back pressure of the gas against the closed meter must have just popped off, and it dropped to the floor. No longer having the flow meter blocking the flow of gas, it was flowing into the pit.

Looking at the floor where he had picked up the tubing, a cold chill undulated through Piehl's body. He moves over to the open door and stares despondently into the pit where he had lain supine on the floor. He exits the lab for a few minutes and returns with a handheld chemical sensing instrument configured for oxygen. Just outside the lab, he checked the display, it read 20.9%, the normal oxygen level in the atmosphere. The same reading is obtained just above the pit. He climbs down one step, with his arm fully extended taking readings as he descends. The display value decreases and an annoying high pitched screech is emitted after the reading drops below its alarm set point of 19.5%. Carefully, he takes a few more steps down and with the sensor extended as far down as possible. Leaving his head above floor level, he watches with dreadful confirmation as the digital value on the display drops to zero percent.

His wife may have just saved his life. Had he not paused when hearing the phone, he would have continued quickly down the steps to the bottom, doubtlessly becoming asphyxiated by the pure gas.

He feeds the long line of tubing down to the bottom of the pit and connects the other end to the vacuum side of a large pump on the bench. The exit end of the pump already is outfitted with tubing long enough to reach the fume hood. The pump is plugged in, and the heavy gas is slowly vented to the outside. Once the oxygen sensor reads 20.9% all the way to the bottom of the pit, he stops the pump.

Unnerved, the repairs in the pit will have to wait until tomorrow, he's going home.

Chapter 4

Monday morning, the ordinarily stolid David Piehl, walks into my office visibly agitated.

"Where is Marcus? I am going to send him to the Mohave Desert for a month to take bag samples along a 50 km transect."

"Oh... umm...I don't know, I haven't seen him yet."

I could have added, 'why what's wrong,' but I know there is no need.

"The miscreant never cleans up after himself and left the CO_2 bench valve open in my lab. While moving equipment around on the bench, I must have inadvertently disconnected his Tygon tubing from a flow meter. The line fell off the bench to the floor near the pit and started dumping gas in the pit."

"Are you saying there was a build up? Did you use the Drager?"

"Yes, I used it." He says slowly with considerable irritation in his voice.

"In three seconds the readings dropped to zero less than

3 feet into the pit."

"Excellent! We finally needed the Drager, now I'm glad I bought it!" I say with some satisfaction, ignoring the big picture. We had debated about whether to spend the money to purchase the unit and since then have never needed it.

"I'm glad you are pleased with yourself. However, I was working in the pit. Had it gone differently, you could have been the first to use it this morning while explaining to everyone how I came to be lying dead on the floor!"

I just stared at him in silence as the potential disaster finally hits me.

"If you were working in the subfloor and it was filling with gas, why didn't you suffocate?"

"Fortunate timing, I exited the pit to get parts. I assume that it was then that the tubing disconnected and started to flow, filling the chamber while I was in my office."

"How did you know the pit was filled with gas?"

"Providence, Liz called me right as I was descended the ladder. I probably was at chin level. While paused and then climbing back up, I noted an acid smell. After I hung up, I looked around and found the gas flowing."

"I've always liked her."

"Me too. If Marcus doesn't straighten out, I'm going to flunk him."

"You know you won't, he's too smart. He's a little distracted right now. He has been disaffected with religion lately. Now our finding has him so excited he can't concentrate on anything else."

"Well, we still have other work to do. While out in the parking lot Thursday night, didn't Marcus tell us he wouldn't be in on Friday because he and Chang were going to take the clarity run?"

"Yes, the regular guy, Jackson I think, was going to defend his thesis why? Marcus should be in any time now."

David starts to say something, and I interrupt,

"Hey, you're not going to believe it, I went down the Chutes on Saturday!"

He mockingly looks around my office and says,

"Failing to see any crutches, you're right I don't believe

you."

"I'm serious, made it all the way without falling."

"Speculation leads me to believe you were following, as you would say, a snow babe, and couldn't stop when she went through the gate."

"Not exactly."

Just then, Dr. Alan Demyan appears at my door. Alan is our Division Director, which technically makes him our supervisor, but since we bring in a steady flow of funding, he pretty much leaves us alone. However, recently he has been under pressure to terminate David.

"Washoe County Sheriff's department just called. They said on Friday evening that our boat was found adrift, about 10 miles south of North Shore, deserted, key in the ignition and a full tank of gas."

"What?"

We say simultaneously, though we both heard him perfectly.

"That's right, they found a list of phone numbers, but

could not reach anyone at the Institute as it was the weekend. There was a Secchi disc hanging in the water tied to the rail, but there was no sign of Marcus. The Sheriff says the engine started right up. I reached Charles, he is in Tahoe City and will be heading over to Incline Village." Dr. Charles Luther is the Director of the Tahoe Clarity study and is therefore responsible for the weekly Secchi disc readings. A humorless man, he is no fan of David and until recently has been indifferent to me.

"David, as Marcus is your Research Assistant, I told Charles that I want you to be in Incline when he meets the Sheriff's Investigator. They are meeting in 90 minutes."

"I better get going then."

"I'll go with you." I say.

While gathering our things to leave, David asks Alan,

"What do they think happened?"

"Right now they are calling it an accident. The assumption is he fell overboard."

"Nonsense, that's impossible. Marcus has been around boats his whole life, and our boat has a high rail." David says.

Alan just shrugs his shoulders as if to say that's all I know.

I chime in,

"Maybe the rope got hung up, and he climbed over the rail to free it and slipped."

David replies,

"Possibly, but it seems unlikely. Let's go."

As we all are walking down the corridor, David asks Alan,

"How did you know it was Marcus out on the lake on Friday?"

After a contemplative pause, Alan says,

"I told Charles that the Sheriff said there was no one on board. He was disbelieving that there was no sign of Marcus. I just assumed he was helping out on this run. Why?"

Ignoring his question David asked,

"Did Luther ask about a second student who should have been on-board as a backup?"

With a quizzical look, Alan says,

"No."

"We'll find out what we can."

With that, David and I turn the corner leaving Alan heading in the opposite direction. David begins one of his patented summary of facts that eventually will end in a rhetorical question.

"According to Marcus, he and Jackson were working after hours Thursday night, and Jackson asked for his help. I asked him if it had been cleared with Luther. He said Jackson didn't think it was unnecessary. These kids loath to talk to Luther about anything, not least of which is Marcus."

David stops and looks at me before stating the obvious question, thus I steal it from him.

"How did Luther know it was Marcus out there?"

"Exactly, and where is Chang?"

"I've got to stop by my office. You're driving right?"

"Since you are coming just to get out of doing any work, I suppose I should."

We stop by my office, then David's and head to the

parking lot. David asks,

"I thought Angela was coming over today to see the instrument we pulled from the field."

"No, tomorrow, but I have the unit in my lab ready for her inspection. I'm not sure what she is looking for."

"Did you ever get her another temporary card key? The front desk wants their guest card returned this week because a VIP from Exxon is arriving on Friday."

"Yes, they have it ready. When she arrives tomorrow, they are going to switch cards with her."

Angela Ward is one of our sponsors for a Long Range Transport study of air pollution extending from L.A. to the Grand Canyon. She is extremely technical and tough when things go wrong. She keeps us on our toes. The head of most funding sponsors have scientific backgrounds but mainly focus on the big picture and the budget, leaving details to the contractors. Angela does it all, including pressing us on the details.

"She dislikes Luther, but has heard his prattle on all your so-called 'failures' and that he wants you terminated for cause."

David maintains a pensive silence as we enter his SUV.

Chapter 5

Currently, we have two exciting projects in progress. Both may lead to David being fired from the Institute. I probably will fall as well for that matter. One is an undisclosed experiment that we are undertaking on our own time that we think will fill a sizeable scientific gap on the origin of life on earth and definitively disprove the religious principle of Genesis. We are using 'Genesis' as a code word when referring to the work. The second is the Transport study sponsored by many power companies. Angela has been designated Program Manager for the project. I am the NRI Principle Investigator, our term for Project Manager. David does all the hard work.

David just finished developing a state of the art chemical tracer analyzer that measures key chemical constituents generated in Los Angeles, sort of an 'L.A. fingerprint,' or signature pattern. Some of these constituents are emitted in other cities, for example, Las Vegas, but not in the same quantity or in the same combination of constituents. When these analyzers detect the L.A. components, we know, with 100% certainty that the air originated from L.A. rather than Las Vegas, Reno, or Phoenix. The L.A. fingerprint can be detected as far away as the Grand Canyon. This is of interest to major power plants in California, Nevada, and

Arizona. It's actually more of a concern for plants along the L.A./Grand Canyon corridor.

Numeric modelers from the U.S. Environmental Protection Agency claim emissions from the plants may reach the Grand Canyon. The pristine air around the Canyon is designated as a Class-1 area which has stricter air quality standards. When the power companies learned that the EPA was interested in our technique, they were quick to get involved and offered to fund a project to answer some of these transport questions. The motivation of the power companies to spend their money to lead the project is simple. They have complete control over the design and details of the measurements and interpretation of the data. EPA still must approve the design and techniques. However, for the private companies, being in a position to develop the Project Management Plan is more advantageous than only being able to provide comments to the plan and data after the fact. For EPA's part, they get a needed research project performed without paying for it, while still maintaining oversite authority. NRI has an excellent reputation, and both sides know that we will conduct the research following sound scientific principles, free of bias and will not compromise our principles. Some consulting firms are not above 'bending' the data to suit the needs of their paying sponsors.

The goal of the project is to assess if emissions from power plants within the L.A./Grand Canyon corridor could contribute to visibility degradation in the Canyon. The companies funded us to produce five tracer units that were built and deployed in the following locations: Cajon Pass in the San Gabriel Mountains, Meadview Arizona, Spirit Mountain Nevada, and Long Mesa on the rim of the Grand Canyon on the Navaho Indian Reservation. In addition to one spare in the laboratory, we operate the fifth unit in the Sierras as a background site.

Regarding the Tahoe Clarity study, our only connection is that David's grad student has periodically filled in to make the measurements. Luther just finished a major project that included a measurement task performed by David. The activity did not go well. He also is a technical advisor on the L.A. transport study which has had some of David's data called into question. He has the ear of the Institute's upper-level scientists and has convinced them to initiate termination proceedings. Now David's grad student is missing. David and I think Luther has somehow learned of our Genesis project and wants this work to be terminated.

During the drive to the lake, I pull out an Institute phone directory and call Chang's cell.

"Hello?"

"Brian, this is Grant."

"Hi, Grant. I'm on campus getting ready to enter class. What's up?"

"Did you meet Marcus on the lake on Friday?"

"I committed to helping him, but went out with a group of friends to the brewpub Thursday night and was 'over-served' at the bar. I was deeper into the bottle than I thought. By the time I woke up, it was way too late. I called him as soon as I woke. He said he was already underway and not to worry about it. As you probably know, he had been on the boat several times and said he could handle it himself. Why?"

"Have you seen or heard from him since?"

"No, why?"

"I'll tell you later, go to class."

I hung up and said,

"Chang was too hung-over to accompany Marcus. Marcus told him he would go it alone."

We rode in silence for a while. As we ascended the Mt. Rose highway, we pass the ski resort and the Chutes. David looks at the mountain, then at me and just shakes his head. I start to defend myself, and he cuts me off and says,

"While reading your email this morning, I take it you saw that Alan agreed to form a termination committee and wants to meet on Friday."

"I did. It's horse excrement. Alan is reluctant, but I guess he is feeling pressured. Luther surely is pushing him. They have requested a list of materials. I put a copy in your box this morning."

"The signature pattern showing up at the background site had to be the tipping point to do something formally." David says thoughtfully.

Not only is transport not expected to be detectable at this site, but the wind patterns at the time the high values were recorded also make it virtually impossible for the air mass to have originated from L.A. Luther learned of the anomaly and brought the totality of ostensible problems to bear on Alan.

"Have you told anyone about our Genesis experiments?" David asks.

"Of course not, but in his excitement, I'm worried that

Marcus took Barbara in his confidence. It would be hard for him not to tell her. They have been sleeping together for at least a year, and he tells her everything."

"My concern as well. If she knows, Luther knows."

"Maybe."

"Likely. Last week Luther made some veiled comments that I was working on unfunded 'pet' projects rather than getting the instruments developed carefully."

I trail off in silence, knowing that David and I have been careful to work on our unfunded experiments after hours. Following a long pause, David asks,

"What's the name of the weird church that Luther helped develop?"

The question catches me by surprise. After a thoughtful silence, I say,

"Rock of the Living Word Church. They took what they like of all the Christian based religions to form their version."

"How convenient." David says with considerable derision and then continues,

"I know you have considered the impact our discovery will have on the religious community, but have you ever considered how the zealots might react?"

I consider this in silence and finally say,

"You think word has gotten out and Marcus was killed... murdered?" It's hard for me to say out loud.

"Well, he didn't fall over the side taking disc readings." David says.

"I can accept Charles going after us professionally for pursuing our Genesis finding if he is fearful of the ramifications." I say soberly.

"But murder is a hard one to accept." I add.

David gravely offers a possible scenario.

"He could have met Marcus, told him, as the Project Director, he wanted to join him. It would have been easy for him to knock Marcus on the head and dump him overboard. Someone could have picked up Luther in another boat."

"I think we are getting ahead of ourselves. Perhaps he had a problem, cut himself or something, then was picked up by another boater and has been hospitalized somewhere."

"For three days? But you're right, perhaps it's premature to speculate. However, consider this. What if I did not bump the tubing connection? Rather, when I left to get parts, someone entered the lab, opened the valve, disconnected the line from the flow controller and placed it near the pit. It could have been done in 30 seconds by someone familiar with the lab."

He sees I'm not bleeding, therefore he cuts a little deeper.

"Admittedly, the timing is unlikely that someone would know just when to enter and leave the lab. However, on Friday afternoon, in the break room, I discussed the solenoid problems with Frank in Facilities. I asked him if he could pull some parts by the end of the day because I planned to go down in the pit on Sunday. Several people were there and could have overheard us."

We both drive in silence as I consider this. We approach Lake Tahoe, and I stare out at the vast beauty of blue water. I see it a few times a month at this altitude, but it still leaves me in awe.

Finally, I say,

"Contemplating these events, I may have a disturbing addition to your theory. Saturday, I wasn't following some hot snow bunny into the Chutes, I was bumped."

David whips his head in my direction.

"Could you have been pushed?" David asks with significant alarm in his voice.

"Conceivably. I was skiing the edge of a rock face and suddenly was slammed into by another skier. The impact sent me over the edge into the Chutes. Actually, it's very fortunate that I'm not rock stain right now. It is improbable that anyone would have been skiing anywhere near me. The area is not used by most skiers. At the time I concluded it was just a weird accident."

"Why would you withhold this information!" he says quickly becoming agitated.

"As I said, at the time, I thought it was a bizarre mishap. It's only in the current context that it makes sense that I might have been pushed. It's the same as you thinking the gas flow was an accident."

After a silent moment, David says,

"Three 'accidents' in three days defies probability. We are

incredulous of one murder over our finding. Perhaps the plan was for *three* Genesis murders. We are beset by known and unknown adversaries. We had better identify the unseen antagonists quickly as they are unlikely to fail again."

Chapter 6

We arrive at Incline at the dock used by the Institute. The Sheriff's department had the boat towed there after completing their onboard investigation. We find Luther, and he introduces us to Sheriff Pierce Taylor, Detective Janis Rollings, and Tahoe Patrol Officer Brad Carr. Despite the disturbing reason for us to be gathered here, during the introductions I can't keep my eyes off of Detective Rollings, a spectacular dark-haired, blue-eyed beauty that filled out her starched uniform perfectly. I feel guilty about this distraction while we are discussing a colleague's possible death, but rationalize that I am sharp enough to process both events at once. Taylor says,

"During his routine navigation of the lake last Friday evening, Patrolman Carr here came upon your research vessel with no one aboard. He boarded the vessel and found the key in the ignition. To test for engine failure, he turned the key, and the motor turned right over. This tells us that there would be no reason to abandon the craft. Dr. Luther just informed us that a graduate student, a Mr. Marcus Kieslar, was scheduled to use the boat on Friday. It's possible that he encountered an acquaintance in another boat, boarded his or her vessel and is sitting in a cabin by a fire somewhere. However, we think this is unlikely."

"Highly unlikely. Impossible really, Marcus would never be so reckless as to abandon the boat." says David.

The Sheriff looks at David impassively in a way that tacitly accepts his assertion. Looking down at his book, he continues.

"Upon boarding your craft, officer Carr wrote down the GPS values on the display: 39deg 10mins 12.98secs north, 120deg 07mins 18.41secs west. We found a laboratory notebook with handwritten columns containing the following headers: date, time, lat, long, cloud cover, and disc depth. Only one line of data was entered and 'disc depth' was blank. The latitude and longitude values recorded did not perfectly match those noted by patrolman Carr which is presumed to be due to the boat drifting once no one was onboard." Patrolman Carr adds,

"The winds were very light on Friday, and the water surface was calm." The Sherriff continues,

"We also found a measurement protocol including an organizational chart with project participant contact phone numbers. We tried to call the numbers on the chart, but got only voice mail messages until this morning." Taylor then produces an evidence bag containing a Secchi disc and says,

"This disc was tied to the port rail submerged in the

water. An early scenario we considered has him working the disc on the side of the boat. He reaches over the rail for some reason and falls overboard."

Pointing up to the parking lot, the Sheriff continues.

"There were only a few cars in the lot Saturday morning and based on some textbooks in the back seat we considered the gray Subaru as likely to be connected to whoever took out the boat. We ran the plates, the owner is a Jonathan Kieslar. Based on what we have learned this morning, we have assumed this is Marcus's father or another relative. We have not been able to reach him as yet. Can you confirm that the Subaru is your students?"

David and I both confirm it is Marcus's car.

"We will be slipping the lock shortly, and the lab geeks will check it out." He pauses catching himself scanning between David and me.

"Uhmm no offense." David waves it off with his hand.

Detective Rollings asks,

"Does this vessel carry an inflatable skiff or tow a smaller boat?"

"It does not." Says Luther.

The Sheriff continues,

"Dr. Luther has told us that it is the Institute's practice, for safety purposes, that a minimum of two people is necessary to take out the boat."

Luther jumps in and says to David,

"Who was supposed to go with him?"

"This is your project why don't you know? Tell me, Charles, how did you know it was Marcus that was filling in on this run?"

Oh hell, I wasn't expecting David to drop this bomb in front of the police. They look at each other with considerable interest and then in unison, all eyes turn to Luther. After an extended delay, he says,

"Well, I didn't know. I learned it from the sheriff here when he called and told me about the plates."

It appears David just caught Luther in a lie. According to Alan, the first Luther heard of a problem was from Alan during their phone call and it was then when Luther said he 'was disbelieving that there was no sign of Marcus.'

Luther looks uncomfortable, and David finally says,

"He arranged to go with his roommate Brian Chang, a fellow student who also works at the Institute. We called and spoke with Chang on our way up here. Chang was hung-over and over-slept. Chang said that he called Marcus and explained that he had just awakened. Marcus told him he was ready to start, did not want to wait, and would go it alone."

Janis, as I like to call her, asks David,

"Do you think it's unusual that they wouldn't have met in Reno and carpooled here?"

I step in and say,

"Thursday night Marcus stated they were going to drive up separately because he planned to go split boarding up at the meadows on the way home. He probably wouldn't have mentioned it, but he asked me which trail I thought he should take.

The Sheriff says,

"We did see some weird looking skis in the car. Alright,

we will want to talk to Mr. Chang, everyone who worked with Marcus at the Institute, and investigate his home." He turns to Luther and asks,

"What was the normal procedure while on the lake?" Luther describes the procedures that are followed in performing the measurements from stepping on the boat to returning to the dock.

When he finishes, Taylor says,

"At this time we are ruling this a missing person. However, I believe it is likely he is submerged out there somewhere." He waves his hand to the lake. "Perhaps he had to hang over the side to adjust the line or clear a snag, it happens. We also can't rule out an abduction."

David says,

"I should point out that Marcus is a very careful yachtsman." I add,

"He also was on his high school swim team."

Taylor says,

"Unfortunately, the best swimmer can't take the cold this

time of the year." I ask,

"If somehow he fell overboard shouldn't his body be floating around here somewhere?" As I say this, David catches my eye and slowly shakes his head no.

Taylor says,

"We have a saying about drowning victims out here, 'Tahoe does not give up its dead.' When a person drowns, his lungs fill up with water displacing the air which ordinarily aids in flotation. With the gas replaced with water, the body sinks deep into the lake. In warm water lakes, when the body starts to decompose, the decomposition results in the production of gases such as nitrogen, methane, and oxygen. These gases force the body to the surface. However, Tahoe is cold year round, the body does not decompose, there is no out-gassing, and therefore, the body stays preserved deep below the surface. Below a depth of around 600 feet, the lake remains at a constant temperature of 39 degrees. I think the Reno Morgue keeps their bodies at 39 degrees to retard decomposition."

A melancholy smile crosses the Sheriff's face, and he continues.

"Before my time, but a favorite story in the office involves a guy who died trying to break the water speed record. During a test run on the lake, his 40-foot-long, rocket-powered boat crashed and sank after reaching a speed of just under 270 miles per hour. Searchers, using an underwater camera and sonar devices, were able to locate and view a section of the boat. His body was viewed still belted inside, at a depth of about 280 feet. A salvage crew was able to bring up the section of boat 10 days after the crash and found his body perfectly preserved."

After a period of contemplative silence, I ask,

"Can you send divers down to look for the body?" Inexplicably I am turning to David while finishing the sentence. He is virtually stoic, but something about his expression tells me the answer is no.

Turning back to Taylor, with a somewhat suppressed irritated look, he says,

"Obviously we would if we could. The lake is just too deep. The average depth is around 1,000 feet. Also, the lake's elevation reduces how deep divers can go. Tahoe is over 6,000 feet above sea level. At sea level, divers with standard equipment can only reach a depth of 130 feet. Even with special tank mixtures, divers can only reach 90 feet at this elevation. By now, it is likely that his body is several hundred feet below that depth."

Out of stupid questions I shut up.

"Detective Rollings here will be down in Reno in a few days to inspect Kieslar's residence and interview fellow students, co-workers, and friends. Please email her a list of any people you think she should talk to." On cue, she starts handing out business cards, and we respond by giving her ours while he continues. "Others on my staff will pursue the abduction possibility."

A little too fast, I say

"I have a spare key to his place if you like I can meet you there." She says inscrutably,

"That will be fine. I will give you a call and let you know when I plan to arrive."

Charles walks back with us to our car. Not a model of tack and decorum, he gets right to the unpleasantries.

"David, did you get the email for the time of the meeting?"

"You know I did."

"Well, I wasn't sure since you seem to be spending all

your time trying to debunk the bible rather than mentoring your grad students, if not keeping them safe, and making certain your instruments perform as advertised."

David, usually the reserved intellectual, appears to be getting riled.

"As usual Charles, your ability to assimilate data and process the most rudimentary information is lacking. Marcus was working for you, on your project. It was up to you to 'keep him safe.'" He uses finger quotes here and then continues.

"Would you care to explain the bible debunking comment?"

With his head shaking back and forth Charles starts to walk away and says,

"God and science are not mutually exclusive, however, our Institute and you soon will be. See you at the meeting."

With that, he was on his way. David says to me with a mocked tone,

"I must say I dislike his pejorative attitude."

"The guy is an impeccable prick."

Chapter 7

Driving back, David and I analyze current events. David offers a theory.

"Well, I think Luther's Bible comment removes any doubt that he knows about our off the books experiment. What would it take for someone to slip into my lab, drop the tubing in the pit, turn on the gas and get out before I return? It would have to be a colleague with knowledge and access to the building and lab and want the three of us dead. This assumes your bump into the chutes was not accidental. For that matter add skier to the list." he says and continues with a rise in enthusiasm.

"Or... a colleague with a limitless number of like-minded minions willing to do any bidding. Since I was working on a Sunday, every entry was locked and needed card key access."

Seeing where he is heading, I say,

"So we get HR to print out a list of all card key activity for Sunday."

He says,

"It should be a short list."

There is a long period of quiet. I drift off remembering a concern that Marcus shared with me shortly after we discovered a potentially new explanation on the origin of life and the potential dangers from religious zealots. It went like this.

"Here's what I think. As our society progresses, there is increased conflict against antiquated religious beliefs on such topics of birth control, homosexuality, abortion, the unworthiness of women, divorce in the case of the Catholics, and so on. In the first century when there were less than 400 million people on earth, few might argue with a church doctrine that only condones abstinence for use in birth control. Now with 7 billion people, even many devout Catholics question or ignore the doctrine. The problem, of course, is that societies evolve and our knowledge of the universe changes, but the bible does not. The bible can't hold up to rational thought and advancements in scientific knowledge. First, evangelicals had to deal with learning that earth rotated around the sun rather than the reverse. Then that the actual age of the earth is almost 5 billion rather than 6 thousand years old. The theory of evolution was a most recent hard pill to swallow. All the religions had to scramble to defend the bible. Some faithful rationalize bible passages to be more like parables of the time or make up catchy terms like intelligent design. If our results hold up, after a period of denial, this will rock all bible based religions. Initially, the Institute will receive negative attention if not death threats...."

"Grant!"

Apparently, David has been trying to snap me out of my reflections.

"What?"

David says

"Is it conceivable that Luther could have somehow sabotaged the Sierra background instrument before we deployed it?" I contemplate my answer for several seconds.

"I can't see how, we oversaw the unit from your lab to deployment in the field. Besides he lacks critical knowledge in how they work. Next to you, I know more about the principle of operation than anyone, and I'm not sure I could sneak into your lab after hours and cause such realistic high values while meeting the quality control checks."

"Well I can't see how the Sierra unit could report false positives, it worked flawlessly in the lab, and I installed and setup that unit myself. And as you said, the calibrations and blank data returning all look reasonable."

"Do you think the calibration protocol could be flawed, or there has been some kind of contamination breaking through?"

"No."

"Of course one could simply bring a cocktail of our target analyses in a cylinder and release them upwind of the sample inlet."

"That's it." He says excitedly. But then his face turns sullen, and he says.

"Actually it's possible but very tricky. Someone would have to be very knowledgeable of our data to get it right."

"We have published the technique."

"Yes, but we did not go into detail on the post-processing of the raw values using calibration standards, spikes, blanks, etc."

We both remain quiet, contemplating David's comments. Then he adds,

"I don't know, that is a lot of work just to get me fired. One thing is certain, we need to visit the Sierra site as soon as possible."

"I agree, and it better be very soon, there is a storm moving in this weekend."

"Let's go as soon as the detective is done with us."

More silence then I voice a new scenario.

"Ponder this concept. Luther has learned of our initial Genesis findings and has discussed it with his Church leaders. They convince him that it's rubbish, that we must be incompetent which plays into his negative opinion of you. To avoid confusion among church members, they ask Luther if there is anything that he could do, within the Institute, to halt this disinformation. I think he is more of a narcissist than a murderer. Luther can't do anything directly to stop our Genesis work since we are operating clandestinely. His position within the institute certainly allows him to sabotage our normal projects. He targets you because he thinks you are the brains behind our Genesis work."

"You're on to something with that last part."

"Shut up. Where was I? He also targets you because of past failures in projects in which you and he both participated. If he gets you terminated that will at least shake us up if not end it. Meanwhile, the church or maybe some radical member sitting in a dark corner decides to take more aggressive action, perhaps unbeknownst to Luther. Luther's action may or may not succeed, but taking out the three of us certainly would end it."

"So you're saying Luther is in charge of getting me fired and some church wacko or wackos are the murderers, maybe working outside the knowledge of the church. It sounds reasonable. However after being under attack by Luther lately it's not a stretch for me to think he would sneak into my lab, turn on the gas and leave."

"Perhaps. There is one thing we need to do immediately." David is of the same mind. I say,

"Increase the security of our samples and data."

"Exactly." I add,

"Some of the things we need require facilities, approval or oversite."

"Leave it to me. We can't secure lab or office doors, but I can design areas inside that will be tamper proof."

"I'll contact Human Resources and tell them we are missing some tools and ask them if they can generate a list of personnel that was in the office on Sunday."

As we walk to our offices, David asks,

“Are you still coming to dinner tonight?

“I’m certainly not going to blow off her birthday.”

Chapter 8

I arrive at David's pretty much on time and ring the doorbell. Liz, David's wife, answers the door. She greets me with a big hug and a kiss.

"Hello handsome, good to see you."

Still holding her in my arms, I see David poke his head out from the kitchen.

I tell her,

"Happy birthday, what's he doing home?"

"He insists on making us dinner."

From around the corner, we hear,

"Ok, break it up you two, do you want a drink?"

"I thought you'd never ask. I'll make it."

Liz and I make our way into their recently remodeled kitchen. They had new concrete countertops and cabinets built and installed but performed all other improvements themselves. I provided some assistance a couple of weekends when ripping out the old cabinets and flooring. I'm better at destroying rooms then building them. They also installed a restaurant grade 6 burner Thermador range with a double oven. As a couple, they complement each other very well. She likes to design the project. He is good at working with her to execute the design but gets bored near the end when the detail work needs to be completed. Then she keeps going and finishes the trim and final touches.

They both are excellent cooks, each going about it with their own flare. Their disparate interests result in a variety of diverse dishes. This makes for excellent dining at their house. They have two grown children living in town but on their own. I make my way to the bar, David is stirring a pot on the stove. Recognizing the familiar technique, I say,

"Even though it is Liz's birthday our real aim only is to bring you joy."

"As it should be. My olfactory sensors are detecting a pork roast in the oven, so if you have made her a chocolate cake, I'd say mission accomplished."

Looking at Liz, David says,

"He has always had trouble detecting sarcasm."

She says,

"It's a strawberry cream."

"Even better." I say.

Mixing myself a double gin and tonic I spot the melting ice in an empty glass on the stove and ask,

"Can I get you another Manhattan? I don't want your attention diverted from our risotto."

He gives me a deadpan look and says,

"Thought you'd never ask."

"Touché."

Picking up his glass I turn to Liz and see she is holding a martini glass. She knows I'm checking on her drink. She smiles and holds up her full glass. David moves the pan off the burner and kills the flame. He and I have done some cooking together. He taught me how to make bread one Saturday. We felt the need to lift weights between dough risings to compensate for the possible lack of manliness in baking bread. From there he went on to show me how to brew beer. No confusion in gender roles there; that's manly stuff. His grandfather was a moonshiner in West Virginia.

"How are the kids?" I ask. Liz answers first,

"Fine, they are out of town. They went together to visit some friends in Oregon. Some concert near Medford. Excuse me for a second"

Once she exits the kitchen, I give David a look.

"I haven't told her yet, not wanting to spoil her day. I'll tell her in the morning."

Liz returns, and David leads us to the living room fireplace where new logs are popping, and yellow flames attack the fresh wood. Liz has brought a plate of hors-d'oeuvres. After catching up on our personal events of the last few weeks, Liz drops a bomb.

"Grant, David has been spending a lot of time at the Institute, after hours and on weekends. When I accused him of having an affair at work, he said the two of you have made a seminal discovery. I'm worried it's more like a SEMINAL discovery with a Coed. Would you care to comment?"

I laugh at her clever double use of the word but find myself in a tight spot.

David looks at me offering absolutely no help. The master

at deflection I say,

"Now Liz you know it's frowned upon for faculty to diddle the students."

It appears David enjoys watching me squirm. She is boring a hole in my head with her eyes. I feign concern and say,

"I'm going to need another drink."

David rises and says,

"We can discuss it over dinner."

The dinner, as always, is delicious. Stalling I say,

"This rice and cheese risotto sure is good." Liz says,

"Don't try and distract me with a tautology." I look for help from David and say,

"Tau what a ogy?" With frustration in his voice, David says.

"It is understood that risotto is cheese and rice; you were needlessly repetitive."

I give Liz a quizzical look, and in return, I can feel real heat on my forehead as she continues to hit me with laser eyes.

After savoring a bite of the pork, I look back at her, roll my eyes and say,

"Alright, alright!" And then begin. Liz has a BS in Science, so I'm going to test her memory of it by not dummying down the material. She will need to stop me and ask questions if she has trouble. "Yes, we have been distracted and tied up on an immense discovery. First some background. There are many theories on how life started on Earth. One involves a prehistoric atmosphere slightly different than the present where amino acids, the building blocks for more complex molecules may have formed by lightning strikes over the ocean. Or they could have been formed by intense heat from hydrothermal volcanic vents. Other scientists suggest that there might have been actual RNA molecules in existence that were able to self-replicate to get the ball rolling. Louis Pasteur generated interest in spontaneous generation for a time. Another popular theory has been around for a very long time, maybe you've heard of it, something about a God that merely creates all life in six days starting with Adam.

There is one that David and I have always liked. It has been speculated that extraterrestrial life forms, AKA aliens, do exist and our first life originated from them. Perhaps aliens crashed, and parts of their body constituents were broken up and building blocks like amino acids or DNA combined with the earth's soup, and here we are. Alternately, perhaps there exists a common set of primitive life components, again amino acids/DNA that was formed when the universe was created. Sort of a life starter kit, if you will. This cluster of materials may be trapped within pockets of meteoroids."

Liz asks'

"Meteoroids?"

"Meteoroids turn into, meteorites upon entering the earth's atmosphere. Anyway, Meteoroids\meteorites impact planets releasing the seeds of Genesis. Any planets with favorable chemistry and physics to support the material result in the evolution of life."

"Wait, you're not going to tell me..." Liz says and then stops. I stop and look at her without speaking and then use the opportunity to take a bite of my risotto.

She stares at me and then David and says,

"Never mind keep going."

"Recall that Darwin's theory of evolution was not limited to the concept that higher forms of life evolved from lower forms and the bombshell that humans are descendants of apes." Liz furrows her brow, and I say,

"Or not. In Darwin's 'On the Origin of Species' he wrote that it was probable that all organic beings have descended from one primordial form. Scientists studying the origin of life have called this organism LUCA, for the last universal common ancestor. If you remember the simplified 'Tree of Life..." I pause to look at her while I take a bite of dinner."

"Yes smart ass. One branch is Bacteria, and the other comprises plants and animals."

"Not bad, but since you graduated a fourth branch has been added, the Archaebacterial or Archaea for short. The plants and animals domain is referred to as Eukaryotes. In theory, there are two branches stemming from LUCA, one branch leading to bacteria and the other to the Archaea and Eukaryotes. The Eukaryota have been placed on the same branch as the Archaea as it appears we are closer to the Archaea than the Bacteria domain. But I'm getting too detailed, we are particle scientists, not astrobiologists." I take another bite and sip of wine. I have Liz's total attention as she eats her dinner.

"Some of our particle samplers draw air through filters

which collect fine particles, say 2.5 to 10 microns in size, and some samplers are dust fall collectors which allow larger particles, up to maybe 100 microns, to simply fall into a container. We perform microscopic analysis on the dust fall samplers to evaluate possible origins of the particles such as wood-smoke or fugitive dust, etc."

I wave my arm at David and say,

"Often your husband becomes bored with tasks germane to our study for which we are handsomely paid, and wanders off pursuing his own interests."

She looks over to him and is greeted with a shrug like some innocent 5 year old. I press on undistracted.

"One day, after processing the dust fall particles and examining them microscopically, some appear to be meteorite-like in origin. He takes more time with these and notices weird spots. They look like some sort of seal almost rubbery. Curiosity drives him to play with it further by moving one particle to a new tray, placing a drop of deionized water on it and setting it aside.

"Wait, you're not going to tell me..." Liz says again and then stops and stares at me.

This time I ignore her and continue.

"Well the 'seal,'" for lack of a better name, doesn't change after keeping it wet for several hours so, he moves it under a UV lamp, keeping it wet for a couple more hours. Well, you know what a rock head he is." This draws a complaint from David.

"Hey!"

Liz says, "I know, go on."

"He goes over to the microbiology lab that has a project involving sea water and asks them for 100 ml or so. He wets the rock particle with sea water and keeps it under the light. Returning after an hour, he found the rubbery material was no longer on the meteorite. In its place was a circular depression. Carefully removing the rock from the original tray, he placed it on a clean tray, and set it aside. He then poured the drops of the remaining seawater off the tray onto a glass slide and installed a glass coverslip for examination under higher magnification." Liz remains completely enthralled as she listens with a scrunched forehead that betrays her incredulity.

"He called me over to look at the slide. There in the field of view was a strange unicellular organism."

"Guys come on, you said it yourself, neither of you are astrobiologists or microbiologists for that matter. You probably are seeing cross-contamination from your materials. Have you consulted other experts?" Although Liz has her bachelors in biology, she works at the Institute as a business manager.

I look at David askance and say,

"Do you believe what we are hearing? Not only are we sloppy, but we are not well-rounded scientists."

David chimes in, finally, and I catch up on some dinner.

"First, for now, we have kept this finding between the two of us, and Marcus, who got his masters in microbiology. Second, I made 20 slides, each with a drop of the same seawater as controls, all under the UV light. Grant and I took turns scouring the drops for the organism and found nothing. Most unicellular organisms like protozoans and amoebas can't survive in seawater, they live in freshwater. Third, I took one of the other particles that we collected in our samples and was able to repeat the process. The seal falls off using seawater and heat from the lamp. Grant took a couple of the other particles we collected in the same sample that did not appear like meteorites, applied the same process and found nothing."

“Holy crap!” Exclaims Liz with excitement, but also with a concerned expression.

“Indeed.” Says David.

He pauses to allow Liz to absorb all that she has heard. She eventually remarks,

“But haven’t astronomers been studying meteorites for centuries? Why have they not found anything?”

David says,

“We don’t know, but hypothesize that these particles are well housed inside larger meteorites and aren’t exposed until broken up into these micron-sized particles. We are unfamiliar with their test methods, but doubt they ground up pieces and allowed them to sit in heated sea water. We have requested a larger piece of a meteorite from UNLV’s geology department. We will run our tests on the large sample and then on successively smaller broken up pieces to see if we can reproduce the same results. As Marcus is gone for a while, we are going to bring in Vanessa in microbiology.”

“So you think you have found this LUCA organism?” Asks Liz.

"Well, we are fairly certain it's extraterrestrial, which alone is very exciting. As you point out, I have had no cell biology courses. The zoologist over there has only had a few courses. But Marcus thought it had features of both Archaea and a Eukaryote. For example, it has a cell wall found in both domains, membranes more like Archaea, but appeared to have a nucleus similar to, but still different than Eukaryotes."

David looks at me and says,

"By the way, you know how Vanessa constantly is bitching at you for one reason or another? She told me to tell you that if you are late one more time she won't wait for you, she is very busy."

"First, she's never bitching at me, she's flirting."

Looking at Liz, I say,

"He has been married so long he can no longer tell the difference."

"That's the way I like it." She says reaching across the table for a roll.

"In any event, she has asked that you stop by her lab to pick up the supplies we requested at 9:00 tomorrow."

"I'll talk to her, she will be fine."

Looking at Liz, he says,

"He thinks he can sweet talk her."

She says in exaggerated loathing, "Oh... my... god."

"No, given our present work, that would be your husband."

"It's not the first time she has referred to me in that way, but it's usually louder."

David jumps as Liz gives him a sharp kick under the table.

"Ok, who wants cake?" Asks David.

As the pleasant evening comes to an end, David walks me out to my car, and I say.

"You really need to tell her about Marcus and our near 'accidents.' She may be in danger."

"I know, she is going to be devastated about Marcus. I'm going to tell her now and come up with a plan to keep her safe."
"Good luck. Thanks for a superb dinner. See you tomorrow."

Chapter 9

The next morning as I pull into an open space in the Institute parking lot. I notice a car slowly entering the lot behind me. The driver takes the row opposite of mine and pulls into a distant open spot. I'm not sure why it has gained my attention. Grabbing my backpack, I exit and lock my car and proceed to the main entrance. There is only one person in the car, a man and I don't recognize him. Normally I would bypass the main entrance and take an outdoor path to my building. Instead, I decide to explore an uncertain curiosity. A quick greeting to the receptionist and then up the stairs to the second floor and a hallway window that overlooks the parking lot.

The man still is in the car talking on a cell phone. Even though I don't recognize him, there are a large number of people that work at the Institute that I have never seen and the turnover rate on temporary staff can be high. Of course, this guy may have just turned into our parking lot to use his phone without driving. He ends his call, stares at the building for a few seconds, and then departs.

Walking to my office this morning I run into Alan. He asks how it went in Incline, and I give him a summary of our conversations, finishing with a grave conclusion.

"Sadly, the bottom line is it does not look good for Marcus."

"Could he really have fallen overboard?"

"I don't believe it, foul play is more likely."

"Who would want to harm Marcus?"

"I don't know. However, lately he has had a lot of anti-religious fervor and has been sharing his views with anyone who will listen, and a few who wouldn't."

"Well, I have received an ear full more than once, but didn't want to kill him."

"You aren't a believer."

"True, I know that Charles got into it with him a few times and the conversation always ended angrily. Still, it's a stretch to think he was out on the lake with someone irritated enough to kill him."

We both get quiet until I break the silence.

"A detective from the sheriff's office will be in Reno tomorrow or the next day and will want to talk with his co-workers. You probably will want to get her a list and see if they can be in the office when she is here. This is her card, I have an extra."

"Thanks. You received my email about this Friday, correct?"

"Yes, and I would like to go on the record that this meeting is premature."

"Look, I'll choose independent people and if they find there is no problem we can drop it. Remember, this is a two-step process. This meeting just determines if there is cause for termination. I'll call you later today to tell you who they are."

After a long silent stare, I turn and head to my office. After getting my laptop out of sleep mode, I navigate to a shared drive on a dedicated server containing data from the Sierra site. Data from all the sites are automatically downloaded to the server via telemetry. Only David and I have security permissions to access the server. I want to review the day that contained the elevated constituents that make up the L.A. signature. The data looked like a perfect hit of an L.A. air mass.

Furthermore, an automated run of blank calibration air was performed an hour before and showed no peaks. Prior to the blank run, calibration span gases also were run, and the peaks were all in the right order, times, and magnitudes. All the quality control data indicate the measurement system was working properly. So how can a measurement system record data that is virtually impossible to exist? If we don't find an answer to that question, all our data from these instruments will be suspect.

My reflections return to my theory that someone may have released a cocktail of chemical constituents near the sample inlet to sabotage our results. I didn't consider the automated zero and spans. They make it even harder to accomplish. During normal sampling, a pump pulls air continuously through the sample inlet. During zero and spans, solenoid values switch, and cylinder gases are introduced to the sampler and, when finished, switch back to ambient sampling. Our quality assurance plan, available to anyone, states we will perform the checks but does not specify the time of day they would occur. These may be different for each site. I only know the times because they appear in the data that David and I review. Each site has a dedicated site operator responsible for the day to day operations. This person would be one of only a few that would know the exact times.

I've known the site operator, Shauna Berkowitz, for five years. She is an hourly subcontractor, not an Institute employee. She works out of her home and rarely needs to come into the office. I doubt she has even met Luther. I decide to call her cell.

"Hey, Grant." Caller ID eliminating the usual salutations.

"Hi, Shauna. How's it going?"

"All is well. I'm at home organizing my field logs."

"Perfect, do you have the log for 10 days ago with you?"

"Let me check, that's the 19th."

I can hear papers rustling.

"There were no site visits on that day. I was there on the 18th. Is there a problem?"

"I'm not sure. We had some high values that day. Any ideas?"

"Nothing comes to mind, the site visit on the 21st shows checks and values to be normal."

"When's the last time you had a visitor or saw anyone out there?"

"Over a month ago when David was here."

"Alright, thanks. I'll talk to you later." I'm convinced only

Shauna would be capable of introducing a foreign air mix of chemicals to the measurement system resulting in the observed elevated values at the site. I'm equally convinced she didn't do it.

"Bye."

There is a knock at my door.

"Hello."

"Angela, come in. How are you?"

"I'm good, I ran into David on the way in and we were just looking at the instrument that was swapped out from Spirit Mountain unit in your lab. That unit has one of the older timers that we use in a sampler at one of our plants. I was wondering if you could loan it to us, ours died."

Having 'asked' to borrow it, she is coyly holding it in her hand smiling.

"Well, I see David doesn't have a problem with it. It's fine, we are replacing it with the newer model anyway."

"Very kind of you. So what's happening with him? Is Charles still trying to have him fired? I don't know any of the alleged problems, but I think David is very talented. I would hire him in a second."

"He is going to be fine, Dr. Luther is out of line."

"Anything new on the false positive data at the Sierra site?"

"No, but we are still analyzing the data, you will be the first to know when we are finished."

"Alright, I'm going to take off, stay in touch."

"Will do." A call to David's office finds him there.

"David Piehl," he answers. Our archaic phone system lacks caller ID.

"Hey, did you talk to Liz?"

"Yes, for half the night. She took it hard, but she's a strong woman. She is going to hang out at Barbara's this week."

"Do you have a couple of hours after work tonight?"

"I suppose, Liz won't be home. What do you want to do?"

"I'll tell you later, stop by my office around 5:00."

"Very well." With that, we hang up.

After lunch at my desk the phone rings,

"This is Stelzner."

"Grant, Alan here, we are set for 1500 this Friday."

"Marking it on my calendar, who do you have?"

"Blake and Wagner."

"Wagner, I thought you were going to choose independent people? Wagner follows Luther everywhere with her nose shoved up his ass."

"Grant you need to be careful with your remarks. We only have a few people with expertise in this field. She is knowledgeable, and in the main, works on her own projects. I'll see you on Friday."

He hung up without waiting for a response from me.

Chapter 10

At 4:30 David walks into my office. I ask.

"Did you hear, Blake and Wagner?"

"Yes, I'm sure Wagner will be impartial." he says sarcastically

"Alan thinks she will be impartial. It never ceases to amaze me that many very smart scientists can be clueless to social nuance. It's that nerd characteristic."

"It's worse at the universities." Recruited NRI scientists are mostly chosen based on their abilities to perform all duties, marketing, budgeting, management, as well as research. Tenured faculty can hide in their lab and run experiments all day.

"Alan is better than most, which he needs to be as a division director. Of course, unlike me, you are kind of nerdy."

"The likeliness of being a nerd is exponentially proportional to intelligence."

I walked into that one.

"Exponentially proportional, you are making my case for me. Anyway, Detective Rollings will be at Marcus's at 10 tomorrow and then will come out here. I just sent out an email to everyone."

"I saw it. I deployed our increased security measures. Our rock samples were moved to a dedicated refrigerator in your lab with a combination lock, it's 4482. The lock hasp is as thick as they make, but if someone breaks in, and opens the door, I will get a text message. Unfortunately, I'll get a text message every time the door is opened, but since only you or I may open the refrigerator, I'll be able to ignore those. I added a pressure switch on one of the legs so if someone tries to place the refrigerator on a dolly and haul it away, I will get a text message."

"Wow, that's really cool. How are you getting the text messages?"

"The door sensor is small and unseen unless you know what to look for. The floor sensor is larger and heavy duty; however, it looks like something used to level the refrigerator; thus if spotted it should be unrecognized as a warning sensor. Once tripped it would be too late anyway. Each sensor is a closed contact when opened, it sends a wireless signal to a data logger, which sets off an alarm on our database computer which sends the text."

"That should do the job."

"So what are we doing tonight?"

"If I'm wrong you will be able to go straight home. Otherwise, I need you to follow a guy."

"What do you mean follow a guy, what am I a spy? I don't know how to shadow someone."

Grabbing my stuff and shutting off the lights, I say.

"Shadow? Really, stop being a wimp, come on let's go the long way."

On the way to the hallway window, I explain my concerns. Now standing at the window, I don't see the Toyota SUV from this morning. This whole business is unsettling.

"I don't see him, but that doesn't mean he isn't waiting. Look for a black, Toyota Highlander with a ski rack, Tulle I think, and a red bumper sticker, I don't know what it says. You go out first and pull over into the lot near the roundabout. Enter the traffic stream several cars behind me. If you see the Highlander or anyone who appears to be following me, stay behind him and let's see what happens."

"You're insane, this will take all night."

"I don't think so, I am going to drive straight home. If someone follows me and sees I'm in for the night, he should leave within a few minutes. If you don't see anyone, follow me home at a safe distance and park up the road and then call my cell. Remember if he is following me, he knows you so don't let him see you following him but don't lose him."

"Look this isn't the movies I don't know the tricks to surveillance. If he sees me, I'm going to abort. Why don't you try and snapshot his face on the way out."

"I will if I can, but if it's the same guy as this morning, I've never seen him. Now get going."

David's reference to a 'snapshot of his face' refers to a strange ability that I possess. It's along the line of the expression 'I never forget a face' but more like a photographic memory. Unfortunately, it only works for faces and some images. I can't read a page in a book and remember everything on the page. That or an idyllic memory certainly would be much more useful. However, this small 'human facial recognition software' occasionally comes in handy.

After a few minutes, I head down to the exit and out to

my car. I walk looking for the Highlander but very discreetly. No sign of it. As I approach the roundabout, I see David in the dirt lot watching the road. He is making a show of talking on his cell phone, a nice touch. I pull onto the highway on-ramp and head to my house. Driving the speed limit, I don't see the Highlander behind me but think I spot David a long way behind me. Finally, I pull into my driveway, hit the garage door opener and pull into my garage. Removing my backpack from the car, I close the garage door and enter the house. Swiftly I climb the stairs and enter a spare bedroom that overlooks the street.

A few cars travel by my house. Cars traveling left to right make the driver challenging to see due to the angle from the second floor. From the opposite direction, I can see the driver clearly. However, it is getting nearly dark, as yet, no Highlanders. This is not a busy street but is one of the more busy times as my neighbors return home from work. Now I see David driving left to right, the more common direction for this end of the street for people returning home. He passes my house and continues out of site up the road. A few minutes later my cell phone plays the theme to '2001 A Space Odyssey', David says.

"Well there was no Highlander but a grayish Lexus SUV was behind you the entire way, he just passed your house and pulled a U-turn a few houses down and is now parked across the street. I did the same thing but am several houses behind him. I noted that the driver is male with dark hair and unneeded sunglasses."

Looking out the window I can barely make out the vehicle through the trees in my yard.

"What do you want to do, I can't stay here all night watching him watch you? I do have his plates and model number. Wait, I think he started his car. Yes, he is pulling out. I will see how long I can follow him."

"Be careful." Fifteen minutes later, my cell phone rings, it's David.

"Are you still in pursuit?"

"He has stopped, and you will never guess where."

"The Living Word temple up on the hill?"

"Yes, how did you know?"

"I got a glimpse of his face, as he passed by the house. It took a while, but I placed him with Luther at John Farnsworth's funeral last year. He too was a member of Luther's Church."

"He pulled into the church parking lot. Luther and some other guy were waiting outside and greeted him. Can I go home now?"

"Sure. What do you think this all means?"

"Let me sleep on it. I'm going to check on Liz at Barbara's."

"Make sure you are not followed. I'll see you tomorrow."

In the temple parking lot, Charles Luther walks out a side door of the church and greets the dark-haired man, Earl Johnson, a member of the Elders Quorum.

"I followed Stelzner from the Institute, he went home and looked like he was in for the night. Last night he went over to Piehl's house for most of the evening."

"Earl, I think we are wasting our time with this surveillance. Why does Roger think Stelzner will go to this woman? Why would he even know her?" Earl works directly for Roger, second in command in the local Church of Latter Day Saints. He will follow his directions despite the opinions of Dr. Luther. He declines to answer Dr. Luther's questions.

"Let me ask you Earl, is Roger up to speed on all that has

transpired since Friday? We have agreed to only discuss events orally, in person but he has been in Utah."

"He is heading back tomorrow morning, and I have not talked to him either."

"I'm going to be tied up all day. Please let him know that Kieslar is dead and I'm working on shutting down their experiments. Piehl soon will be fired from the Institute."

Chapter 11

The next day, after working in the lab since 6:00 am, David decided to accompany me to Marcus's apartment. We furtively scan for a Highlander or Lexus and spot him on the far end of the parking lot. We're in my car, and I say to David,

"Let's lose this asshole?"

"Simmer down Miss Marble, there is no point, everyone at the Institute knows we are going to Marcus apartment."

"Miss Marble?"

"Agatha Christie's, amateur detective?"

"It's Marple, you idiot. What does Luther and or the Church expect to accomplish by this surveillance after we leave the Institute? It's our activity in the lab that I think would concern them. Also, we could alert the world with a click of a computer key."

"Best case is he has discerned we are not ready to go public and wants to learn if there are any other players outside the Institute. Worse case is he has had someone hack into our computers and knows everything we do electronically and needs the personal contacts we might be establishing."

Before I suggest we have our computers checked, we reach Marcus's apartment. We arrive early, we want to have a look around on our own. Rather than use my back up key, we expect Chang to be there as we called earlier to let him know Detective Rollings would be inspecting Marcus' things and that she wanted to question him. Chang is home, and he greets us at the door.

"So am I in fetid feces for not going to the lake with Marcus or am I lucky to be alive?" Chang asks rhetorically.

"Since you weren't on the official schedule I don't see how you can be reprimanded. It was Marcus who broke protocol." I say.

David adds,

"And yes, had you gone with him it is likely that you would have suffered the same fate, these people seem very committed." His body performs a rapid, two-second shake that ends with a non-intelligible utterance.

"That chills me to the bone."

I had drifted off examining the bookshelf and finally ask,

"Brian, are all these Marcus's books?"

"Yes, mine are in my bedroom."

He had a large number of books of a religious or anti-religious nature. All the major tomes: The Bible, the Torah, Koran, the book of Buddhism, the book of Mormon. On the other side of the fence, there also is the 'God Delusion' by Richard Dawkins, 'Under the Banner of Heaven' by Jon Krakauer.

David and I both knew that since, 'nine eleven' and eight years of George Bush, Marcus had developed a strong anti-religion sentiment. He lost a cousin in the towers. He had become obsessed with religious zealots and the power of conservative religious groups. For the former, Marcus believed in the adage that one should study one's enemy. In the latter, he was absolutely incredulous that Americans of faith would blindly vote for a president because they liked the name of his god, even though it was obvious he was incompetent. He believed that Republicans overly pander to the religious right for votes. I remember him saying,

"We went to war because God told George Bush it was the right thing to do. He blocked research on stem cells. What is wrong with these Americans?"

He also could not understand how someone like Dr. Luther, a person trained in science, could believe in the faith which is partly based on Mormonism. One night, over a pitcher of beer at the brewpub, he was rattling off non-stop problems he saw with the Mormon faith and could not believe Luther could be so blind.

"I was talking to a group of Mormons one night, and the age of the earth was discussed. Each agreed that it is less than 70,000 years old. I was shocked. Of course, I pointed out that they were ignoring the fact that proven and accepted dating information has it at least 4.5 billion years. They just shrugged. Did you know that Mormons are not supposed to read certain books and publications? I wonder if his Rock of the Living Word faith adopted this facet of the religion."

Maybe to play devil's advocate or to add balance to the discussion I jumped in and said,

"Luther received his Ph.D. from Stanford. I'm pretty sure he knows the earth is older than 70,000 years."

This only further incited him.

"You are making my point for me, how can he follow a faith with such glaring inaccuracies?"

Undeterred I say,

"Perhaps he accepts the religion in general terms without requiring acceptance of every tenet."

He fires back,

"Again my point exactly, people of faith cannot have it both ways! If you accept something on faith in the face of known truths that dispute the faith, then you may not pick and choose the parts that don't suit you!"

Because I can relate to this argument, and am clueless about what the man really thinks, I lose my desire to continue trying to defend Luther's beliefs.

"Why don't you just discuss it with him?"

"Sure, upstart, Ph.D. student probes Rank 4 professor's religious beliefs and finds himself in the lab cleaning glassware all day. Actually, we have had some indirect discussions about religion which always became heated."

I am snapped out of my musing by a knock at the door. Walking to the door with a sick feeling, I open it, and my sensory detectors shift gears going into instant overload, all synapses firing, at the image of detective Rollings. Held captive by her blue eyes, subconsciously my mind is stretching the limit of my downward peripheral vision bringing in a blurred visage of perfectly shaped breasts straining the polyester of her uniform. All the while knowing if I attempt a glance downward, no matter how brief, the detective will catch me and my inner dog will be exposed. I will be placed in the bin with all the dirt bag men she has met today.

As I remain transfixed, the default length of time allotted for a reasonable person to address a visitor at the door expires, and she says.

"Dr. Stelzner? May I come in?"

A little rattled I yammer,

"Oh ah yes of course. But it is Mr. Stelzner."

"I beg your pardon?"

"I only have a master's degree, no Ph.D." Another awkward pause. Very smooth, what a geek.

"Please come in, just call me Grant."

She enters and turns to David. He has no inner dog and greets her politely while I revisit her perfect form from behind, including a handgun strapped to her side making her impossibly hotter. David introduces the detective to Chang who offers to show her around, but she prefers to proceed on her own. As she turns away from Chang, he looks at me with eyes wide and mouths the word 'Oh my God!' I just smile. She takes a thorough walk through the apartment asking Chang questions along the way. Then she proceeds to question him regarding his relationship with Marcus and his whereabouts on Friday.

"I thought I had way too much to drink because I can't remember much of Thursday night and had trouble walking. Friends had to help me home. But there is something weird. I didn't think I had that much to drink and instead of feeling terrible Friday morning I wasn't that bad I just had trouble waking up. I ended up going into work. My girlfriend had a friend that had been slipped a Rohypnol. She said I was exhibiting some of the same characteristics that she had witnessed in her friend."

"So you think someone slipped you a rufffie?"

"I don't know but I have been drunk a few times but never like that, and I usually suffered a hangover all the next day."

"Can anyone verify that you were home Friday morning?"

"My girlfriend stayed over."

"How can I contact her?" He gave her a cell phone number.

She then returns to us and says,

"While I have you both here, can you tell me where each of you was Thursday night and Friday morning?" We start to react negatively as one, but then, both seem to figure she has to ask. I take the lead.

"Thursday night David and I were at his house with his wife until 11 then I went home alone. I was in the office at 8:00 am."

David says,

"My wife can verify that I was there until 7:00 am then I went to NRI." She was assiduously taking notes.

She finally asks,

"Did Mr. Kieslar have an office at the Institute?"

David responds,

"He had cubical space in an open office area."

"I would like to take a look and talk to everyone who worked with him."

I jump in and say,

"We were going to have a quick lunch and then head back to the Institute would you like to join us?"

She looks at me, expressionless, for what seems like a long few seconds and says,

"Thank you, but I would prefer to head straight there, perhaps a secretary can show me to his space."

I hide my disappointment and say,

"Ok sure, we can get something at the drive through and show you to his desk."

"Good, I will follow you in my car."

On the ride back, David begins to lay upon me the grief that I knew would be coming.

"Allow me to point out some obvious facts. Despite your considerable past successes dating attractive women, I must say that this one is a cut above the rest. In addition, she works with fellow male police officers who tend to be huge, well built, and possess combat skills. You, on the other hand, have been trained in chemistry and physics and although in decent shape, have not been in a fight since high school."

I respond with,

"All true but many of these co-workers are Neanderthals. Maybe she is interested in a change of personality."

"Your rejection for lunch would indicate otherwise. On another subject, do you think we should tell her about the possible attempts on our lives as well as people following us?"

I consider the question and say,

"I don't think we have enough evidence to make a convincing case, we should check on a few more things, like the card key log, and see what we have."

I had another thought.

"You just said 'following us.' Do you think they are following you as well?"

"Oh, I haven't looked."

Chapter 12

Back at the Institute, I lead Detective Rollings to my office, and David returns to work. I offer to keep her coat in my office because I was raised to be a gentleman. Well, ok so that she will return here before leaving. I take her to Alan's office explaining that he would like to lead her around the Institute. Approximately two hours later Alan drops her off at my office.

"How's it going?" I ask.

"Marcus was well respected around here. If you or David think of anything else give me a call."

"I notice you didn't drive a sheriff's vehicle up from Tahoe."

She studies me carefully and says,

"That's right."

Offering me nothing else she leaves me stuck and knows it. After letting me suffer for a long pause, she lets me off the hook with a smile and says,

"I have a sister who lives in Reno, I am going to stay over tonight."

I go with this kernel of encouragement and ask,

"Would you consider going to dinner with me tonight? Perhaps we could discuss the case further."

She drills me with those blue eyes and says,

"Are you holding back some information regarding the case?"

"Well no, I mean maybe, something might come, up or..." I am yammering non-sensibly again, and she is enjoying it.

As she lets me squirm with her hands on her hips, she heads to the door and says,

"You are a person that has been questioned in our murder investigation, and thereby makes you someone I should not see socially."

"But if not for that you would go out with me?"

"I did not say that." She pauses while buttoning her coat and finally looks at me and says,

"I'll tell you what, my sister and I are going for drinks at the brewpub for happy hour. If I happened to run into you there and you think of something more regarding the case maybe we could talk about it." With that, she was out the door.

I go to David's office to gloat over a partial success.

"Guess who's having drinks with Detective Rollings tonight."

"I am."

"That's right... Wait, what?"

"She asked for directions to the brewpub. She thought she knew where it was, but wanted to confirm it. She asked Chang to come by, but he has a test in class tonight but will try and make it over later. She wants to see if anyone who was there last Thursday night might be in tonight so she could question them along with the staff. Perhaps someone saw an extra hand involved in Marcus' drinks. She recognized it's a long shot but was planning to go out for drinks with her sister anyway and it's as good a place as any."

"What's this about YOU having drinks with her?"

"As Liz is out with Barbara, I volunteered to help until Chang gets there. I know a few of his friends."

"What's this about me guessing who is having a drink with her?"

I feel abashed and my face flushing.

"She told me she was going there with her sister and I could stop by if I wanted. I didn't know the whole Institute was invited."

"Are you going to cry about it?"

"I might, what's it to you?"

"Did you receive the card key list from HR?"

"Not yet. Karen said I can pick it up later this afternoon."

"I didn't see Detective Rollings after our brief meeting. Do you know if she learned anything?"

"I don't know, she isn't really talking about it other than to solicit questions. I think we need to tell her about our find and the two 'accidents' we had over the weekend."

"I concur but let's wait until we get the card key information."

I head back to my office and am intercepted by our

Division Director. He follows me into my office and asks,

"Did the detective share anything with you regarding her investigation? She wouldn't tell me anything she just asked questions."

"No, she didn't tell me anything either. Listen, Alan, I want to repeat my objection to this termination process."

"I don't have much choice. Now an instrument developed by David appears to be giving false negatives at a solid background site."

"That's right, at my site. I don't think the problem is with David's design and as Principle Investigator, if I don't have a problem with David's work, it is inappropriate for Luther even to be involved."

"Well, maybe you should have a problem. You are too close to David. The Institute's reputation is at stake, this is a high profile study. You are correct about one thing. As Principle Investigator, if you don't get this problem fixed, you could be next to go down this path. Regarding Charles, he is using David's failures in the Denver smog study, the Mohave Project, along with this current problem to point out the emergence of a disturbing pattern."

I feel a flush of anger wave through my body.

"You know that is a blatant falsehood! As you and everyone else are aware, his role on the Denver project was to try out an experimental instrument. It was understood that the probability of success was no better than 50%."

"Come on Grant you know nominally we can have some failures in the interest of experimentation, but it usually carries a stigma. Three failures in three large studies raise a flag."

"This hearing is premature, and you know it, I am convinced the instruments work and we are missing something."

"All well and good but if you don't resolve this, and fast, you are going out on the same limb. For now, Charles has convinced the other Rank 4's that David falsified his method detection limits to meet the deadline for deployment."

I repeat my equine excrement rejoinder.

"I reviewed the results, and they were all reasonable. Luther has ulterior motives."

"Look I believe David to be a sound scientist but if the method development data are valid why are you getting hits in an environment where it is impossible for those compounds to exist? You are the Principle Investigator for the Long Range Transport study. If you fail to produce credible results and it damages the Institute's reputation your career will be in jeopardy. I can't state this enough."

Trying to suppress my anger I reply slowly,

"Alan, I have been managing projects here for 10 years, and each one has been successful, on time, and on budget."

Alan has moved to my door, shrugs his shoulders and says,

"Look your objections are not falling on deaf ears. I replaced Luther with myself as committee chair. He is now just there to provide information, same as you."

I was surprised.

"Thank you."

He nods and says,

"It still does not look good for David."

He turns and walks down the hall.

As the time closes in at 5:00 pm I walk over to Human

Resources to pick up the list. A clerk hands me an envelope with my name on it. I head to David's office while opening the envelope. There are only 10 names.

As I enter his office, without a word, I hand him the single sheet of paper. He scans the list containing one column of date and time and another with names of card key holders. He looks up.

"Well isn't this curious."

Chapter 13

David and I head down to the parking lot together but will travel to the brewpub separately. This time we don't want to be followed and tip the guy from the church that we are looking for the person who may have drugged Chang.

David says,

"I'm pretty sure I'm not being followed, and it's a little insulting. Why do you rate a tail?"

"Give me a break. Remember the plan, as we pull out you fall in right behind me and drive slowly. I'm going to haul ass and turn right at the yield sign, you take our usual route to the left. I'm going to take a circuitous route to the pub until I know he's not on me. If he loses me make sure he doesn't follow you instead."

"I will let's talk using our car's Bluetooth after a few minutes. Do you see him?"

"No, but let's assume he is out here somewhere. Here we go."

We pull out together, and there are several cars behind David as we drive to the fork in the road. After turning right at the yield sign, I speed up and climb over a hill which hides me from any following cars, and then have an idea. I quickly turn into the community college campus. The parking lot is on a hill. I rapidly turn into a parking row with many other cars, fairly far away from the road, in a spot that points downhill back at the road. I can see any cars that drive by and am camouflaged among all the other vehicles.

Space Odyssey plays through my speakers.

"Hey, we may have someone. A white Subaru was behind me and stayed in the round-a-bout. He may have seen you were nowhere ahead and reversed his direction to find you. Be careful; he is heading your way now."

"I'm in the community college parking lot."

"I'm going to make some additional turns in case it is not him, and there is still someone behind me. Once convinced I'm not being followed, I'll head to the pub."

"There he is." I automatically but needlessly, slump down in my seat. I quickly pull out a pair of binoculars that I had ready for this purpose so I can see his face. I say,

"He just passed, I could see his face I have no recollection of him. Once he is down the hill, I'm going to pull out and come your way and meet you at the pub."

As he disappears over the hill, I pull out of the space and head to the road, all the while looking for him to return. Staring at the empty street fading over the hill, I turn onto the street and speed in the opposite direction. All the way to the round-a-bout there are no cars behind me. I head to the brewpub.

As I enter the pub, there is heavy patronage. Scanning the bar and tables, at the bar, I see David, Janis and another woman who I guess is Janis's sister. This is a college bar, I navigate to them through the humanity of students. Janis, clad in nicely fitting jeans and a tight sweater, greets me and introduces her sister Nicole, another knockout. Carla, one of the bartenders, brings two different draft beers and what looks like a club soda for Janis. I guess she is working and will wait to have a drink. I remain standing next to the three and order a beer and David asks,

"Hey, Carla were you working last Thursday night?"

She repeats,

"Thursday" and looks down at the floor.

"Yes, why?"

"I think you know Brian Chang. Do you remember seeing him?"

"Normally I would say there is no way I could keep something like that straight, but yes he was here. I know because Thursday is my Monday and he lost it, at one point he couldn't even stand."

David says,

"I'd like you to meet Detective Rollings, she works in Incline and would like to ask you some questions."

"Sure I'll be right back, I'm up for a break."

She picks up cash from two patrons, gives them change, and serves two beers to a couple. She says something to another bartender who I don't know and works her way around the bar. The three spin their chairs around to face her as she approaches. Giving me a big smile she says,

"Hi, Grant." And then turns and stands in front of Janis.

"Carla, Mr. Chang believes he may have been slipped a ruffie Thursday night."

"Oh my God! Wait you don't think it was me?"

"I have no idea who may have done it. I would just like to know whatever you can tell me about that night."

She starts by saying,

"Well," and then stops and again looks down at the floor for about 5 seconds.

"It was pretty busy but less so than tonight, the semester just ended today. I don't really remember seeing him until he almost fell and his friends were holding him up. I was working behind the bar and recall that he was not sitting at the bar."

Janis asks,

"So if he was out at the tables who would have waited on him?"

Again looking at the floor, she looks up and says,

"Either Rebecca or Kate."

"Are either of them here tonight?"

"Kate is right there." Pointing across the room.

"Scanning the room, do you see any of the patrons that

were here that night?"

She starts to look around and says,

"Now you are asking a lot of my memory."

After scanning the room for about a minute, she points and says,

"Well, Jeff over there was here. I know because he is a regular and had asked me about ski conditions, I had gone up on Wednesday. I don't see anyone else that I remember being here but I can't be completely sure."

"Ok thanks. Will you ask Kate to come over for a few minutes when she can?"

"Sure."

Meanwhile, Janis hops off her stool and walks over to the Jeff guy. We can't hear their conversation, but she shows him her badge.

Janis says,

"Good evening sir I'm Detective Rollings with the Washoe County sheriff's department and would like to ask you a few questions if you don't mind."

"Sure, I guess."

"What is your name?"

"Jeffery Walker."

She records the information in a notebook taken from her back pocket.

She holds up her iPhone that contains a close up picture of Chang that she had taken at his apartment.

"Do you recognize this gentleman?"

As he studies it for a while, she then swipes to a second wide shot of Chang standing.

"Maybe I do. Was he the guy that got totally pissed and was bouncing off the walls?"

"We have had reports that he was having a problem."

As he says this he too pulls out an iPhone and enters his password and says,

"Check this out."

He starts a video of Chang holding on to a wall and then stumbling into a nearby table before a group of people help him stand.

“He was pretty funny, I had my phone already out and hit the video button in case he went crazy.”

“That video is not that long do you think you could text it to me?”

“I can try what’s your number?”

Janis gives it to him and while she waits to receive it asks,

“Do you remember what he was drinking? Beer, highball, wine?”

“No, I don’t even remember seeing the guy until he started falling into tables.”

She looks down at her phone and sees the text message. Opens the message and hits play on the image. It works fine.

“Thanks for the video. Is this phone number a good way to reach you if I have any more questions?”

“Yes”

“If you think of anything else will you call me on my number?”

"Sure."

With that, she walks back over to us, and Kate joins us. Janis asks her all the same questions, but Kate doesn't know Chang.

Janis says he may be memorable because he was reported to be really drunk and needed to be escorted out by some friends.

"Oh yeah, I remember. I waited on him because after he was stumbling around, I thought back to how many drinks I had served him. It was three."

"What was he drinking?"

"Bourbon and water."

"Where was he sitting?

"He wasn't he was standing around talking to a group of people, watching Thursday night football on that TV."

"Was he holding his drink the entire time?"

"I don't remember, but you see how those people standing there use that shelf to place their drinks. He could have rested it there at some point."

"Chang claims that he was drugged that night. First I have to ask, did you spike his drink with anything?"

"Absolutely not! Why would I?"

"Did anyone ask you or pay you to spike his drink?"

"Absolutely not!"

"Alright, I believe you. Do you remember seeing anyone near his drinks?"

She paused to consider the question.

"No, but if he placed his drink on that shelf, you can see that it would be easy, to slip something into it."

"Ok thanks. Here is my card if you think of anything else, please call me."

"Sure."

Kate returned to her tables and Janis to her stool. Janis turns to David and me and says,

"When confirming Chang's alibi with his girlfriend, she told me she could not remember seeing anyone lingering near his drinks that night. I'll ask him if he ever put his drink on the shelf but his memory of that night has all but disappeared."

Janis's sister had a friend come up to her, and they were chatting. Janis gets off her stool and walks between David and me.

"Take a look at this." She says, and she starts the video.

It shows the group standing and several glasses on the shelf and then the besotted Chang almost falling on to the nearby table. He righted himself and then stumbled in one direction nearly falling and then stumbled and fell into the group, two people holding him upright. The camera held there for several seconds and the video ended. I say,

"I saw someone I've seen before but can't remember where or who he is."

"Show me." Janis restarts the video.

"The best shot is toward the end."

I grab the phone ready to hit pause and do so when his image is the clearest.

"This guy."

Janis touches the image to make it full screen and then

takes a screenshot of it to save it to her photo library. I'll text you a copy.

"Do you think you recognize him from this bar?"

"No."

"You are sure?"

"Very. It's not from here, I think it will eventually come to me. I will tell you this, I am getting an ominous feeling about him."

Janis stares at me and then turns to David without speaking.

"He is extremely good with faces. If he has portentous feelings about him, you can count on it."

She looks back at me with a perplexed look when Carla walks up and serves my draft. Janis shows her the picture.

"Do you know this guy?"

She studies it thoroughly and says no, and she doesn't remember him from that night. Janis walks over to Kate where she is taking an order, gets her attention but waits for her to finish. She shows Kate the picture, and she too does not remember him from that night and doesn't recognize him. Just then Chang enters the bar and walks over to David and me.

"Hey guys, did detective hottie show up tonight?"

David says,

"As a matter of fact she is over there, and this is her sister Nicole."

Nicole gives him a big smile having heard his remark, and Chang grimaces and holds his hands to his face and then says,

"Hi, nice to meet you." Behind him, he hears,

"Mr. Chang, we have much to discuss."

Janis tells him all that she has learned and shows him the video.

"Yes I was drinking bourbon, I recall resting my drink on the shelf a few times while checking my phone. I don't remember seeing the guy, don't know who he is and my memory falls off precipitously with no recollection of anything on the video except stumbling around and having difficulty standing."

"Alright, I am buying the ruffie theory and believe it is likely that one of these people may be involved in Mr. Kieslar's disappearance. If Grant's 'feelings' have any merit it might be this guy. Nicole and I need to go, if anyone has any other ideas call me."

Janis looks at me, a little longer than feels normal. What was that? Is she interested? Oh wait, it probably was because I told her I would eventually remember the guy. The girls gather their things and head for the door. They stop as Nicole readjusts her beanie. And then it happens, Janis throws a look my way and holds it. Then they were out the door.

Chapter 14

The next morning I call Janis.

"Rollings."

"Hi, this is Grant are you still in town?"

"Yes, I am on my way to the Washoe County morgue on another case."

"There has been a development, some isolated events that we now believe may tie together with Marcus's death."

"Can you fill me in, over the phone, I have another 10 minutes before arriving at the morgue?"

"The explanation is rather intricate."

"Well I have a meeting all afternoon downtown, and then I was going to head back to the lake."

I decide to go out on a limb and say,

"If you could stay over one more night we could meet tonight and go over what I need to tell you in a few hours. In fact, I know a nice quiet place that has decent food."

After a long quiet moment, she says,

"I guess that will work, I will call my sister and let her know. Where did you want to meet?"

Here goes nothing,

"My place."

She is quick to protest,

"I don't think that is a good idea."

"Look I have a fairly complicated series of events that may tie together, and I need to discuss it with you where we will be undisturbed. We can have a quiet dinner and see what you think of some theories that David and I have put together." Again dead air that I intrude with,

"You can bring your gun."

I hear suppressed soft laughter.

"I suspect it will be safe enough. Where do you live and what time should I be there?"

I pack up my laptop so I can work at home in between preparing dinner. I stop by David's office to let him know I am leaving and that I am having Detective Rollings over for dinner tonight. I like to gloat, it's a character flaw.

"She agreed to come to your house? Inconceivable."

"Oh, not only is it conceivable, it's been conceived."

"I hope that while you are trying to engage her in your litany of depraved activities, you might find some time to discuss Marcus's murder."

"I resent the term depraved. Only a few things on the list can be considered fringe, most are totally mainstream."

He just stares at me with his patented 'stink eye.'

"I've got to go."

My house is on the edge of town along the foothills of the Sierras at an elevation right at one mile. There is a panoramic view of the city and the surrounding basin. In my opinion, Reno is the best-kept secret in the west. It is in a bowl half surrounded by bare desert mountains and the other half by the Sierra Nevada Forest. Our closest ski resort is only 30 mins away, and we can be at Lake Tahoe in 45 minutes. One of the coolest cities in the country, San Francisco, is only a 4-hour drive over spectacular Donner Pass. Pyramid Lake, a unique desert lake on tribal land, is a 30-minute drive. The western entrance to Yosemite is 3 hours and Mammoth Mountain about 3.5 hours.

I have just prepared the bread dough for some Parker House rolls, set it in a warm corner to rise and have resumed analyzing data on my laptop. As I was schooled in chemistry and physics, cooking is a natural extension of the myriad lab experiments I performed in college. Particularly recipes involving yeast such as breads, beer, and yogurt. As much as I like to experiment in my kitchen, David takes it to another level, fearless in attempting complex recipes, even making a wedding cake for a mutual friend. He makes wine and brews beer, using his own keg design involving a carbon dioxide cylinder, refrigerator, and specialized tap. I would put his beer up against the finest brewpubs in the west. My beer making is in its infancy.

I starting cooking simply to feed myself and the food was as basic as it comes. Slowly I branched out and fine cooking became sort of a hobby. I was surprised to discover that most women really are pleased to have a man cook for them. Usually, the law of unintended consequences bites me in the ass, but for once there is a positive outcome.

For Detective Rollings, I have made the preparations for a shrimp pasta with a homemade Caesar salad. The pasta will have all the ingredients of pesto but without being ground up in a sauce. Hopefully, all of this won't backfire on me with the tough cop viewing me as too metrosexual. What the hell! We have to eat and I'm reasonably manly right? Right. As my father would say,

"If you don't take a chance you don't got a chance."

On my laptop, I am analyzing time series data plots from several sites. Preliminarily it looks like transport from L.A. to Grand Canyon is occurring under favorable synoptic weather patterns. More data are needed to confirm the finding. Of course, this assumes David's instruments are working correctly.

All the while processing graphs and statistics I can't get the card key list of personnel out of mind. It showed 10 different cards were used but only 4 in our building, David's, Barry Franks, a technician that works in the third-floor soils lab, a visitor card that I think is an hourly working with Franks, and Charles Luther. The fact that Luther was there at the same time that David was working in the pit, filled with carbon dioxide is very disconcerting, if not a smoking gun.

The shrimp, or prawns as they are called in the west, have been peeled and are in a mildly spicy marinade. The salad dressing and pasta fixings have been prepared. Bread dough has been shaped into crescent rolls, and they are on their second rise.

A fire is burning in the fireplace in my great room consisting of a combined family room and kitchen, both of which look out over the city. Chris Botti is playing on the stereo and the doorbell rings. As I walk to the double glass front doors and see Detective Rollings, I can feel my heart pounding in my chest. Easy now, calm yourself. Opening the door, I make my greeting,

"Hi I'm glad you could make it, did you have any trouble finding the place?" She forms a lovely coy smile and says,

"Well, I am a detective."

"Right, good point."

We walk from the foyer toward the living room/dining room. The table is set fairly plainly compared to those laid out by women I know. I don't want to appear prissy to a girl who wears a gun. It may be too late. The living and dining room north wall consists of floor to ceiling windows also exposing the lighted Reno skyline.

"Wow, nice view."

"Thanks, let me take your coat."

She is wearing those perfectly fitted jeans from last night and a blue top that highlights her more than full breasts and brings intensity to her blue eyes. There is no sign of her gun, but I have a feeling it is on her somewhere.

I lead her to the kitchen/family room, and she is drawn to the warmth of the fire. As she takes in the entire room, she says,

"Very nice."

"Thank you, Detective, may I get you a drink?"

With a smile she says,

"If I don't say anything would you really call me Detective all night?"

I smile and say,

"Honestly, I probably would wait for your permission to call you Janis."

"You have it. How about Scotch rocks."

"I think I can find a bottle somewhere."

"Thanks. Nice horn", referring to the music from multiple speakers,

"Is that Chris Botti?"

"Good ear." I say.

She continues,

"I love his music, I saw him last summer at an outdoor concert."

I ask,

"Were you at his concert up in Truckee?"

"I was, were you there?"

"Yes, I became a big fan that night." I hand her the drink, start to make a gin and tonic for myself and see her peaking under the towel where the rolls are rising.

"Hey get out of there!"

She ignores my command and says,

"They are beautiful, did I miss your chef on the way out?"

"Not on my salary."

"I'm impressed."

I lead her to the sofa in front of the fireplace carrying some cheese, crackers, and an artichoke dip and then retrieve my drink.

She says,

“You have made such a comfortable atmosphere I hate to disturb it with talk of the disappearance of your colleague.”

Sitting next to her where we can both look into the fire I say,

“It does make for a somber mood change. I notice you always refer to his disappearance rather than death.”

“Without a body, we are reluctant to call it a death. Perhaps your new information will persuade me otherwise.”

I start from the beginning with me getting pushed over a cliff and then the attempted gassing of David. To head off any aggravation on her part for not telling her this at the lake, by explaining in detail that we both thought they were accidents until we finally got around to discussing with each other about our respective experiences. Noticing her empty glass I rise, pick it up and walk to the counter, all the while continuing the summary of events. I return with her drink and put another log on the fire. She silently listens as I begin to describe our research on the meteorites. I start talking about DNA and catch myself.

"Without boring you with too much detail in the science..."

"Too late." She mumbles due to a piece of cheese and cracker in her mouth. Having to keep her mouth closed she manages a big smile and her amusement breaks out through her eyes. It is adorable.

"Gorgeous and funny."

She swallows her food, performs a mock showing of straightening up and says,

"Sorry go ahead, it must be the scotch."

"I can go into more detail later if you're interested, but essentially we think we will be able to answer the question on how life first formed on earth."

"Damn that's huge! I'm guessing it is going to be inconsistent with the Old Testament?"

"Most definitely."

I explain about Luther; that he is a Christian of a cult-like church which is gaining in popularity in Reno, is trying to get David fired, and that someone from the church is following us.

Then finally, that we just learned Luther was in the office on Sunday when David was nearly suffocated. As she is sipping her drink and staring into the fire, I can see in her face that she is processing all of the information. She eventually says,

"And now it appears that Chang was drugged to get Marcus alone on that boat."

Taking her hand, which was soft with long slender fingers, I say,

"Why don't you move up here, I'll get dinner started."

I lead her to the granite bar in the kitchen and pull out a barstool, and she says,

This has always been my favorite color granite, white with black speckles. There is a lot of it in Yosemite." She has a glorious scent, faint though bringing all senses to attention.

"That's amazing. Exactly why I chose it. No one has ever made the connection. I spend as much time as I can backpacking in the backcountry." Removing the salad bowl and mortar and pestle containing the dressing she says,

"Hey, I used one of these in chemistry class."

"Me too."

I resume the discussion of our work.

"Now where was I? Ok, we have tried to keep our discovery secret, working on it on our own time.

Tossing the salad with the dressing and grated parmesan cheese, I say,

"However, David and I are concerned that our results have leaked out, probably through Marcus. Furthermore, based on comments he has made, we believe that Dr. Luther knows of our findings."

I open the oven, slide in the sheet of rolls, set the timer, set the burner under the pasta water to high, and dish up two salads.

"So you think Dr. Luther or his people killed Marcus on Friday, pushed you over a rock in the chutes on Saturday and tried to suffocate David on Sunday, making the actions look like unrelated freak accidents, albeit very coincidental. All to stop your research on the origin of life."

I take a break from eating my salad while she resumes hers.

"Yes. We know Luther is involved but how deep into the murder attempts remains a question." I add the pasta to the boiling water and start a flame under a sauté pan.

Janis says,

"First, this is an excellent Caesar, and those rolls smell fantastic. Second, have you had any more thoughts on the guy at the bar?"

"No. The problem is I've probably only seen him once and then for a short time. Otherwise, I would have placed him by now."

"How can you be so sure?"

"I have sort of a photographic memory for faces."

"That's weird,"

"I know. I may come across another face that was at the same location where I have seen him or someone associated with him, which will allow me to place his name." I say while starting to sauté shrimp, pine nuts, and garlic in olive oil.

Getting up to watch me at the stove, she says,

"You have given me much to consider."

After draining the pasta in a colander, I dump the shells into the pan with the shrimp and then add basil and cooked pre-chopped artichoke hearts. I finish it off with some diced tomatoes and grated parmesan.

"Let's eat."

I place the bowl of pasta and shrimp on the dining room table and toss some rolls in a cloth-covered basket.

"Would you like some wine with dinner?"

"Yes please."

"Pick a white from the fridge would you."

She grabs a chardonnay, and we sit facing the lights downtown. I open the bottle, and as we settled in at the table. Janis says,

"This all looks so wonderful."

"Thank you. So tell me about yourself, are you a native Nevadan, how did you get into law enforcement?"

"I was born in Reno and went to UNR's criminology program after high school. I had always been fascinated with investigative work. I entered the academy and after graduation was assigned a position in Winnemucca then Ely and now Incline Village. This pasta is delicious, and I love the rolls. I can't believe you made all this."

She reaches across her chair and kisses me on the cheek, sending a jolt down my spine. Her lips are warm and soft.

"What about you?"

"I was born in New York, my family moved to Florida when I was a kid. I got a bachelors at the University of Florida, Go Gators, and my masters at the University of Nevada. During grad school at UNR, I worked as a graduate assistant at NRI, got a job at a local consulting firm and then came back to NRI as an Assistant Research Scientist, at the urging of David who was an NRI scientist. David and I had worked together when the consulting firm hired NRI to perform some particle measurements. After a few years, I was promoted to Associate Research Scientist."

She nods contemplatively and eventually says,

"I'm struggling to accept that your research was worth three murders. The church has had to deal with scientific discoveries disputing religious doctrine as far back as Copernicus. They always find some way to spin new information to suit their doctrine."

"How many deaths do you think occurred before Copernicus's ideas were accepted and also during the evolution debate." I say rhetorically and then continue with,

"Marcus was concerned that there could be trouble. He has been studying religion as much as science lately. He went on in great depth how the religious faithful, not just zealots have been killing people over issues regarding their faith since the beginning of time and it has not really slowed all that much. He cited Muslims slaying any form of infidel including fellow Muslims and Iranians that would kill you if just disagree with them or showed any disrespect of the Koran. Of course, he had become something of an anti-religion zealot since 911."

We finished dinner, had a couple of small chocolate mousse cups I had experimented with last night, and returned to the fire with a couple of Irish Coffees. She said she had someone in the Reno office comparing a print of the picture of the man from the brewpub to mug shots. She also had a few items to run down and loose ends to check.

"Your Dr. Demyan can call Sheriff Taylor in a few days and he will either want to ask follow up questions or may be able to provide an overview of where he thinks the investigation is heading."

I leaned next to her and got within her personal space and quietly said,

"So with all the Marcus investigative work now on hold, I was hoping to investigate something else."

"And what might that be?"

I slowly moved my face into the crook of her neck and kissed her on the neck.

"The perfume you are wearing."

She reached over, placed a soft kiss on my lips, held her lips on mine for a long beat and said,

"I'm not wearing any."

We kissed passionately on the couch for a few minutes, and both broke it off, looking into each other's eyes both panting when the moment was interrupted by a horrible shrill coming from her purse. She fumbled for her phone and was able to answer before it went to voice mail. Looking at her watch and then apologetically at me she said,

"Hi, Nicole. Sorry I am on my way." A period of silence and then,

"No, I am just leaving." She hung up, stood and said,

"I'm sorry I have to go, I promised my sister I would babysit. She and her husband never get to go out, and when I told her I was staying over another night, it enabled them to attend a late party."

I stand and say,

"Sure, I need to go up and take an ice bath anyway."

"I wasn't going to sleep with you tonight."

I shuffle my feet and stare at the wood floor.

"Well sure, I mean, everybody knows that."

She smiles at me and says,

"You are pretty funny. But listen, I am too busy to start a new relationship right now."

That kiss on the couch told me she was interested in something.

"Well maybe we could keep it loose for now; you pop in

you pop out."

"Oh, sure every man's dream. I know all guys think they can have casual sex, even prefer it. However, once you have been with me, you are going to be buying me flowers and whimpering for me to come over every night."

"Been there before have you?"

"Twice, with big strong macho cops. A thoughtful intellectual like yourself won't stand a chance."

She could be right.

"I have an idea, let's try it once but you don't bring you're A-game, hold back a little, and I'll wear my big boy pants. Which of course I'll take off right away, well you know what I mean."

"So you want to turn me into one of your experiments?"

She walks to the door and then looks at me for a long time.

"Don't say I didn't warn you. Since I was staying in Reno, yesterday I scheduled a meeting on another case. I should be done by noon tomorrow and will be heading back to the lake. I'll come over here around 12:30 and, we'll see what happens. Save those leftovers."

"Excellent."

"Buy a box of tissues."

She leaned into me, gave me a long passionate kiss and was out the door. Am I in trouble? Nah I can do this.

Chapter 15

If I was coming home at noon, I needed to get in early to attend to one critical task and email a guy. I found David in his lab early the next morning, he says,

"You're in early, must have been an early night huh. You can't win them all."

"For your information, we shared a lovely evening."

"Lovely? I was unaware that adjective was in your vocabulary. Your self-stated sexual proclivities usually run along the lines of 'monkey nasty,' or 'incorporation of yoga poses' and the like."

"This woman is different."

"Yes, Ms. Rollings has a gun."

"Well she didn't pull it out last night and unfortunately neither did I, she was called away early."

"Don't women prearrange such calls?" he asks.

I didn't tell him about my upcoming nooner. I think about that for a moment.

"Maybe but not this time."

"I'm leaving at noon but will email the data to Adam before I go and will be back for the committee meeting."

"Why noon?

"Janis is coming back over for lunch."

"Now you are worrying me. No bravado or braggadocio, no strutting around like a peacock. Are you getting serious with her?"

"It's too early, but I like her."

"By the way, Chris at UNLV is now not sure he can ship us the meteorite."

"Was he expecting that we were going to use non-destructive testing techniques?"

"No I had told him that we were going to pulverize the rock and it would not be returning. His supervisor is questioning why a couple of air pollution guys need a meteorite. He pointed out that we really are interested in atmospheric science which includes atmospheric particles of which meteorites would be included. He also pointed out that their collection from the

Mohave site were all similar and one rock would not be missed. His supervisor was not placated but did not forbid him to send us one either."

"How did you leave it with him?"

"He is going to get back to me. Do you think Luther could have made a call?"

"Shit, probably. Get that rock! I'll see you this afternoon."

I sent my data to Adam and took off for home, I need to re-floss and brush my teeth. At 12:20 the doorbell rings, I check video from my doorbell camera and see Janis there in uniform. She is just so sexy. I open the door give her a smile and a jocular greeting,

"Hi, what's going down?"

"Your face in my lap."

"Oh my."

She deftly turns toward the front door, locks the deadbolt, grabs my hand and pulls me upstairs. I nudge her in the direction of the master bedroom. In the room, she places her hands on my face and puts a firm but soft kiss on my lips. After a minute, she slowly parts my lips with her tongue while caressing my back with her hands. She reaches down and feels for my erect penis and says,

"Thought so."

I try to say something, but there is an excess of tongues in my mouth. Janis nimbly pulls my shirt over my head, leaving my mouth at the very last minute then returning when the cloth just clears our mouths. Still kissing me, she begins working on my belt buckle, and my pants are undone without her ever looking. Backing away from me, both of us panting heavily, she pulls down my pants to my knees. She can't hide a small surprise in her face in the form of a tight smile when realizing there is a lack of underwear. She starts undressing while perusing my body from shoulders to toes.

"Nice abs for a scientist. Very considerate of you to save me time by going commando this morning."

"That's the kind of guy I am."

Then looking at my erection greeting her she says,

"I can work with this."

I feel a little insulted, but before I can complain, she

pushes me on the bed and finishes removing my jeans. I move up on the bed while engaged in studying her progressively naked body. She really has a perfect body. Caught like a 12-year-old looking at his first Playboy magazine, she spins around and says,

"What do you think? I don't have enough blood in my brain to form proper sentences, my mouth is making only grunts.

"Never mind, I know."

At this point, I'm just following tacit orders. With my head on the pillows, she stands on the bed, walks over to my face and crouches. In due course, she slides down my chest, breasts in my face and slides onto me. She rides up and down on me and before long, her body tenses and then slowly relaxes as she noisily climaxes. Gradually her quivering body slows to a gentle stop. She kisses me softly and then drops her head on my chest and goes totally limp. After a few minutes, she lifts her head, looks at me and says,

"Did you climax?"

Finally, my mouth once more is operating.

"Absolutely, it was magnificent."

"You hardly said or did anything."

"I came with you. I was just a little quieter, enjoying your response."

"That's a first, the cowboys I'm usually with like to holler and pay scant attention to what I'm doing. But it was good right?" I decide to test her sense of humor.

"You are about to find out when you get up."

I reach over for the tissues and hand her the box.

"Is this why you wanted me to get tissues?"

She smiles and laughs quietly and finally puts on a stern face and says,

"Sure you're a stud now but just wait."

"That was all very fast."

"That's the girl version of a quickie, we call it 'Slam fur thank you, sir.' "

"Well, there wasn't a lot of fur."

"You get the idea."

"Indeed I do, I liked it. Though, I wouldn't mind a little post-coital cuddling."

"Here we go. You are starting already."

She cleaned herself and then hopped in the shower.

If that was her B game, I'm a dead man. I place my forehead on the shower door, remove any sound of a whimper in my voice, and a little too deeply say,

"I'll warm up lunch."

She came down looking like she did when she arrived and we sat down to the leftovers.

"This pasta tastes even better than it did last night."

"The flavors have had the opportunity to meld overnight."

"Wonderful, and you even rewarmed the rolls." We ate rather quickly, as both of us had to get back to work.

"This was fun, last night was sweet. I need to go."

She gave me a big kiss and a long hug and was out the door. Damn, I did want to buy her flowers.

Chapter 16

After everyone is in the south conference room and settled, the termination meeting started at 1515. This first meeting would determine if there was cause to terminate David. If there were insufficient evidence, the process would end, and no further action would be taken. Should the committee rule that he be terminated for cause, then the committee would convene to make the final judgment that would include the original participants here today and the addition of the head of Human Resources and the President of the Institute. The President makes an individual determination to terminate after weighing recommendations from the committee. This process doesn't happen very often but everyone who has gone to the second stage has been terminated.

We all know each other so, there is no need for introductions. The three voting members are Alan, Dr. Richard Blake, and Dr. Melissa Wagner. David, Luther and I are only there to provide information and answer questions. Dr. Blake is an expert in gas chromatography. He provided significant assistance in our transport detection instruments. He has been involved in numerous field experiments, some of which involved David. Overall he is a reasonable person and should exhibit no bias.

On the other hand, Dr. Wagner, a particle expert, is not so reasonable. She is a hardnosed, tireless researcher that thinks everyone should work a 60-hour week. Not believed to be unrelated, she is unlovely and has almost no personal life. Any social life seems to be associated with University events or dinner with Luther's family. She has not worked directly with David or on my projects but has collaborated in numerous projects with Luther. A bias against David is almost a certainty. They only needed a majority vote to take the next step in the termination process. I do not like his chances.

As committee Chair, Alan begins with opening remarks.

"We are here to determine if there is sufficient information to continue with formal termination for cause proceedings of Dr. Piehl. Dr. Luther alleges five cases of incompetence. Mr. Stelzner is or has been the Principle Investigator or participated in some of the projects and will be heard where appropriate. Charles, please describe each complaint in turn and David, please respond to each in turn. Charles, please proceed."

Five projects is a surprise. David and I look at each other, we were aware of only three complaints. Luther begins while simultaneously handing out packets of information to the group.

"Over the last five years, there have been at least five projects that Piehl has been assigned to make specific measurements that have resulted in either zero useable data or data that has been judged as suspect. In chronological order, these projects are Denver Smog, San Joaquin Valley Air Quality, Mohave Study, Nevada Test Site Modeling Project, and the current Grand Canyon L.A. Signature Air Mass Study."

The two unexpected projects are the San Joaquin Valley and Nevada Test Site modeling project. We understood that the San Joaquin Valley study was a complete success. I managed the Nevada Test site project, hence I am certain it was a success.

Luther continues,

"Let's take them in chronological order, shall we. I draw your attention to packet one." There is a shuffling of papers, and then he continues.

"Piehl was funded to set up and deploy two sulfur analyzers as part of the intensive smog study. He deployed instruments in the field, they did not work as advertised and no useable data were collected. You have before you, the scope of work and detail breakdown of the budget. No data were collected; thus there are no data to provide you. "

Of course this last part, regarding the lack of data, is said for emphasis, well played. Luther was the Principle Investigator, I was not directly involved in the project but was helping David with aspects of the development of the instrument. Unfortunately, I was not present when Luther asked David to participate in the project. Back then we had not learned to cover our asses in paper, thus there is no email trail. Alan looks from Luther to David and says,

"David."

"Charles, you have conveniently left out the part of our conversation where I warned you that the low sulfur instruments were experimental and that the two instruments had never been field tested. They worked fine in the lab, but they had only been operational for two weeks. You also failed to mention that you told me it was worth the risk of failure because my part would be only a very small portion of the overall budget, but if we could acquire the low concentration data it would be important information."

Luther erupted,

"You said the instruments would work. Yes, the data were important; it's a shame none were obtained."

David turned to Blake and Wagner,

"Look, there is no dispute here regarding the lack of usable data collected during the January intensive experiment. The units were deployed in remote mountain locations in 6 m of snow. It took a guided snowcat to deploy them. I had essentially one shot at getting them up and running, it was too expensive to return to the sites to verify their operation until after the intensive period. The power service at the distant field sites was limited, and both units popped a breaker after less than a day of operation. These units were deployed the following summer at field sites with proper power and worked well and without failure."

"It's a simple case of you obtaining funds to make a measurement, and you failed, just like the committee will see in the next four projects.", cried, Luther.

"Charles please state your problem with the next project." Alan interrupts to limit the contentious back and forth between the two.

"The next project was another one of mine we conducted in the San Joaquin Valley. Again Piehl setup a specialized instrument, we deployed three of them, they seem to work fine, but once we incorporated those data with values from our other instruments, it was determined that his data were anomalous."

All eyes turn to David who is flipping through the material. He looks up at everyone staring at him and says,

"I was not given a file for the San Joaquin Valley Study." Luther looks at him and offers a prevaricating statement,

"Oh, since it was your data I didn't think you would need a copy." David turns to me and gives me a wry smile. I say.

"If that were the case why did you give him any information, all the projects involve his data." I don't add, 'you vomitus mass.' I look at Blake and Wagner. Both have their heads down reviewing their information. They didn't get it or choose to ignore the interaction. Alan clearly sees that this is theatrics but remains silent. Ignoring my comment Luther smoothly says,

"It's fine, I have an extra copy." Luther slides a file across the table. Staring down at the 20 pages of information David says,

"This project is at least four years old, I certainly don't remember many of the details. The instruments were fabricated in my lab using proven principles that had been used in commercial units. My instruments were tweaked to improve the detection limits. They worked flawlessly in the lab, I was not involved in the deployment or operation in the field. Until today I was unaware of any problems either during the field study or during the data validation and reporting."

Dr. Blake turns to Luther and says,

"Charles why was this not brought to David's attention during the data analysis phase of the project?"

"We needed to meet a final report deadline. I just scrapped the numbers, there was no more time to spend on specious data. We reported our results, published a couple of papers and moved on to the next project. I hope all of you are noticing a pattern here. According to Piehl his instruments supposedly work in the lab but then not in the field. It is in the field where we need the data."

I can tell that David is cool on the outside but boiling beneath the surface. He says,

"According to *you* the instruments didn't work in the field." David says with emphasis and then continues,

"It is an incompetent Principle Investigator who waits until writing the report to evaluate whether instruments were working properly. Your students were trained by me to interrogate the instruments throughout the study. Numerous quality control checks were designed to alert the user of any problems. None of them came to me with any questions or problems so they must have believed the instruments were performing as designed."

"You can make all the excuses you want, but data from your instruments were obviously inconsistent with multiple other parameters. The analyses are in front of you. See for yourself."

Wagner asks David a series of technical questions, all are reasonable, and then Blake has a few of his own. When it appeared they were finished, Alan keeps us moving.

"Next project Charles."

"The Mohave study is very similar to the San Joaquin Valley issue. Piehl set up two ozone instruments, off-the-self-commercial units this time, and trained our technician how to use them. Although the values all looked reasonable on their own when compared to similar data collected at or near the same site, it was clear that his data were anomalous."

Even though the collocated instruments measure parameters other than ozone, data from certain instruments may be expected to rise, when ozone increases and others may decrease. These inter-parameter quality control checks were cause for concern. We made some assumptions, one being that he improperly calibrated the units before they were deployed in the field. We performed post field calibrations, used those calibration values to rescale the data, and reported the numbers. This issue, taken alone, seems minor but when combined with all these other failures, it shows a pattern of incompetence."

I create an uncomfortable mood in the room by saying,

"If there is a pattern of incompetence, it's due to you as the manager for these projects."

"Not quite smart ass, you were the Principle Investigator for the next two."

Again Alan attempts to bring order and says,

"Let's eliminate these personal attacks and get through this. Charles, the next project."

"I was in a bidder's conference with EPA last month regarding one of their Request for Proposal notifications. My contact advised me that I might not stand a good chance on the proposal because he had heard that the data collected at the

Nevada Test site were not fitting well with a new dense gas dispersion model the oil companies were developing."

I interrupt with,

"There's a shock, a modeler stating measured data are flawed because the model prediction doesn't match his results."

That got a chuckle out of Blake while Luther and Wagner remained stoic. Numeric models are basically computer programs that attempt to predict downwind concentrations of a given gas or particle based on meteorological data and the known upstream concentration of gas or particle. Of course, if there is a discrepancy 'the model can't be wrong.'

"The bottom line is that David ran the experiment out at the site, and the data reported from his efforts are now being questioned by EPA to the point that I had to pass on a proposal." I forcefully respond,

"David led the field experiment, but as Principle Investigator, I was responsible for everything that occurred out there as well as data acquisition, validation, and reporting. Our EPA supervisor oversaw the entire experiment and was pleased and impressed with the results. The project was a complete success, and I have not been told of any complaints from EPA."

Luther starts handing out copies of a single, handwritten sheet of paper and says,

"Here is a copy of my notes from the telephone conversation and contact information for my EPA Program Manager."

Alan reviews the sheet and says,

"Charles, let's have the final alleged issue."

"Finally we come to an ongoing project run by Mr. Stelzner. Piehl professed to have invented a technique that would be able to distinguish a Los Angeles air plume as far away as the Grand Canyon. He has generated a lot of attention with his claim, and Grant here has obtained a large contract to deploy these instruments. Unfortunately, like the other projects just discussed, it appears they don't work in the field. This project will bring sizeable negative attention to this Institute."

I don't let David speak.

"Again, as the lead investigator for this project, I'm responsible for every aspect of this study, including these measurements. I am investigating the inconsistency in the Sierra values and believe the issue will be resolved soon. Since this is an active project, its inclusion for your evaluation is inappropriate."

"Nonsense! You have nothing to investigate. His instruments don't work, again! Case closed!"

"Unlike you Charles, I know how to manage projects. We catch potential problems when they occur not when writing the final report. So if you don't mind, I'm investigating the problem, and I will resolve it within the next week."

Staring at Blake and Wagner, I say,

"Look, you do what you want, but if you recommend termination of this guy based on this project and we resolve the issue favorably, you are going to appear foolish."

Alan intervenes again and says,

"Very well, I think we have what we need to make a decision. We are going to deliberate for as long as it takes. I will come to talk to you David, either when we finish today or first thing on Monday. We also will provide everyone here with our written finding."

With that David and I push back our chairs and exit the conference room. While walking back to our offices, David appears pensive and says,

"I appreciate your support in there, but if you weren't before, you now are Luther's enemy. His Rank 4 status affords him more power than we have as Rank 3's. I'm concerned that you will be taken down with me. You would be better off staying out of the negative limelight."

"Everything in there was fallacious and distortion from reality. I can't just ignore his comments."

"Well, thanks. I certainly share your view, but I think they have me. Certainly, they will vote to terminate, and even if we resolve the Sierra background issue, it may not be enough for the President to overturn their decision."

"We need to go to the site and unravel what is going on out there. We must go first thing on Monday! There is a major storm developing for Tuesday."

"Agreed."

Since it is after five, David and I work on our meteorite particles in my lab. Approximately 30 minutes after we left the committee meeting, Alan pokes his head through the door and says,

"David can I have a word with you?"

"Come in Alan. You can talk in front of Grant. I'm just going to turn around and tell him what you are about to tell me." He sighs and steps into the lab allowing the door to close behind him.

"The vote was to take the next step and allow the President to make the final decision. I made a motion for the Denver Smog Project, and the current L.A. Signature Air Mass Study, be withdrawn from consideration. We all agreed to drop the Denver study. It seemed clear the problem was due to the power failure which was the responsibility of Charles, and I told the other two that I had recalled you warning Charles that the instruments may not be ready. However, Blake and Wagner voted to leave the L.A. Signature issue as part of the complaint as it has given the Institute positive publicity. If it is later revealed to be a failure, the negative notoriety will hurt us. If you can resolve the problem that will only leave two complaints that seem weak to me, and the President is likely to vote against termination."

Alan pauses to scan our bleak expressions and adds a final comment as he walks to the door.

"So get busy and resolve these false positives at the Sierra Site."

Chapter 17

I arrive at my house with a brain strain and tension in my neck. Picking up the mail from my mailbox, I can't decide whether to go for a run or make a stiff cocktail. I go through the garage door leading to the kitchen flipping through the envelopes and newspaper type ads. Using the light from the city, I place my backpack at the base of the stairs to bring up to the master bedroom once I get a glass of water. Living alone, no pets, I've acclimated to the quiet and stillness of an empty house. At this time I am registering an untoward feeling that I can't readily identify, and my subconscious has engaged my sensors into anxiety mode. My dull front brain registers a massive dark mass rise from my couch in the living room, and finally, the impetus for my pounding heart is identified.

I flip on the kitchen light as a huge man in a large cowboy hat slowly moves from the darkness into the light. My flight mode is fully engaged, but for some reason, I can't move my feet. I want to ask him what the hell he is doing in my house, but the terror I'm feeling has paralyzed my vocal cords. He steps up within a few feet of me, my eye level even with his chest, and breaks the noise of my pounding chest by saying,

"I'm sure my uninvited visit has jacked up your nerves. If

you don't do anything stupid and listen attentively, I will leave shortly, and you will survive the night."

I'm still trying to calm myself before having a heart attack and don't move or say anything.

"Good. It has come to my attention that you and your colleagues have engaged in activities that fall within God's domain. Our concern is that just because you may be able to reproduce God's actions, you, of course, are not God. You are not a prophet; you do not speak to God. Based on our observations you and your colleagues are in fact Godless. The worst of you, Mr. Kieslar, has paid for his Godlessness. I would advise you to avoid a similar fate."

"Our concern is that your activities could be misunderstood by faithful Christians. Therefore, we believe it is in the best interest of all concerned that you cease these Genesis experiments. After all, God has brought us this far, nothing is served by your activities other than to confuse good faithful Christians."

Still mostly terrified, anger also is being added to the mix, I say my first words.

"Please leave my house."

The giant cowboy, who I surmise is acting on behalf of the Living Word Church, slowly closes the gap between us even further. It would hurt my neck to try to look him in the eye, so I look toward the living room. He says with significant menace,

"Think hard about what I have told you."

Thankfully, he backs up without turning around and then turns for the front door. As the front door closes, I quickly walk to it, turn the deadbolt and set the alarm, albeit a little late. Definitely going with the drink over a run. I make myself an extra-large cocktail and start thinking about how the behemoth got into my house.

"Hello," David says answering his home land-line, the only person I know who still has one.

"So I had someone waiting in my house when I got home tonight."

"In your house, that sounds ominous, anyone I know?"

"Doubtful, I don't know him. A Gigantor, not the guy in the bar nor my follower. Ostensibly he was here to represent Christians. He did not claim to represent any group, but he wore cowboy boots and a big ass cowboy hat."

"Indoors, how rude."

"I know, right?"

"So you are thinking Rock of the Whatever?"

"That's my guess."

"Given their previous attempts, I wonder why he did not arrange for you to have a home 'accident.'"

"I know, I thought he had me. I was frozen just a few steps out of the kitchen and kept calculating how fast I could get to a knife."

"Have you ever stabbed anyone?"

"No."

"Me either, but a guy that big probably would have defended whatever you tried. It sounds like you handled yourself as well as possible under the circumstances."

"Why, because I didn't piss myself?"

"Oh, we both know your underwear has a wet spot right now. So no, what I mean is you remain alive, therefore you did everything right. How did he get in? I thought you had that fancy alarm system."

"He broke in through a side window. The windows aren't alarmed, they are not at ground level. He probably reached around the upper deck railing. In any case, it would not have mattered since I hadn't set the alarm this morning."

"May I assume you now will set it every morning?"

"You may."

"And the windows."

"I've already left a message with the alarm company. You need to watch your back as well. Is Liz still at Barbara's?"

"No she is here tonight, but after hearing this, I'm going to send her back tomorrow. Should you call Janis?"

"I've thought about it. It's a Friday night, she will think I'm calling her for a date."

"Seriously. That will stop you from calling her?"

"No. She will want me to call Reno PD, and I'll be tied up all night, and they won't find anything. He was wearing gloves the entire time. I noticed both my neighbors' houses are dark so they will not have seen anything. You should remain vigilant, it's not out of the question they may visit you as well."

"I'll be careful."

"By the way, I forgot to tell you, Angela called to check in today. I told her we were going to the Sierra site on Monday to see what was going on out there, she was pleased. Talk to you later."

"Good night."

I head to the bar for another drink trying to shake off the cowboy's threats. Thoughts of past conversations with Marcus intrude...

"If you discuss the Mormon faith with some southern Baptist on how ol' Joe Smith put his face in a hat filled with rocks to get messages from Jesus, they will admit how ridiculous it is and mock the idea as strongly as any atheist. If you discuss with them the view of the Hualapai tribe that their people first originated from reeds along a river orchestrated by their 'Creator,' they laugh at such primitive thinking. But if you bring up life originating from the rib of Adam, that's believable.

If you tell a Catholic or Baptist, etc., you are an atheist, they will side with Mormons over an atheist even though they firmly believe the Mormons claim to be able to communicate with Jesus is ridiculous. It is this phenomenon that allows them to act as a large unit. This is how you get the statistic thrown around that '95% of all people believe in God' and politicians pander to the people of faith. Except for Muslim fundamentalists, as long as you believe in something called God, you are better received than an atheist. It doesn't matter if it's a 'Creator' or 'Ra' or if you can talk to God's son through a hat full of rocks.

Only Muslim fundamentalists have the commitment to lump Catholics and Jews with atheists in their hate."

Marcus, a proud atheist, is, was, a devotee of Richard Dawkins. His copy of Dawkins' bestselling book 'The God Delusion' is well thumbed, and if allowed, he would discuss its virtues for hours. He had purchased many copies of the book so that it could be readily handed out to any fence sitters who he believed he could convert. Marcus, like Dawkins, concluded that there are many more atheists out there than are reported. Marcus felt negative connotations of the term kept atheists silent regarding their belief and therefore were not counted.

I'm snapped out of my daydream by my phone ringing. Seeing the caller ID, I feel a rush of excitement flow through my body.

Chapter 18

"Hello."

"Hi, Grant this is Janis."

"How are you?"

"Good. I'm at Squaw Valley attending a conference this weekend. I was wondering if you would be interested in coming up tomorrow. You could ski while I'm in meetings and we could both ski Sunday."

"I am interested."

"I've got a suite at the resort."

"Very interested."

"Good there is a fold-out couch in the living room."

"Less interested." An extended silence makes me nervous, so I add,

"Just kidding, I'd love to ski tomorrow."

"Watch yourself buster, I'm here at this resort which is filled with of cops. A few of them are chasing me relentlessly. If they learn that I chose you over them, they will want to take you out to the woods and make some red snow."

"They will have to get in line."

"Why what happened?"

"I'll tell you tomorrow."

"If you say so. I'll leave you a key at the desk, room 616. I'm out at 4:00 and that's when the lifts close."

"Sounds great. I'll see you at 4:00."

I need to tell David I will be out of town.

"Hello.", answers David.

"Hey, I wanted to let you know I'm headed up to Squaw Valley tomorrow so don't worry about me."

"I thought you were working this weekend."

"Change of plans, Janis just invited me up to Squaw to stay with her."

"Oh and you didn't call to brag, you just didn't want me to worry."

"Yes, of course, I'm not sure I'll have cell service there."

"Thank you, very considerate."

"That's me. Of course, I won't mention how extra safe I'll feel lying naked next to a gorgeous deputy sheriff."

"And there it is."

As my half day of skiing comes to a close, it has been a perfect day, blue sky, no wind, cold enough to preserve the snow while allowing a comfortable body temperature with proper ski attire. New snow had dropped yesterday resulting in tree branches heavy with thick powder and an undisturbed white flooring meandering its way through the woods. I end the last run around 3:45 and not a minute too soon, my quads are burning. The trail brings me back to the resort very close to an outside bar/lunch patio with fire pits and a musician playing guitar. I ski up to the steps leading to the patio, remove my poles, skis and unlatch my boots. As I check my skis with the outside valet, I see Janis walking over to me with a couple of drinks in her hand, and she says,

"Hey, we finished our meeting early so, I have been hanging out by the fire, listening to music. I caught you coming down the hill there, nice form."

Looking at her I thought nice form indeed. She hands me

the unbidden gin and tonic and takes a sip from her scotch.

"Sweet, you remembered. First a perfect afternoon on the slopes and now a greeting from a stunning woman holding drinks."

"I'm not finished yet." She leans into me and gives me a long soft kiss.

She guides me over to where she was sitting near a fire pit, and I notice a group of large guys at the bar staring at us; doubtless, her crime-fighting colleagues. It seems each is sizing me up and finding me unworthy. She sees me looking at the bar.

"Oh yeah, those guys asked what kind of pussy drinks gin and tonic."

"Did you tell them someone who is completely comfortable with his masculinity?"

She smiles and says,

"Something like that." I bet those Neanderthals are all scotch drinkers. It's sexy on her though.

I asked her about her conference, and we make light conversation, listen to music, consume hors d'oeuvres and order another round of drinks as darkness pushes out the remaining light.

Janis asks, "Are you starving or can we go for a swim before dinner?

"A swim sounds good and maybe sit in the hot tub."

"Let's go."

We walk up to the lobby of her building and take an elevator to her 6th-floor suite. As we enter the suite, it's nicely appointed with a fireplace and a large bay window overlooking Olympic valley. There is a small kitchen, but it has all the essentials. A separate bedroom and really nice bathroom.

"Man, this is beautiful."

"Definitely, but I had to upgrade to this room on my own dime. You haven't been up here yet?"

"Well done. No, I picked up the key and left a bag with the bellhop. I wanted to get right on the mountain."

Just then there was a knock on the door, the bellhop. I had asked the ski valet to have my bag sent to the room. I tip the guy and receive my bag. We change into bathing suits and flip flops. She in the bathroom with the door closed and I'm in the living room. Given our last encounter, the level of modesty is a bit of a disappointment. She comes out wearing a robe provided in the room and hands me one. Exiting the room and entering the elevator, the descent to the lobby has that familiar awkward feeling where she looks up at the ceiling, and I suddenly am captivated with the carpet. What is it with elevators? We exit the lobby and are hit with the cold night air and look at each other with tacit concern that our robes may be insufficient to stave off the 20-degree temperature.

The pool area is spectacular with a waterfall running down from the third story lobby. At night, the series of pools and hot tubs embedded in walls of snow presents an eerie sight as columns of steam rise into the darkness. At the pool edge, Janis looks at me with an expression that questions if the water is warm enough and perhaps we should head straight to the hot tubs. First dipping in her toes, she removes her robe indicating a commitment to entering the pool. I pause to revel in her beautiful body barely covered by a bikini. I'm just going to say it if she is going in so am I, no matter the temperature. Placing her robe on a pool chair, dauntless, she eases in and then submerges completely. I follow after her.

"Oh my God!" She exclaims.

After we swim around and become acclimated, it's comparable to entering a pool in the summer where it feels cold at first, but then you get used to it. However here, surrounded by snow, the steam, and cold ambient air, the water seems colder.

We swim around aimlessly. After a few minutes, I roll on my back staying afloat by gently treading water with my hands and arms.

With my head floating just above the surface, through the steam, I see a bright crescent moon with Venus just below it; the centerpiece of a star-studded display.

Two hands gently grab the bottom of my floating head, slowly pulling my floating body along the surface of the pool. I'm drawn to a distant, dark corner of the pool and my legs drop to the pool floor. Janis rolls around and sits on my lap while I hold us up in a crouched position my back up against the wall. Submerged to our necks, I am forming sort of a chair. Janis presses her full breasts against my bare chest and places her soft full lips on mine. Slowly our lips part slightly, and warm tongues meet softly, extremely stimulating. Interesting, kissing her in this position is generating excess heat that offsets any feeling of cold water.

She pulls back a few inches from my face, stares into my eyes and forms a smile rich with mischief. With small short kisses, she moves along my neck up to an ear, caresses it with her lips and slowly laps it with her warm tongue. Of course I'm already as hard as Chinese calculus, and she is gradually dry humping me, or in this case wet humping as it were, riding back and forth over our suits. I look over her shoulder and don't see the other couple that had been at the opposite end of the kidney-shaped pool. The turn in the pool and rising steam would hide us in any event.

She reaches down to my lap and grabs my very stiff member. She says,

"Jesus, I thought these things got smaller in the water."

I say coyly, "It has baby." Her whole body shakes with laughter.

She looks over her shoulder, seeing no one, her hands find the fly in the front of my suit. Her fingers deftly navigate to my erection, and with a soft, smooth motion she pulls me through the opening. Apparently, her other hand pulled her bikini bottom to one side because in one fluid motion she shifts her body and guides me to her opening. I slide in effortlessly. Somehow I still have the wherewithal to glance over her shoulder for any new swimmers, not knowing what I would do if I saw someone. Well, I'm pretty sure I would ignore them. She places her mouth back on mine and begins a slow rhythmic motion. Within a few minutes, her arms are wrapped tighter around me and with her cheek next to mine, I can hear quiet moans and then a building climax. This arrives at a propitious moment as I am hanging on for dear life. Feeling her release, I react in kind, and we finish together.

After several minutes of a warm, tight embrace, my legs begin to tremble. I crab walk the both of us around the edge of the pool, still holding each other with me still inside her. She leans back on the surface of the water with her arms floating above her head. Staring up into space and remarks,

"Wow, I'm seeing stars for the second time tonight."

After a while, we return our parts to their respective bathing suits and plan an exit from the pool, which seems to be rapidly cooling. We quickly move with considerable interest to an empty hot tub and are greeted with shocking, but welcome hot bubbling water. After a long period of blissful silence looking at the stars, Janis says,

"I'm hungry, but I'm not sure I can walk to the room. My legs feel like jello, and I'm not sure my heart can take the cold walk back to our room."

"I know. I'm still waiting for blood to reenter my brain."

After another 5 minutes or so I say,

"Listen, our towels and robes are right there on the chair. We just need to step out, quickly dry off and put on our robes. Are you ready?"

"I guess."

"On the count of three, we go. "3, 2, 1 go."

I move to the stairs, make it out of the water, but notice she is not behind me. Looking back I see her still submerged to her neck laughing. I reenter and say,

"What the Hell!"

"I can't."

I return to the spa and resubmerge into the hot water.

"So, I'm going to get out first, dry off, and put on my robe. Then I will have your towel ready and dry you off right as you exit, then help you with your robe. Your body will sustain its heat even in the cold air. Remember, I've been trained in thermodynamics."

This gets her out of the water. We remove our suits under our robes, and the walk back is surprisingly comfortable. Once in the room, privacy is no longer an issue. Janis removes her robe, and I see her for the first time tonight naked. Grant junior instantly comes to attention. Her back turned to me she says let's take a shower and steps in and starts the water. Junior, in all his splendor, enters the shower first as I follow. She now sees my condition and says,

"Are you kidding? You are ready again? We are never going to get anything to eat."

Chapter 19

We finally make it to one of the on-site restaurants shortly before closing. She looks incredibly beautiful, but thankfully little Grant appears to be in a coma, hence there is no physical reaction just an emotional one, Uh oh. We order two draft beers and peruse the menu. After ordering, Janis asks me about my previous veiled comment about people wanting to beat the crap out of me. The nice thing about being totally, if only temporarily, sexually sated is you can finally concentrate on other things.

I told her about my visitor, and she was agitated. She said she would talk to Reno PD about having someone watch my house and follow me to work. We talk about her end of the investigation regarding fingerprints and interviews with Institute personnel, particularly Luther. Our meal arrives, along with a bottle of chardonnay, and we decide to pause talking of the case and fill in some blanks that we had with each other's personal history. After an excellent dinner, we return to the room and crash into each other's arms.

The following morning I partially wake up with Janis playing with my erect penis. Usually, that would be a good thing. However, I need to pee. I excuse myself and sleepily head to the bathroom. It's not easy to urinate with an erection, but I battle it and stumble back to bed. Outside it's still dark.

"You know, I didn't cause your erection, it woke me up by poking me."

"Yeah, it does that."

"Why?"

"Oh, it's some sort of auto maintenance systems check. Totally out of my control."

"That is a blatant fabrication."

"No, see it's over now. I'm in total control."

"That's what you think."

She slides down and takes me in her mouth. Within a few minutes, her statement was confirmed, I was not in control. Of course after finishing I pass out. About a half an hour later I wake and see Janis is just starting to stir. She asks,

"There is something I could never understand. Why is it that men become unconscious after sex?"

"Based on my own research, in general, men are

genetically programmed to wake up with only one objective, to procreate. Everything that happens in between, work, golf, whatever, is just killing time. Immediately after sex, our bodies sense that the objective has been met and shuts down. After a sufficient resting period, the cycle begins anew."

"How long does it take for the cycle to begin again?"

"It is directly proportional to our age. Unofficially, in minutes, it's one's age divided by 500, then this number times the age squared."

"You are making this up."

"You might have missed this when we met, but I am a scientist."

She reaches for her phone, navigates to her calculator and checks the math.

"So a 16-year-old can go again in 8 minutes. That seems right, how old are you?"

"34"

She enters the data.

"So subtracting 30 minutes that you were asleep, you

can go again in 49 minutes?"

"Give or take."

She climbs on top of me and places her breasts in my face.

"Forget that, I'm hungry, we need to head down for breakfast before going skiing." With her naked body writhing on top of me, I'm ready, and she slides back, meeting resistance. A slight adjustment with her hips and she rides slowly for a time and then grabs me, and we roll 180 degrees with me now on top, and she says,

"You drive for a while."

"If you insist."

She takes a little longer to climax than previous encounters, and there is much more tenderness involved. Finally, she climaxes for what seems like a very long time. I follow a few minutes later and drop on top of her.

"So much for your calculations." She says.

"Well, I'm still fine tuning the equation," I say with heavy breath.

Then with large gaps between words, I manage to say.

"The logic is sound I just need to add a negative coefficient to the equation that considers the hotness of your partner. I'm going to call it the Janis factor."

Panting she laughs and then whispers in my ear,

"You say the sweetest things."

We enter the shower together and wash each other. I wash her hair using my fingernails to work into her scalp. This causes her feet to get wobbly. I sit on a short ledge at one end of the tub/shower and position her so she is sitting on my lap and I resume working my fingers through her hair. She hands me the removable shower head, and I rinse her hair and body. When finished I say,

"You're done, hop out and dry off. Then I'll rinse off and join you." Leaning back on my chest she mumbles,

"I can't move."

I help her to her feet and then out of the tub. Seeing she is stable I rinse entirely and shut off the water and say,

"Woman you better find some strength in those legs if

you want to ski today."

"I'll cowgirl up in a minute, I'm just so relaxed."

We dress in our ski underwear. While I put on some jeans, she plans to wear her tights to breakfast. With our coats on, we head outside the lobby through an outside breezeway to the restaurant. I tell her,

"I am in serious need of some coffee."

"You read my mind. But I'm ready for some serious food as well."

We are seated at a table by the window overlooking the top of the waterfall that was running by the hot tubs last night. After downing our first cups, we head to the omelet maker and pick up some bacon and sausage while we wait. Back at the table, I say,

"So your sessions start at 2:00 this afternoon and end at 8:00 tonight?"

"Correct. Then we end at noon on Monday. Can you stay over tonight?"

"I wish I could. David and I need to be at a Sierra site

trailhead by sun up. Accordingly, I need to meet at the office an hour before then. We have collected some weird data from there, and if we don't determine the origin of the problem, David will be terminated, and I won't be far behind him."

"While I was waiting for you yesterday I called Reno PD. They are shorthanded and can provide some surveillance help, but we are going to have some large gaps. So I have enlisted the services of a Reno private detective."

"Hey, I'm just a state employee how much would that cost?"

"You're in luck, this guy likes me so is willing to work cheap." I had just taken a big bite of my omelet and had to finish it before responding.

"What do you mean he likes you? I would rather defend myself."

"See what I told you, there you go getting all jealous."

"Well no, I was just worried about the cost."

"Your sad puppy dog face tells a different story. Relax, he is my brother. He just got his PI license and is working this job for me Pro Bono to get experience."

"Oh, that's great," I say and then quickly become interested in my breakfast. I sneak a look at her, and she is doing that laugh with her eyes, and I say,

"Shut up I'm fine."

"Whatever you say, tough guy."

We finish an excellent breakfast and head back to the room. Despite all of Janis's show of being aloof and accusing me of falling for her, I notice she has become very affectionate. Always grabbing my hand, putting her head on my shoulder, pulling me in for a kiss. I'm getting the feeling she is not the emotionally aloof woman she pretends to be.

We get to the room and put on our snow pants, helmets, and ski boots, only partially fastened to make walking easier. We had called down to have our skis brought out to the valet, and when we arrived, they were waiting for us. I ask,

"So how good of a skier are you?"

"I can hold my own. I've been skiing since I was 7. How about you?"

"Well, I grew up in Florida. I water skied and surfed, but this is different. I've been skiing for 10 years and mostly like to hang out on the blue terrain. I can ski the single black diamond runs well enough, but struggle with moguls when it's steep. And of course, I've skied the Chutes, I'm pretty badass."

"Ha-ha right. I have skied every run on this mountain including the rocks under the Tram, but at age 20, the blue and single black diamonds are fine with me."

With that, we were off to the chairlift. Today was just as beautiful as yesterday, cold enough to keep the snow nice, the lack of wind and sunny blue skies making it very comfortable. The Squaw Valley resort is a fun ski area, lots of varied runs, plenty of open terrain and a state of the art gondola, cable car, and lifts. Janis and I skied well together, she has much better form than I, but I don't seem to be holding her back very much. She says,

"This day went by so fast. I need to head back to the Squaw Creek Mountain runs so I can change and get to my first session by 2:00." We are at the top of High Camp and need to ski all the way down to the base. From there we will take a lift back up Squaw Creek Mountain and ski back to the resort.

"So do you want to race down to the chair lift?"

"Sure old man."

"That really hurts. You better fix your ski pole; it's all tangled." I pretend to straighten it, but quickly remove it from her wrist and throw it behind us and say,

"See you at the lift." and take off down the hill. I can hear her yell,

"You shit!"

I head down the trail as fast as I can while remaining in control and not running into anyone. I want to look behind me, but it will cost me speed, so I just concentrate on making efficient, safe turns. There are a couple of run choices that branch off on the way down, but I don't see her taking any of them out of my peripheral vision. Coming up is a hard choice on which path to take. I choose the one with fewer people. While concentrating on making smooth, efficient turns without giving up any speed, I hear a loud smack sound followed by a stinging pain on my ass. Then comes the unhappy conclusion as I see Janis fly by me. She just smacked my ass with her ski pole and was pulling away from me down the hill at high speed. Nothing to do now, but cease making cuts and let my skies stay straight downhill.

I swing way wide left of her and make a half tuck, my skies begin to chatter, but there is no one in front of me, so I let it fly. She makes a mistake and turns slightly to her right to look for me behind her. I'm in her blind spot and pulling away. Now she straightens up and can see me just ahead of her. She plots a straight course and tucks slightly to catch me. One problem, we are approaching the base of the hill with multiple runs all funneling together. We must slow down to avoid the crowd. I turn left, and she turns right.

I realize my mistake. I'm heading straight for a hill, and she is going to miss it by staying high right. I come to a slow halt needing to use my poles to keep going as she flies toward the chair lift. I crawl up the hill and then ski down to the lift as she mockingly acts bored. We both enter the gate and get on a chair together, and she says,

"Cheaters never prosper."

"Who are you, Gomer Pyle?"

"Who?"

"Never mind. I needed a head start. I'm five years older and grew up in Florida."

"Poor baby. What do I get for winning?" I whisper in her ear through her helmet as others are on the chair.

"Deal!", and she shakes my hand to seal the arrangement.

Our skis hit the ground, we push off the chair and start down our last run to the resort. At the bottom, we check our equipment with the valet and head to the room. Janis says,

"I'm running late. I'm going to get in the shower and change."

"Go ahead, I'll shower at home, I'm just going to change out of my ski clothes."

With Janis out of the shower and dressed, I have my things pulled together in one bag. I grab my boot bag, and we head down to the lobby. She needs to walk to her meeting, and I will traverse to the valet for my car and skis. Janis wraps her arms around me, stares into my eyes and says,

"I wish you were staying tonight."

"You're not going to get sloppy on me are you?"

"Maybe."

"Get out of here before you make a spectacle of yourself." She reaches up and whispers in my ear,

"This strong man façade is fooling no one. Good luck getting me out of your mind on the drive to Reno." She kisses me, gives me a lascivious smile and starts to walk to her meeting. Yeah, this is going to be rough. After a few steps, she turns and says,

"Oh, I will let you know when the surveillance begins and will send you a picture of my brother, so you know what he looks like." Then she turned down a hallway and was gone.

Chapter 20

I arrive at the Institute and am surprised to see Angela working on a laptop in the lobby.

"Angela, what are you doing here so early?" She lifts up a suitcase sitting on the floor.

"David calibrated my flowmeter last week. I'm flying to L.A. this morning to work at our power plant today. My staff is getting some weird flow rates. I hope this meter will help find some answers."

She resumes keyboarding her laptop.

"I'm checking my flight status. Currently it's on time. Are you guys hiking to the site this morning?"

"Yes, we want to be at the trailhead at first light."

"Good. I don't need to tell you how critical it is to figure out what is going on out there. Maybe you'll find an easy explanation like the calibration system leaking during ambient sampling or something. I talked to Alan about the termination meeting results, it looks bleak for David."

"Yes, this issue is important for both reasons. I'm certain

we will resolve the problem at this site. That, in turn, will remove their strongest complaint. The other incidents really are unworthy."

She closes her laptop and says,

"Well, I better get to the airport. Good luck to you guys."

"Thanks, we'll let you know how it goes."

She exits the building, and I head to my lab. Shortly thereafter, David arrives in the lab.

"Good Morning, the storm is now supposed to arrive early afternoon."

My response is,

"You have to love modelers. Since they first predicted this storm would arrive tomorrow maybe they have it wrong, and it will arrive late."

"More likely it will arrive even earlier, let's get out of here."

I grab the GPS from the shelf, install fresh batteries, turn it on to verify that it works, and then turn off the unit. David packs the data download equipment and various electronic calibration gear used to interrogate the samplers. We both pull snowshoes, poles, and backpacks. Just in case, and as a matter of course, we pack the survival gear. Our ski pants, gloves, etc., are moved from our respective cars to the NRI SUV.

With all our gear loaded I volunteer to drive and we make our way to I-80 west. Our destination is the trailhead to the monitoring site which is located in the Sierra Nevada mountain range near Cisco California. The location is in the vicinity of Monumental Ridge. As we pass Truckee California, David peers at the horizon and says,

"That looks nasty. I hope it is slow moving." He holds up a thermos and asks if I would like more coffee. I hand him my cup and say,

"Yes, please. Oh, I forgot to mention that Angela picked up her calibration kit this morning."

"You ran into her? Why so early?"

"She is catching the early flight to L.A. She already has talked to Alan about the termination meeting."

"That was fast."

"She is playing it cool, but I can tell there is a real concern there."

We mostly remain quiet on the way to Cisco. At the trailhead, we put on all our snow clothes and load up our gear into backpacks then put on snowshoes. The snow is thick, but firm so the snowshoeing is not very difficult. With the sun still more dominant than the clouds we don't need the GPS to navigate to the site, we are very familiar with the trail. It is about 4 miles from the trailhead in a small opening surrounded by dense woods in either direction. There is a 6-mile long dirt road that is accessible via a 4-wheel drive in summer. Now, covered in 17 feet of snow a mudcat or snowmobile is needed. Both of ours are out at other sites. Consequently, since only light equipment is required, we hike the shorter trail route.

We arrive at the site in just under 2 hours. The shelter consists of a 10-foot by 20-foot wooden structure built on site on a raised platform 15 feet above ground to allow for snow accumulation. A ramp was made that switchbacks from ground level to the entrance to facilitate carts and cylinder dollies. The site operator has been diligent in shoveling the snow off the ramp.

David says,

"Shauna still is the site operator here right?"

"Yes."

"She doesn't hike in here weekly does she?"

"Sometimes, but usually she uses a snowmobile."

"That's what I thought, but I don't see any tracks."

"I think it snowed since her last visit, or she may have hiked."

We unlock the door, flip on the lights, and enter the instrument filled room. The only window is blocked by an instrument rack. There is a small desk with tools for working on equipment and another one for setting up a laptop and writing on field logs. The roof of the site, containing multiple particle samplers and sample inlets, is surrounded by a safety railing and is accessible via wooden stairs at the entrance level. Typically instruments are added and removed during non-winter months.

Our tracer instrument is located inside and draws outside air from an inlet designed much like regular heating vents in houses. The inlet caps prevent snow and rain from entering or blocking the sample tube. Straightaway David begins to inspect the sampler. He reviews the current chromatograph on the PC screen. The calibration peaks look good, well resolved and above the baseline. Zero air calibration responds with a flat line and zero peak height. Ambient sample periods are flat as expected, with zero peak heights. He navigates the software to previous runs. Everything looks fine, and all quality control, including blank data, are nominal. Sample blanks contain zero air and are designed to detect any carryover of calibration standards or contamination.

We start a manual calibration using known calibration gases and zero air. This is a lengthy process, so I break out two turkey sandwiches that I made this morning and a couple of waters. The sandwiches are masterpieces if I do say so myself. They are on homemade bread, with onion, tomato, lettuce, avocado, and mayo. This run takes even longer than usual because David is carefully examining the detail of every peak even though the overall results look within acceptance criteria. Meanwhile I manually download this latest calibration and the past month's data for backup. David says,

"I cannot find anything wrong with the instrument. All calibrations are within specifications, the chromatographs look clean, the data written to final storage match the chromatographs." These data in final storage are those that get sent to our lab via telemetry. I ask,

"What about the time stamp on the PC?"

"It's within 2 seconds of those written on the chromatographs and within 1 second of Naval Observatory Time." David and I are both time nerds. Instead of Rolexes, we have these cheap plastic watches that are thrown out when the batteries die. They keep excellent time however and have stopwatches, timers and his, for slightly more money, even has a barometric sensor. We routinely check them against the atomic clock available over the internet.

"When was the storm supposed to arrive?" David asks. I walk to the door, start to open it while I'm saying,

"Not for a few more hours..." The outside is a complete whiteout with large flakes falling silently in rapid succession.

"Or, how about 30 minutes ago." I say.

David tries to mask his obvious concern and says,

"Swell." Then mutters,

"Modelers are using complicated mathematics to make wild ass guesses."

We both start moving with determination. It takes another 20 minutes to shut down our activities and pack our gear. While putting on our coats, backpacks and getting ready to don our snowshoes, David asks,

"Is the GPS ready?"

"Batteries are new and fully charged. I've set our route to travel from here to the trailhead using the fixed set points." When the site was established, we set up these waypoints and have used them for several of our trips. We exchange a look and a sigh and head out the door.

As we begin to head back, the snow already has lightly covered our tracks from our hike to the site. Having spent several years growing up in Florida, I still am struck by how quiet a heavy snowstorm can be. An equivalent storm in Florida, falling in the form of rain, would be incredibly loud on the roof requiring raised voices to be heard. Not to mention you would at least know that precipitation was occurring. Outside, the raindrops would be heard slamming into the ground, trees, and leaves. During this storm, conditions actually are quieter than before the snow started because there is no bird noise or the rustling of leaves.

The wind begins to swirl, and we are hit with horizontal

flakes. Even though the visibility is low, we continue to navigate by our memory of the forest formations. Apparently, we have drifted from our original path because we don't see any snowshoe prints. Nevertheless, even in the snow we recognize the familiar terrain and are confident of our position.

However, we will shortly need the GPS in the middle section of the return route because this stretch contains a dense stand of ponderosa pines lacking any point of reference. When visibility is good, visitors to the site rarely take the same route twice leaving no visible trail but follow a general northerly direction then the trees thin out, and recognizable markers appear.

As we approach the dense forest, everything looks the same. I remove the GPS, pull up our route which is highlighted by a green trail. I take the lead and keeping my head down from the snow blowing in my face, walk, so the arrow is on the green path while navigating around trees. We continue this way for approximately 30 minutes, visibility nearly zero. David stops and says,

"Something is wrong."

Chapter 21

"What's the matter?" I ask.

"Do you remember last summer when we went off the path to do a little exploring? We found the precipice with a view overlooking the valley?"

Looking around in a 360-degree sweep of our surroundings I give a skeptical drawn out,

"Yes."

Pointing behind me, he says,

"Observe that rock formation just left of and behind that large pine."

Peering through the falling snowflakes, I see the formation David is referring to, and its distinct markings do look familiar.

"You think the overlook is at that tree. If you are right, we are way off course."

While removing his pack, he says,

"Wait here, I will keep you within line of site and hike

over there and confirm that the overlook is there."

"Fine. Be careful near the edge, with this much snow it can give way in chunks."

"Right."

David shoes in the direction of the location while I retrieve the GPS from my pocket. I dig further into my pack for my compass. Looking back at David, at 30 yards he is disappearing in and out of a shifting whiteout, but I can still make out his form, and his blue jacket is well contrasted in the snow.

Holding the GPS, with the trailhead not in view, I zoom out until it appears. Then I center the waypoint on the screen and zoom back in to see the detail around the trailhead.

"Son of a bitch."

Looking for David, he is barely visible, mostly just the fading shape of his coat. As I start to look back at the screen, the blue figure drops down and out of site. Did he just trip? Staring into the white mass, I don't see him stand back up, and a pang of fear washes over me. Trying not to panic I remind myself that David is too experienced to allow a snow precipice to give out from under him, even in these conditions. I call out to him, not surprised at the lack of a response. My sound waves must be getting absorbed by the thousands of snow particles between us. Examining his snowshoe path, I note that the falling snow is covering the track, but his prints are still discernible making me believe that if we don't dally, we will be able to return to our packs following back both our trails. I prop David's pack up higher in the snow, rest mine on top of his, and head off in David's tracks.

Nearing the half-way point, I call to David and again am unrewarded for my efforts. Just before reaching the expected drop off, the only sight of David is snowshoe tracks that cover a wide circular area with a path that ends at what appears to be the cliff. My stomach seems to be ahead of my brain at processing this information as my lunch is backing up in my throat. Perhaps my mind can't comprehend the conclusions running in the background. David is nowhere in sight, and snowshoe prints lead to the edge.

Against the protestations of my stomach, I shoe over to a pine near the large granite outcropping. Grabbing a long branch while easing my way near the cliff, I'm able to peer over the edge. While holding on to the thick branch for stability, my vision is filled with a sight too horrible to comprehend. With both atmosphere and earth colored white, blending as one, coming into focus is a morbid image consisting of a pool of red stained snow radiating from a blue mass. I could make out black pants at the other end of the blue coat. I couldn't tell if the body was face down or up. The depth of the fall had to be at least 75 yards.

Based on the volume of blood, there is no doubt that my best friend is gone. How could this have happened? My legs are shaking, and I just want to sit down. Still holding tightly to the tree branch I withdraw from the edge. Safely away from the cliff, I place my hands at the base of a tree while dropping to my knees. My lunch finally gives way.

I experience a conscious stream of rapid, disjointed questions. Did he stand too close to the edge and slip or did the snow cliff give way? What am I going to say to Liz? How will I get him out of there? How will I be able to work without him? How will I be able to live without him? What was he thinking on the way down? Why am I so cold? This last question slaps me back to my current predicament.

My eyelids, covered in tears are starting to freeze. I must start moving to get my own blood pumping. Getting to my feet, I start hiking back to our packs. My snowshoes feel like cement blocks while a total numbness has taken over the rest of my body.

I can only concentrate on lifting and dropping one foot at a time audibly sobbing and shaking. Barely noticing, I arrive at the packs.

Part of me wants to find a trail down to David and haul him back to the car. The rational part knows I don't have the gear to repel down to him. If I'm not careful, I may not make it back myself. I put on my pack and glance one more time back to the cliff. The snow ceaselessly tumbles from the sky. I think I see a blue mass near the ground in the distance. Doubtless blue and red images will infiltrate my vision when looking into snowstorms, for my remaining years of life.

With my pack on my back, looking down at David's, I can't leave it here. I remove my one arm and place the pack back onto the ground. From a side pouch, I remove a 3 feet section of rope and begin tying his pack on top of mine.

During the menial task, I can't push Liz's reaction of David's death out of mine. I can't conceive of even how to tell her he is gone. My mind is inundated of memories of the two of them laughing and loving each other. Of their kids responding to the death of their father.

Not sure if I'm chilled by my thoughts or the snow storm, probably both, but I'm shivering uncontrollably. Snow has been getting underneath the collar of my coat. Clearing out as much as I can, I pull up the zipper of my jacket all the way to my chin and place both packs on my back. I remove my goggles, rub my eyes, clean off the snow from the plastic, and return them to my head. The only thing remaining is David's poles. I grab them and place them between both packs.

Pulling out the GPS from my pocket, I almost forgot, I need to make an adjustment. Some asshole adjusted the trailhead waypoint. I only checked that the point was still there, not its exact location. I hadn't noticed the change because it was zoomed out too far and this unit doesn't show a large amount of geography, since the screen is relatively small. I didn't verify the location because of the stupid assumption that it had not been altered. We are the only ones that use this unit. Now David is dead because of it. He trusted me to be smarter than a piece of electronics, and I failed.

This is too painful to endure, thus my mind proposes reasons why I didn't check it. For example, it is rare for others to use the GPS. David and I are the only NRI staff that are working in this region, therefore if someone else borrowed it, there would have been no reason to change the point. Unfortunately, my stomach isn't accepting my mind's lame excuses. It wants to heave again. The changed location was leading us straight over a cliff, and David detected it. Irony is a cruel bitch. In taking measures to make sure we didn't fall off a cliff he did precisely that.

I relocated the point to where we parked the car and headed in that direction.

Chapter 22

With my first step, I cast one more mournful look toward the cliff. The blue spot on the white horizon remains but now seems higher off the ground. I shake my head to clear my mind with no success. The image is moving and looks more real than a creation of my imagination. What the hell?

I throw off the two packs and started running in my snowshoes with my eyes trained on the blue image appearing to rise above ground. I am really losing it. What sick tricks my mind is playing. Am I supposed to believe that David shook off the massive loss of blood and free climbed up the cliff with no gear?

As I draw nearer to the cliff, clearly there is a man in a blue coat and black snow pants walking in circles, his back turned to me. No kind of comprehension is occurring in my brain. As I approach the man I call out,

"David?"

He turns, removes his goggles and chatters out,

"Oh man, I am freezing."

I come to an abrupt stop and stare at the face of my best friend, brought back from the dead. I can't speak, can't move, my mind is a jumble of confusion.

He says,

“Where have you been?”

With some considerable agitation, I say,

“Where have I been? Where the fuck have you been? I just saw you lying in a pool of blood on a rock 75 yards over this cliff. I’ve been trying to visualize a world without you in it”.

Shivering he says,

“Pretty hard isn’t it.”

“Shut up! Get moving before you freeze and start explaining yourself.”

David starts dusting the snow off his clothes and lifting his legs up and down. Rubbing the back of his neck, he begins to explain what happened.

“I’m sure you did see a body down there, and it was supposed to be me, and then you. I was looking at the drop-off from a safe distance. Behind me, I heard a sound and thought it was you. I started to turn right, lifting my left shoe out of the snow and I saw this guy with what looked like a club or baseball bat in the fully cocked position. As he started to swing, I just barely moved my head out of the way, and he caught me on the back of the neck. I went stumbling to my left and fell over that log."

He points to a snow-covered log and continues.

"My head was spinning. Lying behind that log, I tried to pull myself up. I lifted my head just above the log and saw him looking over the edge. I assume his next move was to throw me over. Suddenly, the earth gave way, and he vanished. Then everything went black. I woke up behind the log shivering, pulled myself to my feet and saw you hiking over. You didn't see him hit me?"

"No, I could barely see anything in this shit. I did see what I thought was your blue coat disappear downward. I thought it was you over the edge. Wait a minute."

I worked myself back along the edge using the tree limb again. I could see the body just starting to disappear as snow blanketed the rock. I looked back at David, similar blue coats with black snow pants.

"Who was he?" I asked.

"I didn't recognize him, he was wearing a ski mask and goggles."

"Could it have been Luther or the guy from the pub? Or Gigantor from my house."

"Not Luther he is a munchkin. I don't know if it was the man from the bar. I didn't see the guy from your house but based on your description, this person was not as large."

"Doubtless a Church member, Luther could call on an army of the faithful to do his bidding. Let's get out of here before we freeze to death. I did confirm that this was near where we were last summer, and I know how we got off course."

"Let me guess." David says,

"Bad GPS?"

"The GPS is ok, bad waypoint." While walking back to the packs, I explain that the waypoint was changed, why I didn't catch it, and that the GPS was now properly reset. I untie the rope to separate the packs. David watches and says,

"I can't believe you were going to abandon me." The very same thought passed through my mind. I look at him and while putting on the packs say, with a little too much agitation,

"Give me a break. You were dead." I hand him my compass and say,

"Let's go. Double check my course."

We hike in silence for about 5 minutes, savoring the warmth from our increased metabolic rates. David breaks the silence and says,

"What do you think of this theory? Many people knew we were going to make this hike. Luther or someone grabs the GPS and moves the waypoint. The dead guy on the rock programs a similar GPS, we have many of the same models at NRI. He follows us along our route, just out of sight. Watching me heading for the cliff, he makes his way over to me, making a wide arc to remain unseen. He intends to knock me out and then throw me over the edge. When you come to investigate what is going on, he hides and then we both share the same death. In the spring, when they find our bodies, they find an errant GPS. Nice and tidy."

David lets me contemplate the theory as we hike in silence. Finally, I say,

"These guys sure go through a lot of trouble to make it look like a plausible accident. It would have been much easier to smack us over the head and bury us in the snow somewhere."

"That would look like foul play and result in a lengthy investigation. All he had to do was get us to hike over here, and the rest is easy."

We eventually make it back to the car, mostly in silence and by a circuitous route. We miss the car at the trailhead by a half a mile. While shoeing through the deep snow, in whiteout conditions, I had trouble forcing the image of red snow surrounding a body in a blue coat out of my head. Both exhausted, we load our gear in the SUV. I fire it up while David is brushing off the accumulated snow from the windshield and windows.

In the car waiting for it to warm, I say,

"I should call Janis and report the guy over the cliff."

"They will want us to wait here for hours and then show them the scene, do you really feel like going back out there?"

"Hell no. I don't think they can require us to hike in there, it's dangerous. Besides there won't be anything to see, he will be covered in snow. Besides I dropped a pin on my GPS, I can give them the precise lat/long."

David stares at me silently.

"What?" I ask.

"We were out there freezing, you were recovering from seeing me not dead, and you had the presence of mind to drop a pin?"

"What can I say I'm a cool character."

He shakes his head.

"Let's get out of here. Call her when we get back to Reno, I don't want her to demand we stay here and wait. We can plead ignorance, something at which you excel."

"I try to excel at everything I do."

"Would you just go!"

David clearly is not in the mood for my nonsense. I can't blame him so I remain silent while we drive back to Reno. Again at the Institute, I call Janis and recant the entire story.

"You should have called me when you got to the car."

"Oh, well, we were freezing, David had been hit in the head, it was snowing, and we wanted to get down to Reno in the event they closed I-80."

I left out the part that she is a cop and we were afraid she would want us to stay until one of her brethren arrived. I gave her the location of the trailhead and our latitude and longitude at the rock edge.

"That is the Placer County Sheriff's office jurisdiction. How is this for a coincidence, I just met a guy at the conference from their office. They can't get a chopper in there now anyway and won't attempt a rescue if he is dead. Are you sure he is dead?"

"It's more inference from my observations than certainty. He was splayed on a large rock after a fall of at least 75 meters, ah yards, and had lost several pints of blood. That with the cold, I don't see how he could still be alive."

"Reasonable. Do you think this was the guy that was waiting for you at your house?"

"We doubt it. According to David he only had a second but judged the man to be close to his own height. He would have been able to tell if it was the massive guy from my house. The guy from the brewpub is still a possibility."

"He knows it was a man?"

"Oh, he might have assumed that. The guy, umm, the person was wearing a ski mask and goggles."

"We women have come all this way, but you men just assume we are too weak to be able to overcome a man."

"No, our first reaction is that women are not homicidal assholes."

"Oh, well, ok then. I'm back in our office, I'll call the detective from the conference and explain what you told me and that I believe it may be related to an open case of mine. When are you leaving today and are you going straight home?"

"I plan to leave at 1700. David and I have been through much today. And yes I'm going straight home."

"I have arranged for a friend of mine, Blake Perdue, in the Washoe County Sheriff's office, right down the road from your Institute, to come by after you get off work. I'll call and tell him to meet you in the parking lot at 5:00. If the person who has been following you is there, point him out, and Blake will do the rest. If he is not there, Blake will follow you home and go in with you. Lock up and set the alarm, my brother Josh is going to pay a few visits later in the evening. Josh drives a Black BMW SUV, I just texted his picture to you. Is David going to be alright?"

"He should be fine, he and his wife are home tonight, and they borrowed a friend's nasty guard dog."

"Good I'm going to call Blake now, call me if you have any problems."

"I will, thank you for everything. And for a fun weekend. You were right about my ride home."

"Ha-ha good. I'll be in touch."

My phone's text tone went off, prompting me to navigate toward the messages icon and open the messages window and then Janis's message to see a headshot of her bother. With the text 'This is my brother Josh.' I stare at the picture at length with concern. I run it through my card catalog of faces and find a match. Finding Janis in my favorites the call goes straight to voice mail.

"Hi, Janis. Received your picture of Josh. We have a problem, call me back please."

Chapter 23

In David's office, I catch him up to speed on Janis's surveillance plan and ask him if he thinks he and Liz will be safe at home.

"With the dog and our old school alarm system we should be fine. Also unlike you, I have a shotgun. Besides all the action seems to be around you."

"They must know I'm the dangerous one."

"I'm fine with it."

"Here is the weird thing." Showing him my phone and the picture of Janis's brother I ask,

"Do you recognize this man?" David scrutinizes the image for several seconds and says,

"No. Who is he?"

"Janis's brother, the person who is going to trail us for a while looking for bad guys."

"Fine, am I supposed to know him?"

"You probably won't remember him. He was the guy that

tried to follow us to the pub."

"Are you sure? This is an insane paradox, Janis has arranged to have a guy potentially watch himself. What did she say when you told her?"

"I called to tell her, but got her voicemail, she doesn't know yet." I look at my watch and see it's almost 5:00.

"I've got to go meet the sheriff, I'll let you know what happens. You should ice your neck." I rush to my office to pick up my backpack and lockup. Slowly climbing the steps, I scan the parking lot for Josh or the first follower. I don't see either person, but a sheriff's car is parked at the far end of the lot near the entrance.

I walk to the sheriff's car all the while openly looking at every car for any occupant. Only two had someone preparing to enter the vehicle, all NRI personnel. Reaching the car, he rolls down his window.

"Hi I'm Grant, you must be Sheriff Deputy Perdue."

"Yes good to meet you. Is the person who has been tailing you present?"

"I don't see him."

"I have your address and cell number in case I lose you. Once you head out, I'm going to stay a fair distance behind you to see if anyone drops in. Start out slowly and then stay at the speed limit." He hands me a card and says,

"Here is my cell phone number, call me if you need to."

"Will do." I walk to my car and drive out of the parking lot. I slowly drive to the highway never seeing anyone behind me. On the freeway, several cars back, I can see Blake. I arrive home, pull into the garage and walk to the mailbox and don't see anyone until Blake pulls up in front of my house. He exits the vehicle and walks over to me and says,

"I did not see anyone following you, how about you?" He turns to face the street.

"No."

"Have you gone inside your home yet?"

"No, I was waiting for you." I pull out my iPhone and disarm the alarm system, and we enter through the garage. We walk around turning on all the lights, there is no sign of anyone.

"Nice view."

"Thanks. I'll run upstairs, but everything looks fine." All is well. I thank Blake for driving over, he leaves and I lockup and set the alarm. Blake looks around 30 years old, very fit and good looking. Well, not to me, but I wonder how good of 'friends' he is with Janis. Geez, I need to get a grip.

I'm beginning to feel like a prisoner once I set the alarm. Instead of heading out for a run, I grab one of my books in progress and step on to my step climber. After 30 minutes my cell rings and by the recently assigned ring tone, 'Love her madly' by the doors, I know it is Janis.

"Hey, girl."

"Hi, you have a problem with my brother?" I explain that my personal facial recognition ability detected him as one of two followers. He tried to follow me from NRI the night we all met at the brewpub, I managed to lose him. I believe this was the only time he was on me."

"Well, this is incredibly weird and totally unexpected. Damn, I tried to get him to meet my sister and me at the brewpub that night, and he said he was working. He was planning on hanging outside your house tonight. I'm going to call him as soon as we hang up. On another matter, you caught a break. The

Placer County detective that I met at the conference had business in Reno tomorrow, thus he is up there now and is willing to come by your office and take yours and David's statements. This will save you both a drive to Auburn."

"Well, that's something."

"Blake told me there was no one following you tonight."

"Yes, you probably think I'm crazy. There has been someone in our parking lot every night, and now that you have someone to intercept him there is no one there. Can they be monitoring my phone calls somehow?"

"No, it probably was just a coincidence. Tyler will call you tonight to make contact and ask some preliminary questions." At that moment a call came in.

"I think he's calling me now."

"Ok, I'll call you back after talking to my brother."

"Hello, this is Grant."

"Hi, Grant. I'm detective Tyler Owens of the Placer County Sheriff's office. I believe Detective Rollings told you I would be calling."

"Yes, she did."

"I would like to meet with you and Dr. Piehl tomorrow at your office to take a report. What time would be good for you?"

"Any time you like we are both in all day and will stop what we are doing to meet you."

"That's great. How is 10:00 am?"

"Just fine. Park in the lower parking lot, come in the main entrance and check in with the receptionist I will pick you up from there."

"Sounds good. Since this incidence occurred today, I would like to get an overview for my report rather than wait until tomorrow."

"Sure whatever you need."

"Would you call what happened an accident?"

"I was about 40 yards away in whiteout conditions and did not see what happened. According to my colleague, it sounded more like attempted murder gone wrong where the perpetrator accidentally went over the cliff."

"I'm going to call Dr. Piehl next. You saw a body lying

prone on a rock with a voluminous amount of blood, and in your judgment he was dead?"

"Yes it seemed so, but I've never before seen a dead body. However, I don't expect anyone can fall 50-75 yards, land on a rock and survive it."

"Right. Detective Rollings gave me GPS coordinates that she said you provided her, is that correct?"

"Correct"

"I will get the rest of the information I need tomorrow. Normally I would want you to show me the location, but given the weather conditions, I will take your coordinates and as soon as we can, investigate the site. I will still need you two to accompany someone to the scene as soon as the weather clears."

"It shouldn't be a problem."

"Good night Grant. I'll see you tomorrow."

"Good night."

I move to the kitchen to whip up some dinner. I'm thinking oven fried chicken and broccoli. With the chicken in the oven and the broccoli ready to steam 'Love her madly' can be heard from my back pocket.

"Hey, how's it going?"

"Fine. I talked to my brother. Apparently, he was hired by someone in Luther's Church to follow you for the night. You made him look bad by losing him straight out of the parking lot where the other guy never lost your tail."

"In defense of your brother, it was the first time we purposely tried to lose a follower. Does he have a steady job with the Church?"

"Apparently he has done some occasional work for them, mostly character references, never surveillance. If you are not busy tonight I was going to have him pay you a visit instead of watching your place from outside. I would like to see if he can identify the cowboy that paid you a visit."

"Sure that's fine."

"So no hot date tonight?"

"As you are not coming over, no."

"I like that answer. He should be there at 8:00. Talk to you later."

I finish dinner and am almost finished cleaning up, and the doorbell rings. I take out my iPhone, navigate to my security app to view the live doorbell camera. It's Josh.

"Hi, I'm Josh."

"Hey come in."

We shake hands,

"I'm Grant."

I lead him to the living room couch.

"Nice view."

"Thanks. Can I get you something to drink?"

"I'm fine, thank you. So how bizarre is this, first I'm hired to follow you, and now my sister 'hires' me to watch anyone who may be following you."

"Yes, do you feel like it is a conflict of interest?"

"No my sister comes first over all others. Plus I'm just getting started, and the work I was doing for the Church is not really what I'm looking for. Let me ask you, did you know I was tailing you that night?"

"Yes, we knew we were being followed a week ago. I had my colleague, David, drop in behind me to block all cars until I could speed up and hide. We didn't know you were there until he saw you turn back in the round-about. I was up in the community college when you drove by."

"I'm missing something. You didn't know I was following you but guessed it might have been me when I turned around. Presumably, David gave you my make of car. You then see my car drive by, and you quickly exit the parking lot in the opposite direction. From that encounter, how could you possibly know it was me just by looking at my picture on your phone?"

"Good question. I got a good view of your face when you drove by the community college parking lot using binoculars.

"Wow, good memory."

"Let me ask you, in your work with Church personnel have you interacted with very many people?"

"Not all that many. Janis wanted me to get a description from you of a man who invaded your house."

"Yes. He never said he was from the Living Word Temple, but it was certain he was concerned about Christians."

"This is the type of work that interests me. Tell me everything about him."

"He was tall. Hey, come over here for a second." We rose from the couch and walked over to the kitchen where there is an open rectangular entrance separating the living room from the kitchen. I pointed to the top of the entrance and said,

"His head came to about right here." Pointing about an inch below the top of the entrance. I went to a kitchen drawer and pulled out a measuring tape. Holding the end down with my foot and pulling the tape up to an inch from the top. I say

"That's 79 inches. So he was approximately 6 foot 7 inches tall." I notice Josh now has out a notebook and mechanical pencil. I tell him about his hat, boots, and clothes.

"He looked like he was in his early 40s and was once very fit, but has put on some pounds."

"It seems you are good with faces, I'm pretty good at drawing. Do you have a couple sheets of printer paper?"

"Sure hold on." I return with the paper, and we repaired to the glass table in my kitchen. I described in detail the man's facial characteristics and hair as it appeared under his hat. Josh with amazement says,

"I can't believe you can recall such detail about this guy."

"I'm good with faces."

"I'll say." Josh was skilled at drawing, and after almost an hour he had an excellent likeness of the man. He laid the sketch on the table, took out his phone and snapped a picture.

"I'll send this to Janis. I don't recognize this man from my few visits to the church, but this Wednesday I am going to provide an oral report regarding a previous unrelated assignment. I'll take a look around and study everyone I encounter. I might also attend next Sundays worship called a Sacrament meeting, visitors are allowed to attend."

"Sounds good, thanks for your help." I walk him to the door, and he says,

"Unless I need to ask you some questions I probably won't be in touch with you, I will report all my results to Janis. It's better that way. If you need to get a hold of me though, here is my card."

Locking up the house I head to bed to do some more reading.

Chapter 24

Arriving at the office around 07:00, there are no signs of anyone trailing me. Perhaps they have given up the surveillance. After dropping off my lunch and backpack in my office. I walk the halls reconnoitering Luther's office. He is in there alone working on his computer. I don't knock, just walk in and plop down in one of his guest chairs.

He looks at me sitting in the chair and says sarcastically,

"Please, come in, have a seat."

"Don't mind if I do. I don't think I need to tell you coming home to your goon sitting in my living room last Friday was rather unpleasant."

"Am I expected to be able to decipher this obscure comment?"

"I'm talking about murder, threats, scientific sabotage all due to scientists simply following their curiosity, a process that has advanced our understanding of the universe for millennia."

"Murder? Please, Stelzner, spare me your hyperbolic paranoia."

"Do you deny having me followed by your church faithful?"

A reaction of surprise is not well hidden in his face. I say nothing, allowing the silence to linger. Finally, with resignation and a sigh he says,

"You overestimate my position with the church. Look, Marcus was shooting off his mouth a few weeks ago at lunch where he was overheard by a few members of my church. Yes, it concerned them, they grilled me relentlessly for my understanding of what you are doing. Am I leading an assault of churchgoers to follow and threaten you? No."

"So you claim to be uninvolved in orchestrating the church's actions, but I noticed you don't deny their involvement."

"Do I think they were involved in Marcus's disappearance? No. Look, they, as am I, are concerned that you two amateurs are going to get lay people upset and confused for no reason."

"Do you no longer believe in the scientific principle?"

"I'm not following you."

"Certainly astrobiology is not our field, but currently we are simply engaged in non-complex chemistry, and we have postulated a refined extraterrestrial origin of life on this planet. You know how this works, these ideas will go nowhere without first being confirmed by specialists in the field, with others being able to repeat our work. What appears to be happening is a group of people is attempting to squelch the work before it makes it to the scientific community."

"In most organizations, there exists an overzealous few that may overreact to events which run counter to deeply held doctrine."

"What do you and church leaders do to control such zealots?"

"They are dealt with, that's all I'm willing to say. Also, that I am just a member of the church, I'm not involved in the leadership."

His office phone rang, he looked at the caller ID and said, "I've got to take this."

I rose and left his office. After a break in the restroom, I stopped in my office, checked messages and email and left to look for David. I found him in his lab tinkering with a pump.

"Hey, where have you been?" he asks.

"Luther's office."

"Uh oh."

"He's undamaged. I just decided to confront him directly. As expected he was pretty cool. He denied any involvement on his part but did not try and defend any actions by church members other than to say he did not 'think' they were involved in Marcus's disappearance. Surprise, surprise."

"What about the guy that broke into your house."

"The way I posed the question, without admitting anything, it appeared he knew I had him on that one. He didn't deny that the guy was from the church."

"Interesting he doesn't want to outright admit to homicide and attempted homicides, but doesn't deny the church is involved."

"He went a long way to sway my opinion that perhaps he is not the mastermind of the attacks, but is providing them information. When they pull the corpse off that rock and identify him, the church is going to have a lot to answer to."

"Unfortunately, the way these storms are rolling in, that is going to take a while. The Sierras are getting hit hard right now. In the meantime, further assaults should be expected."

"Yeah, we need to stay vigilant. Did the Placer Sheriff call you last night?"

"Yes. He asked several questions on what happened out there. He said he would have the front desk call you when he arrives, as you know. He wants to talk to you alone first and then me."

"He wants to see if we can keep our stories straight."

"I suppose. Hey, guess what arrived yesterday. David asks rhetorically and then continues.

"A tech from our Vegas office drove it up yesterday I forgot to tell you. I have it locked in your refrigerator."

"Cool let's check it out after 5:00 today."

"Sure. I reviewed the data from final storage that we downloaded from the Sierra site. I might understand what the problem is out there, but don't quite understand how it happened." He is interrupted by my cell phone ringing.

"This is Stelzner."

"Hi, Grant. This is Joe down at the front desk. I have a Detective Owens here to see you."

"Thanks, Joe I'll be right there." Hitting the end call button on my phone, I say to David,

"The detective is here."

"He's early." As I start to head to the door of the lab, I say,

"So you think you might have solved the problem with the bad Sierra data?"

"Maybe. However, there is something strange there, I need to verify a few things."

"I hope so, let me know soonest. I'll bring Tyler to your office when he is done with me. Are you staying in for lunch?"

"Yes." I depart the lab and head down to the receptionist. There is a tall uniformed man examining photos of past scientists that have won awards. He turns when he hears me descending the stairs. When within a few feet I reach out my hand,

“Hi, Grant Stelzner.” He shakes my hand.

“Tyler Owens, glad to meet you.” I lead him to the stairs from whence I came and wave to the receptionist.

“Thanks, Joe.”

“See you, Grant.” We ascend the stairs, and Tyler asks,

“What do you guys do here?” I give him an overview of the Institute, our affiliation with the University of Nevada, and activities of our various divisions. We arrive at my office, Tyler takes a seat, and I offer him coffee or a drink. He declines, and we get right to it. He pulls out a tape recorder and says,

“If you have no objections I need to record your statement.” I wave my hands in a show of no problem. He begins with preliminary information such as date, time, location, my name, etc.

“Mr. Stelzner, we spoke on the phone last night, and I obtained a preliminary summary of what happened in the mountains near Cisco. Please describe in detail what happened once you left your car to hike into your monitoring site to the point of your return.”

I discussed snowshoeing into the site, the storm arriving

earlier than predicted, leaving the site, finding we were off course and then stopping so David could verify our suspected location. I told him, that David disappeared into the whiteout and how I mistakenly thought he was dead on the below rocks. Until now he listened without interruption occasionally taking notes.

"So you thought David had gone over the cliff, but he was really knocked out behind a log."

"Yes"

"You never saw the man who now lays dead on the rocks."

"I may have seen him, both he and David were wearing blue snow jackets. At some point, I could have thought I was seeing David may have seen the other guy and vice versa."

"So you think your friend is dead. What happened next?"

I describe the rest, where I hiked back to the packs, fixed the erroneous GPS location, and prepared to walk out of there. I omit the part where I was crying like a baby. That I saw movement of the blue jacket, returned to the cliff, found David, and the two of us hiking back to the car.

"You are sure you don't know the man?"

"Absolutely. Well, I may know him, he could be my next door neighbor or mailman for all I know, but did not see enough to recognize him."

"Right of course. David told you the guy hit him, and then disappeared over the cliff."

"Yes. That reminds me, Janis suggested that we confirm with David that he is sure it was a man, as opposed to a woman."

"Sure ok, I'll ask him. Now, you think he altered your GPS monitor, tracked you to the cliff to kill you both because of ongoing research on the origin of life."

"Yes, or he has a contact within the institute that made the change."

"Why didn't you call 911 when you got to the car?"

"I didn't really think of 911 since we were no longer in danger. We thought of calling Janis since she has been investigating our case, which we did once we got back to Reno. We wanted to get out of the storm, fearing they might close I-80."

He turns off the recorder.

"That should do it thanks. We still can't get to the site, there is another storm up there." I walk him over to David's office. He is not there.

"Have a seat, and I will go find him."

"I'd rather you two not talk until I take his statement."

"Oh, sure. I'll call his cell." I do so.

"He is on his way."

"Thanks." David arrives within the next minute, and I leave them to it.

Chapter 25

Since Marcus's death, and yes I am confident that is his earthly state, I have neglected many tasks for all my projects. This afternoon I am catching up on this backlog of duties when my office phone rings.

"Stelzner."

"Hi Grant, Vanessa."

"Hi Vanessa, how are you doing?"

"Fine, I'm calling because David told me last week you guys were going to need some microbiology work on a few slides. I may not be able to analyze them."

"What's the problem? Other than we are not paying you?"

"That is a problem. I told him I could analyze a couple of slides gratis because I know you are running some unfunded experiments. However, I bid on a job last month that was just awarded, and I am going to be swamped in a few days. With a paying sponsor."

"All reasonable concerns on your part. How long does it

take you to analyze one cell?"

"I'm not sure, I haven't seen your bug. At least an hour maybe three."

"Would you consider the following? You give us 8 hours this Thursday before your new project hits. Bill us for any costs incurred for supplies and expendables, so you are not out of pocket any funds. To compensate you for your time we put you on as the third author for a publication in Science."

"Science! What are you guys working on? I thought you were just screwing around testing a theory and would not be publishing the work in any journal, certainly not Science."

"If this next batch of analyzes gives us the same results as the first samples it will definitely be in Science."

"If I'm going to be a co-author I need to know what we are doing."

"You will need to keep it secret for a little while longer. Do you have a few minutes right now?"

"Sure."

"I'm leaving now." I tell her about the meteorites and

our theory. She is very excited and more than willing to perform additional analyzes. As I arrive back to my office, the detective and David are talking in my office door. I say,

"You guys look finished."

Tyler answers,

"Yes, I have what I need for now. With this second storm out there the crime scene will be destroyed. We will get out there tomorrow using your coordinates to compare your statement versus the environment and determine how to retrieve the body. I will try to avoid dragging you both out there again, but can't guarantee it. So far we have no missing person reports in Reno or Northern California."

David and I don't really have anything to say and just nod silently.

"That's it then, can you walk me out of here?" We go out a side door, and I point to an outside path leading to the parking lot that is a quicker route and doesn't require an escort. Back in David's office, I ask,

"How did it go?"

"Fine, I think he believes us, but he is diligent in verifying our story. When I told him I was struck on the back of the neck, he got up and inspected me. By the way, I have a lump, and there is a large black and blue mark."

"Yes, he seemed competent. I have a 'by the way' for you. Vanessa is going to be a co-author on any journal article that we publish."

"I hope you did not bestow this honor on her to get in her pants."

"How dare you. I think I can do that on my own, maybe. Besides I'm seeing Janis now. Wait did you just stutter, honor honor?" First I'm thrown a frustrated look then he says,

"Did you advise her to keep quiet lest she makes the Genesis Murders list?"

"She knows to remain silent. Also, we may need to pay her lab some money out of your personal account."

When we secure a grant or contract a small percent of the total revenue goes to the Principle Investigator's personal account. The funds are used to sustain investigators during lean times but are mainly there to allow investigators to follow their scientific muse when no funds are available.

"Why not your account! I assume to avoid labor charges you had to negotiate a deal."

"And Luther thinks you're dumb."

"So does Vanessa know everything?"

"Pretty much."

"Well, it's not like the whole world doesn't know already anyway. The only people we didn't want to learn of what we are doing were those that would want to kill us over it. How is that working for us? Perhaps we should just hold a press conference and notify everyone officially, then they might be reluctant to make any more attempts on our lives."

"I actually think it's a good idea. But, if we announce before confirming our theory and we are wrong we will be ridiculed. We will be relegated to counting tortoise holes in the Mohave Desert."

"Right now that doesn't seem so bad."

"Oh, one last issue. We need to give her all our samples on Thursday."

"Next week?

"Uhh..no the day after tomorrow."

"Why would you agree to that?

"She is starting a big project next week that will have her tied up for a few weeks. We need to get in there before those samples arrive."

"Then we better get in early tomorrow. Do you think we can stay alive that long?"

"Man you really are a downer right now."

"How boorish of me to allow myself to become dejected over people either trying to kill or fire me."

"That's the word I was looking for boorish, that's you. Hey, I know what will cheer you up, let's go take a look at the rock."

"Lets. I almost forgot, Liz invited you over for dinner tonight, she is making her famous Coq Au Vin."

"Absolutely, put me down as a definite." We go to my lab, unlock the refrigerator, and remove the box containing the meteorite. I open the box, dig into the packing material and lift it out wearing plastic gloves and place it on the bench. It's slightly larger than a golf ball, but of course, has a less uniform shape. I say,

"It feels heavier than I expected."

"It looks like a nice specimen. This is one from a large group that impacted just outside of metropolitan Vegas. It was widely reported, and the guys from UNLV's geology department were out there the next morning collecting the samples. Thus earthly contamination should be limited. They have been processed using gloves and kept in sterile containers."

"I see our box of microscope slides and coverslips were delivered."

"Right. When will Jackson arrive from San Francisco with the carboy of saltwater?" I ask.

"Tonight. So we should be able to get started first thing tomorrow." We wanted to repeat the tests with fresh seawater from a second source.

"What did his trip cost us?"

"It didn't cost me anything. He stayed with my friend Mark in North Beach and went out with a friend of Mark's girlfriend. Apparently, she was attractive and fun, consequently he is happy."

"He said 'fun'?"

"No something coarser."

"Thought so."

"You, on the other hand, owe him a case of Sierra Nevada Pale Ale. Actually, we both need to reimburse him for gas and a large quantity of ice. Hey, we better get going."

We arrive at David and Liz's house with no sign of anyone watching us. Liz has cocktails already prepared for us as we enter the door. I could get used to women greeting me with drinks at the ready. Coming around the corner is a small horse that is glowering at me with malicious intent. I freeze and say,

"Oh hell, this must be Butch. Is he going to eat me?"

"Watch this." says David. Liz claps her hand twice and says,

"Friend!" Butch starts wagging his tail, and the menace leaves his face.

"So behave yourself, Grant, if I give him an alternate command your girlfriends will be disappointed."

"They'll be disappointed?"

"This dog has been trained extremely well. We have absolutely no control over Zoey." Says David. Zoey is their chocolate Labrador.

"Something smells really good." I say.

"We can only hope. You guys are late so let's sit down at the table." The dinner, as always, is delicious. We resist discussing shop, limiting our conversations to family, friends and an upcoming trip they have planned to Connecticut. We finish and make it an early night.

"Thanks, Liz you are the master of that dish."

"Thank you, that's very kind."

"Tell Carl Sagan over there to get in early tomorrow we have a full day." I holler at David doing dishes in the kitchen.

"Good night David."

"See you tomorrow."

Just settled in at home, Janis calls, and I answer with,

"Hey, how are you?"

“I’m good and you?”

“I can complain, but I won’t.”

“Well good then, I guess. If you are free tomorrow night, I would like to bring my brother by he has some information to discuss with you.”

“Yes please do, I’m available. In fact, come for dinner.”

“Oh, well, I don’t want you to go to any trouble.”

“These days trouble is my middle name.”

“I can attest to that. Also, I suspect you are having trouble getting me out of your mind.”

“That is the most of my troubles. Come over any time after 5:30. I will make something simple, and it will keep for as long as it takes for you to arrive.”

“Sounds good. I’ll see you tomorrow then. Goodnight.”

“Goodnight.”

Chapter 26

David and I get in at 6:00. Yesterday we sent emails to Alan that we were taking vacation days today. We usually never notify him like this, we just take the day off and record the time on our monthly time sheets. Given that David is under attack, this is an ass-covering measure. I enter David's lab carrying a lapidary saw that a geology colleague agreed to loan us for a few days. Placing it on one end of a bench, cleared off and cleaned, for today's work I say to David,

"Vanessa plans to stop by today to review our techniques and check out the meteorite."

I receive some inaudible grunt that may have been something like 'fine.' He is scanning the meteorite using a stereo microscope also borrowed from a colleague. We have the bench organized for an efficient division of labor for today's activities. In addition to the stereoscope for use with the larger pieces we have our compound scope when we get down to the hair size pieces. We have started a new page in our logbook with date, and time and have written headers that include: sample identification number, circumference, cut number, weight, digital photograph filename, and the number of 'seeds' observed. The circumference will be measured at its longest axis. We needed a better name than the ‘rubbery looking seal thingy’ so we decided to call it a seed.

We plan to make consecutive cuts along the short axis into equal halves. One half will be stored in a clean zip lock bag, and the other half will be processed. If it contains seeds, they will be counted and the seeds extracted. When complete, this half will be halved again, and the process will be repeated until the rock can no longer be cut. All data will be logged in the log book. It is our practice to record all data, old school, with a pen and a bound book and then later enter the values into a digital spreadsheet. It would save time to input the data directly into the laptop, but we feel that things can still go wrong with a digital file. It happens much less frequently using today’s hardware and software, but we were burned earlier in our careers with computers that unexpectedly generated corrupted files resulting in irretrievable data.

Once the rock is too small to cut with the saw, we will place it on a small press and carefully exert pressure until it breaks up into various sized pieces. To avoid fatigue, we will take turns at the microscopes. We don’t expect to find any seeds until we get to the smaller pieces but won’t know until we go through the process.

Waiting for David to finish his scan of the original rock, I review the logbook. He recorded that the meteorite has a weigh of 145 g and a circumference of 160 mm.

"Hello, gentleman," Vanessa says as she comes through the lab door. I whisper to David,

"She uses that term loosely." No reaction, he lifts his head from the scope, stands up, and handles our reply.

"Hello, Vanessa." He turns to me and says,

"Why don't you take a look at the scope and double check me and I'll show her what we are doing."

"Sure." I sit down at the microscope, and he catches her up on our protocol.

After covering our plan, he explains a concern we have been discussing between the two of us.

"We theorize that when the universe was formed, somehow, maybe during the Big Bang, rocks containing these life starting seeds were sent hurling through the universe impacting planets and moons. However, not all meteorites that impact earth will contain these seeds. We receive meteorites from planets and moons that exploded or where pieces were sent into space after colliding with an enormous rock." She interrupts him with a question.

"Why do you think that exploded planets or moons wouldn't contain the seeds?"

"Of course we can't be certain, but hypothesize that these seeds were not originally present on earth. Ergo, if the earth exploded and sent meteoroids to Mars, they would not contain these seeds. We only have checked one rock from earth and didn't find anything, hence we need more data."

She says, "So you may work all day and not find anything."

"Correct. Regarding that, we have received some criticism about working on a 'hobby' and charging time to our projects. Grant and I are on annual leave today. You may receive the same negative attention. I think Grant asked you to keep this work private for now."

"Yes, and it's not a problem. Regarding billable hours, I run my own lab 60 hours a week on average so screw them. Anyway, for today, I just came by to see your setup and take a peek at the meteorite. I'll come back over if you find any seeds, just text me." Hearing this and finding no seeds, I rise from the stool and grab a pair of gloves from the box.

"No problem, take a look. Here are some gloves. As we are looking for extraterrestrial DNA, we will make every effort not to contaminate the sample with DNA originating from Earth." While she examines the meteorite and has further discussions with David, I move over to the lapidary saw and begin wiping it down with alcohol and then install a new blade.

"Thanks, guys, let me know if you find any seeds, and I'll come right over. I'll be here until around 7." We both issue our goodbyes. David asks,

"How long did Fred give us on the saw?"

"I told him I would return it in a few days, but it didn't seem like he was going to be using it this week. I'm ready to make the first cut."

"Here we go, now the fun begins." I move the rock from the microscope and bring it to the saw. I place a piece of aluminum foil on the base to catch cut fragments and align the stone along its shortest axis and begin the cut. When finished, David picks up one of the halves, shakes it over the foil, brings it to the bench, places it over a new piece of foil and makes the physical measurements He takes photographs and logs the data.

As he examines the piece on the microscope, I label two bags with this cuts ID number, place the other half in one bag and pour the cut particles off the foil into the bag.

This process continues past the lunch hour until we reach a stopping point and then take a break. We take turns going out to get our lunches while the other guards our samples. Paranoia is an unwelcome presence in our life these days. After a period of silence, while we eat, David says,

"What is the first name of Dr. White that just started in Archeology working to extract DNA from ancient bones?"

"Prudence, Prudie to her friends." I wait to see where he is going with this. He continues,

"How would you feel about adding a fourth to the author's list?"

"No problem as long as I remain the first author." He looks up from his leftovers and gives me a very nasty stink eye. Sure, now I get a reaction out of him.

"Just kidding relax. I assume we will include Marcus, he makes five?"

"You're right."

"So you want Prudence to run a DNA analysis on one of the cells?"

"If she'll waive her costs, I don't think we can afford her rates."

"I've heard she's feisty. I can see her performing the work for a piece of the action."

"People are examining the DNA code, working backward, trying to reconstruct the code for LUCA. If we indeed have LUCA it would be incredibly interesting to obtain the DNA information."

"Unquestionably. I have to think that Prudence would be very interested in becoming involved in the endeavor. Assuming we find more seeds in this rock. In addition, if we should find more than one seed, it would be huge to know whether or not they are exactly the same organism using the DNA data. However, if we don't find any seeds in this specimen, it will be a major setback."

"It certainly will slow our progress. I'm not sure we could come up with another meteorite. We could reexamine other particles from our sample archives, but I don't like our chances."

"If we run out of options we can publish what we have. It

should generate interest from astrobiologists and NASA to test their samples." David puts away his dirty dishes and says,

"Let's go find some seeds." We restart our duties, and my last cut appears to be as far as I can go.

"I don't think I can cut this one in half. It's time for the press."

"That's fine, as we discussed, you can't let any particles explode off the press. These next sizes are critical, I have not seen anything so far. How are you going to proceed?" I show him a pan and a box of plastic wrap.

"The sides of this sterilized pan are 5 cm deep." I place the remaining piece of the rock in the pan and start pulling plastic wrap from the box.

"I thought I would loosely stretch the plastic over the pan allowing it to drape down over rock, like so. Now a second piece for double the strength. I agree with your concern that as I exert continuous, increasing pressure, once it fractures the pieces will become projectiles."

"That looks pretty good. Maybe a third layer of plastic."

"No problem." David has moved over to the press to

watch. I place the pan under the ram of the press and bring down the arm to align it with the rock. With the ram in contact with the plastic layers on the rock, I slowly apply pressure. David holds the pan to secure it, and I increase the pressure. I have the arm pulled down to the point where the strength of my arm is in equilibrium with the rock without it breaking. I release the pressure, and David walks to the other side of the lab.

"We need a lever arm." He goes to a box in the corner and inspects a couple of pipes. Pulling one out, satisfied that it has the correct length and diameter, he brings it back to the bench.

"Try this." I slide one end of the pipe over the arm press and restart the pressure application. Now when I reach the point of failure that I had with my arm alone, I'm able to apply additional, gradual pressure slowly and the rock fractures. All particles are trapped inside the pan. We tap the plastic and carefully remove it. David reaches over to some tools near the microscope and grabs a pair of forceps.

"Let me have this peppercorn sized piece." He places it on a slide on the compound microscope, adjusts to the lowest ocular, sets the focus and studies it for a few seconds. He looks up at me with a wide grin and says.

“Call Vanessa.”

“Yes! You have one? You better not be toying with me.”

“Take a look.” We switch places, and I adjust the focus.

“Oh my God.”

Chapter 27

According to the scale on one of the oculars, the diameter of this piece is 1800 microns. It is covered in seeds. They all look incredibly similar in size and shape. I finally say,

"This is amazing. Inside the original meteorite, there must be thousands of these seeds. They are all protected by the impervious outer shell."

"They also are all well-hidden. To be released they must get broken down to 2 mm or less. Although the odds of this happening on earth seems unlikely, the fact that we all are here and have found some in our air monitoring equipment is evidence that it occurs. Do you want to call Vanessa? I'm going to attach the camera to the microscope." I do so.

"She will be over in five minutes." With the camera attached, David is able to obtain several high-quality photos. My thoughts turn to cell biology, and my memory fails.

"So if these cells are all the same, they must have the ability to replicate asexually. They may have the ability to undergo cell division and also recombine their DNA. There are organisms on earth that have that ability."

"I'm ill-equipped to weigh in on these topics. I'll let Vanessa, and you address these questions."

"Did I hear my name?" We both turn and greet her.

"So you found another sealed capsule?"

Davis says, "See for yourself."

Vanessa sits at the stool, refocuses the microscope and studies the rock for several seconds and says,

Gees there are a lot of them, this is great!" Without looking up, she continues.

"Previously you placed a drop of seawater on the sample and heated it?"

"That's correct." Answers David.

"The last sample was, what 100 microns. This one is almost 2 mm. I don't think working with it on a microscope slide will work. I have very small cuvettes that work better." She looks up, faces David and asks,

"What do you think?"

"Sure. We are relying on your expertise here."

"Good let me call my tech." She turns to me, smiles, and starts dialing her cell phone.

"Hi, Kathy. Can you bring three 5 mm cuvettes over to David Piehl's laboratory?" In between short periods of silence, we listen to the one-way conversation.

"They will be fine, I need them right now. His lab is on the first floor, room 116." A pause and she continues,

"Perfect, thanks." She again turns to David to ask a question. I'm feeling like second banana here. Well maybe I am; he started all this.

"Are you concerned that instead of repeating the successful extraction process with the previously used seawater, that the introduction of another variable, new water, may not yield successful results?" This was my idea, therefore I field the question.

"Normally we would be systematic and use the original solution and then try different seawater, but time is against us. We don't like to make assumptions but have made a few in this case. We hope that if the San Francisco seawater fails to release the seeds that we will be able to change to the original solution and achieve success. If San Francisco water somehow interferes in the process to liberate the seeds, this, in itself, is an interesting finding. We can continue to use the original water on the remaining seeds. However, if the San Francisco water successfully extracts the seeds than that is a significant verification and we will have jumped a step."

"That's reasonable, as you know, I too am short on time." Vanesa's technician enters the lab, sees her and hands her a sterilized bag containing 3 small glass cubicles.

"Thanks, Kathy, I'll be back in a few minutes."

David takes the bag, removes a cubicle and brings it over to the stage of the microscope. Using forceps, he lifts the lid and places it on clean aluminum foil. He sets the meteorite into the cubicle. While he does this, I remove a covered jar of the seawater from the refrigerator and place it on the bench near the microscope. He takes out a pipette, transfers water into the cuvette until the piece is just covered and askes Vanessa,

"How is this?"

"Fine, go ahead and put on the lid. I will leave you the remaining cuvettes in case you want to soak some more." Still looking at David, she says,

"I don't have any spare lights perhaps Grant could bring this one over and help me get set up." What is she doing, I'm right here. I guess I'm just a lackey now. David is amused.

"Of course, he would be glad to." She looks at me.

"Of course, I would be glad to." I say using his same tone and inflections adding a big smile to seal the deal. With that, we gather our material and head to her lab. Setting up the cuvette under the UV lamp and her equipment we engage in small talk.

"This is an incredible discovery, I'm very excited. Thank you for including me."

"Of course, we absolutely need you. Do you want to go over what our goals should be?"

"Yes, you start."

"We know it's a unicellular organism. First, we want to see if you can identify the cell as a known earth organism. If not then we need to learn all we can. You know, does it have a nucleus, chromosomes, cell wall, mitochondria, etc. anything you can learn. We need a count of how many cells there are and if they all are exactly the same."

"Sounds good. I would like to isolate a few for cultivation

and then take a few and stain them to identify structures."

"Good, follow any course you think prudent. Speaking of prudent, what do you know of Prudence's work?"

"I was going to ask you about DNA sequencing. We do extractions here, but she is better equipped to sequence the code. Are you willing to bring her into the project? If so maybe you should let me discuss it with her."

"Why is that?"

"She is gorgeous. We wouldn't want you to be distracted from our important work here."

"Ha-ha, well you are very hot, and I am managing to sustain my concentration." This causes her to flush read.

"Stop it."

"I'm actually seeing someone right now."

"I heard that you were dating a cop."

"Yes, and how we met is an apt segue to discuss security with you. We have touched on the need to keep our activities secluded, but did not elaborate on the forces behind the requirement." With the meteorite piece soaking in seawater under the lamp, I summarize the series of events involving Marcus's murder, the multiple attempts to kill David and me and the visitor to my house.

"The sheriff detective that I'm seeing has a lead that may put an end to the violence, but for now we need to remain vigilant. It would be best to keep your name out of this work. Similarly, if we decide to involve Prudie. I don't really know her, what do you think about involving her?"

"She has a gap between projects right now so she should have the time. From what I know about her she would not wane in the face of potential threats. If we really have LUCA sitting in that cuvette right now, I guarantee she will be interested in participating and would not have a problem waiving her costs for the opportunity to co-author a publication on the results."

"Sounds good. Prudence dictates that we wait to engage Prudence until we see what you find. You see what I did there? That's two."

"Lame."

"Ha-ha, seriously though, perhaps you could see what her schedule looks like for the next week without giving her any details. I hope we are going to have a cuvette filled with numerous unicellular organisms, but there is no sense in bringing her up to speed until we are certain. If she is booked for the next two weeks or so we may have to go to an outside lab."

"That's reasonable. We often have clients check our schedule to see if we could handle samples for a given period and then we never hear from them again. She will need a couple of days to complete the work, I'll ask her if she has that block of time for some samples that may be received."

"Perfect. How long have the seeds been incubating?"

"Almost an hour, let's see if anything is happening." She places the cuvette under a stereomicroscope and makes the necessary adjustments. After a minute she says,

"There are a few empty pockets, but many more have not changed. That is so cool, it looks like it is going to work, but we should give it more time."

"Dr. McFadden?" We both turn to her tech, but then Vanessa returns her attention to the microscope.

"What is it, Kathy?"

"The fluorescent stains are finished." Without looking up from the scope, she replies,

"Very well, I'll be right there to take a look." Kathy retreats to the other side of the lab, and I say,

"Well, I better return to David's lab and see what he has accomplished. Will you check in with us later?" Rising from the stool, she says,

"This is so much fun. Yes, shall I come by around 4:30 and update you guys?"

"Sure"

"I'll go talk to Prudie in a few minutes." Back at David's lab, we compare notes.

"I performed a cursory look at the particulate matter that was broken up by the press." Pointing at a larger irregular piece on a slide he continues,

"That piece is 3.7 mm. I found no seeds. Thus far all pieces below 2 mm have had at least one or more seeds. I think we are narrowing in on the size range that contains seeds."

"Very cool. How are you storing the separated particles?" He points to an area on the bench.

"I'm placing them in labeled Teflon filter holders."

Examining the stored particles in the holders, I say,

"Excellent idea." In one type of particle sampling, we use thin filters composed of Teflon, quartz or nylon. They have a diameter of 40 mm. Air is drawn through the filters and particles of 2.5-10 microns are trapped on the filters. The net weight of the filter along with the flow rate and the length of time air is drawn is used to calculate the concentration of particulate matter in the air. The filters are stored and shipped in these holders. They are well suited to storing the smaller meteorite particles as they are about 50 mm in diameter, only about 10 mm thick, are made of clear plastic and have a tight-fitting lid.

"How is it going over at Vanessa's lab?"

"It's going well. After just under an hour, some seeds have fallen. She is letting them soak a while longer."

"That's great news."

"She is going to come by around 4:30 and give us a progress report. Also, she is going to call Prudie to check on her schedule. For now, she is just telling her that she may have some DNA coding work for her and just wants to know if she is available."

"Sounds good."

"Oh, I forgot to tell you Janis and her brother are coming over for dinner tonight. She has some information to share."

"Interesting, keep me informed."

I head back to my office to work on project budgets. At 4:45 Vanessa calls my cell.

"Grant, I have fantastic results but need to finish a few things tomorrow morning. Can I come by first thing tomorrow morning? I need to go rescue a girlfriend."

"Come on you are going to leave us in suspense? Give me something."

"I need to check a few things, but there is a 95% chance that these organisms do not exist on earth. I've got to go." I pass on the exciting if cursory results to David and also need to exit.

Chapter 28

The bell rings, and the security panel indicates it's Janis and Josh.

"Hi, guys welcome." Josh moves past me, and I say to Janis,

"Let me take your coat." I slide off one arm and then the other. With the coat off, I find she is wearing a figure-hugging dress with long sleeves, incredible.

"You look lovely." She reaches up and kisses me on the lips and holds it for a few seconds. I wasn't sure what she was going to do in front of her brother. I take Josh's coat and hang up both in the living room closet.

"Can I get anyone a drink?" They both raise their hands, look at each other and laugh lightly.

"What are you two related?" Which earns me another giggle from Janis. Josh weighs in,

"Do you have the means to make a margarita?"

"I have the means and the wherewithal. Blended or rocks?"

"I don't want to put you to too much trouble."

"If you make them blended, I'll join him."

"Blended it is. Regular, strawberry or mango?" Janis replies,

"Now you are just showing off. Regular is fine."

"Salted rims or regular?"

"That's it. I'm going to shoot you."

Josh intervenes. "Hey leave him alone. Salted would be great."

"Very well." I move past Janis, scrunch my face and stick out my tongue at her.

"Don't take that thing out unless you plan to use it."

Josh complains,

"Ew, you aren't going to be like this all night are you?"

Janis says, "Maybe, tough luck." I intervene with,

"You two remind me of my brother and me."

"We have always been close, but he won't admit it

because he's angry about the constant beatings by a girl." Josh looks at me in protest and says,

"She's older."

"Just two years." Having all the ingredients in the blender, I put an end to their mock fight and turn it on high. While the blender crushes the icy mixture, I line three margarita glasses rimmed with salt. They have moved to the balcony windows to look out at the city lights. Once the blender is off, they turn back to the kitchen and see me pouring the drinks. I place their two glasses on the breakfast bar next to some chips, salsa, and guacamole and they sit down on bar stools. Josh says,

"Those look delicious, Thank you."

"You made an excellent choice in cocktails, we are having tacos for dinner."

"It's my detective's intuition."

"I see." I look over at Janis, and she just rolls her eyes.

Over the drinks and dip, I learn that Josh was a detective in a small town in California and their father was a detective in the Bay Area. Josh quit after only a couple of years saying it was boring, that nothing ever happened there. Instead of getting in with a larger town he got his private investigator license in Nevada and California.

While we talk I leave them sitting at the bar and get up to make another pitcher and start pulling out taco food that I had prepared. Ok, white man's taco food. If my friend Juan were over, he would have been displeased. I did buy some marinated chicken, peppers and onions from a local Mexican store and had blackened the meat earlier and cooked my own black beans. Now I am just rewarming everything and creating a mini taco bar. I remove flour tortilla shells warming in the oven and add them to the bar.

"Make a taco and then let's sit over at the table." While they made their tacos, I refresh our drinks. Settled at the table, Janis decides to get down to business.

"Josh why don't you brief Grant on your activities today." He had just taken a big bite from his overstuffed tortilla shell and just nodded yes. We ate while waiting for him to finish his bite and then he says,

"These are delicious by the way."

"Thanks."

"I gave the report to my contact at the church. All the while scanning everyone I saw for your large visitor. He never appeared. On the way out I stopped by the secretary in the office, she and I have been very friendly in the past. No one else was in the room. I chatted her up briefly then told her I had seen a man at the church a while back that looked like he may have been a rancher. I told her my cousin was looking to board her horse, but everyone was too expensive.

"Very plausible." I say. Josh gives me half a nod to express mild agreement and then continues.

"She asked if he was really tall and pretty fit. I said yes, then she said it was probably Jake Barnes. But he is not a rancher. He owns the store, Boot Country located south of town. I thanked her and told her I would keep looking. I paid Boot Country a visit, but he was not there. I looked around for a while holding off a couple of salespeople trying to decide how to ask one of them if he was in the store." He takes a long sip from his margarita and then continues.

"These are so good." Before I could respond, he continues.

"As I'm working on a story to tell the salespeople, he

appears from the back room. He was all decked out in western gear but was not wearing a hat. While pretending to be reading text messages or something on my phone I really was taking pictures of him. I always have my shutter sound off, so it's not revealed that I'm using the camera."

Josh pulls out his smartphone from his back pocket, hits a few buttons and shows me a picture.

"Is this the guy?" I study the phone carefully and then say,

"That's him, 100%." Josh displays a satisfied look and resumes eating his taco. I say,

"That was fast work Josh. Nice job."

"To be honest, it is never that easy. I got lucky."

Janis says,

"I like your modesty, but not everyone would have gotten the information from the secretary."

"Thanks."

I look at Janis. She smiles and says,

"I notified Tyler, he is coming up tomorrow. We are both going to pay Jake Barnes a visit tomorrow."

"Are you going to arrest him?"

"Yes, for home invasion. Of course, we really want him for Marcus's murder if we can get it. Failing that maybe we can get him to give up someone else. I'm concerned that there are many people involved in the murder and murder attempts. This is not the person who pushed you over the cliff skiing, correct?"

"I never saw who pushed me, but there were only three people nearby, and none were of his size."

"So we have Jake Barnes and the skier. The dead guy that wanted to send David and you over yet another cliff could be the skier or a third guy. Jake Barnes doesn't seem likely to be the person who stealthily manipulates gas values in David's lab. So it's either the skier, the third guy or a fourth person."

"I see your point. Do you guys want any more food?" Josh and I already have had seconds.

"I can help you out and finish those avocado slices and tomatoes." volunteers Janis. I grab those dishes and bring them over to her. Josh says,

"May I borrow your restroom?"

"Of course, right around the corner there." Once the door closes, Janis asks,

"What are you doing tonight after all this?"

"No plans, clean up, go upstairs and read or something."

"Any girls coming over to spend the night?"

"No."

"Want one?"

"I would love it. Can you?"

"Yes, Josh and I took separate cars."

"Excellent," I say goodbye to Josh, and Janis walks him out to their cars. She returns with a small overnight bag and a garment bag. While loading the dishwasher, I ask,

"Would you like an after dinner drink or some coffee."

"No thanks, those margaritas were excellent, they have a kick. I'm buzzed. Let me help you clean up and then, if you don't mind, I'd like to take a shower."

"That's Ok, I've got this. Let's go up and get you situated, and I'll come back down and finish here." I grab her bag, and we climb the stairs to my bedroom. Entering the room with the lights off, she exclaims,

"Oh my god, you have even a nicer view up here. And in the bathroom too, this is spectacular." Turning on the lights, I say,

"Definitely why I bought the place. So you didn't notice the last time we were up here?"

"Ha-ha I was a little distracted, and the lights amplify the scene."

"There are soap and shampoo in the shower and here is a fresh towel. I'll be back up in a few minutes."

"Thanks." I walk over and kiss her. Finishing up the dishes, checking the doors and setting the alarm I join Janis upstairs. She finished her ablutions and is now wearing a short, lightweight silk robe. Extremely sexy. I turn down the bed and join her in the bathroom to brush my teeth.

"Nice robe."

"Thought you might like it." I undress down to my underwear, thinking I'm on equal footing with her attire. I turn off the lights allowing only city lights to illuminate the bathroom. We remain in there kissing and caressing for about 20 minutes. I finally lead her to the bed, remove my underwear, but make her keep on the robe.

We made love and then dropped off to sleep. Our lovemaking has become tender with longer caressing, without losing any intensity.

"Good morning. I'll get you some coffee. Can I make you breakfast?"

"Thanks, maybe something light?

"Yogurt with raspberries and granola?"

"Perfect. I'm going to hop in the shower."

Once the water from her shower ends, I bring up her coffee and yogurt.

"That looks great, thank you." She takes a couple of bites and says,

"This is delicious, what kind of yogurt is this?"

"Homemade."

"Stop it."

"It's actually fairly easy. But of course, I'm deploying the same temperature control devices David and I constructed for our experiments. It's probably overkill, but since we already have the technology, it also was easy to set up." She gives me a stern look and asks,

"What about the granola, is that homemade also?" I just shrugged my shoulders and gave her a look to say well yes.

"You're killing me. If you tell me these raspberries are grown in your garden, I'm going to punch you in the throat."

"Take it easy, those were purchased. So how does it feel knowing you are going to arrest a guy today?"

"I'm pretty comfortable. I am not anticipating that he will resist."

"Are you going to go to his store?"

"Yes, I have a junior colleague in plain clothes staking out the store. He is going to call me when and if he arrives. At some point you may need to come in and identify him, we'll see how it goes." We both get dressed, she in her uniform that was in her garment bag. After a few more cups of coffee, we prepare to leave. She walks up to me and gives me a hug and kiss on the lips.

"Thank you for a nice evening. You are a beautiful man."

"I'm flattered. That's very sweet thanks. Be safe today and call when you can."

Chapter 29

Working in my office my cell phone rings, it's Vanessa.

"Hi Grant, I'm ready. It might be better if you two come over to my lab, I'm alone right now."

"Will do, I'll grab David, and we will head over in a few." I find David in his office.

"Vanessa is ready, she wants us to come over to her lab." Without a word, he saves some documents on his computer and rises from behind his desk. Her lab is in another building, so I take the opportunity to tell him the news.

"Regarding my meeting with Janis and her brother, they found the guy! She is going to arrest him today."

"Outstanding that was fast. Who is he?"

"He is with the church. Her bother learned that he is a member of the church and owns a local western store."

"That's a relief." We enter Vanessa's lab and are greeted with,

"Good morning. Before I get started, David are you familiar with the current concept of the Three of Life?" He says,

"Since this started I've been studying the concept of a common ancestor. There are three branches, Bacteria, Archaebacterial, and Eucaryota. Plants and animals are Eukaryotes. The three branches are believed to stem from LUCA."

"Good. One reason for this theory is that organisms in all three branches share 23 common proteins. It's reasonable to conclude that they all got them from a common ancestor. One problem with the tree is it is oversimplified. There is evidence of gene crossover between domains."

She turns a laptop so that we can see the screen. There is a photograph of the familiar looking single-celled beast that appears like the one we initially found.

"I found hundreds of this guy." She takes her mouse and moves it to the center of this oblong creature.

"This right here is a nucleus. All Eukaryotes have one, bacteria and Archaea lack a nucleus. From an evolutionary standpoint, it is more likely that LUCA would have lacked a nucleus and then evolved one later in the Eukaryotes. It's less likely that the other domains evolved to drop the nucleus. Similarly, this is mitochondria, and here is a Golgi apparatus. None of these are present in the other two domains, and again it's unlikely they were dropped. Don't get me wrong it can happen, many animals have vestigial parts, our appendix for example." I jump in and say,

"Crap, so it's not LUCA. But you thought it was not of this world." She gives me a quiet glance, then one to David and without answering clicks on another photograph.

"I also found several of these. Note, no nucleus, mitochondria, or Golgi apparatus, and it has a cell wall." I respond,

"Whoa, an early Archaea?"

"Looks like it to me." Now David is intrigued.

"Are you going to bring up another photo of an early bacterium?" She smiles and clicks on an arrow that slides in a third photograph.

"I found several of these as well. You can see it's much smaller than the other two. I need more time to enhance the image, but it looks very primitive. Based on its smaller size, it could very well be an early bacterium." I propose an obvious conclusion.

"Perhaps then there is no single LUCA, but one for each

of these major branches."

"It's a plausible conclusion. We could strengthen the argument by testing for the 23 proteins and getting the genetic code. I spoke with Prudence, and she said she has a one week window and then is out of town for a couple of weeks. She could start work tomorrow. To this end, I have started the process of separating out the DNA from each type of organism. I might be able to finish today. How would you like to proceed?" I turn to David as a gesture for him to offer his view.

"This is all good stuff. Any data that we can obtain to lockdown our theories will be critical. The sooner we can get the data, the better. I'm glad you got started, let's get Prudence on-board today. Who should we send to go talk to her?"

"Well, you guys are going to need to negotiate a deal with her, so count me out. After that, she and I can get together to discuss details."

"Grant you got Vanessa to join us why don't you talk to her." I turn to Vanessa and give her an exaggerated wink. And without taking my eyes from her say,

"I would be glad to take on this task."

"You're a dick."

"Yes. Yes I am." And I turn and exit the lab.

"What was that all about?" Asks David. She points at the space just occupied by Grant, and then her arms go limp.

"Nothing."

"How are you processing the samples to extract the DNA?"

"Kathy is working on it next door. An oversimplified explanation: first we crack the cell and then use a surfactant to 'wash' out the DNA. We will keep it in a solution of Purdie's choice."

"Is it likely that you will be finished today?"

"It is likely, I'll check with Kathy and give you an update this afternoon."

"Sounds good, talk to you later."

Prudence was not in her office. As I head to her lab, she turns the corner walking toward me with her head down. As we get closer, she looks up at me.

"Prudence I don't know if you remember me..."

"Grant Steelzner, over in atmospheric sciences?"

"Close enough. Vanessa mentioned to you that she might have some DNA samples for analysis?"

"Yes."

"The project is sensitive, do you have a few minutes to discuss it."

"Sure, let's step into my office." I start with the latest finding of the three types of cells and work my way backward.

"Vanessa said you were working on a seminal discovery, but LUCA, that's unimaginable. And three different versions. Impressive for a couple of air pollution guys."

"Well..."

"I will want to see these things in person and will discuss specific preparation requirements with Vanessa."

"My cell biology knowledge has been clouded amidst golf muscle memory and sports statistics. Will you be able to list the proteins present in each organism. We are keenly interested in whether each has the 23 proteins present in current cells."

"Yes, I can provide this information. I will list them out separately for each cell."

"Regarding security, we have had attacks on our lives." I give her a summary of all that has happened to us.

"The detective working the case is making an arrest today. Accordingly, I'm hoping it will end the murderous actions. However, for now, it would be best to keep this work secret."

"It's unimaginable that the church would kill people over a scientific discovery. First, do they think we are cowards? Do they reason we are simply going to say, 'oh lets shut down, so these ass holes don't hurt us?' This kind of thing makes me more determined to complete the work and find the truth. Second, we still don't know where LUCA originated. Perhaps some God created them and sent them off into the universe."

"I admire your determination and desire to seek the truth. It's why we were drawn to science. I think the problem evangelicals might have in this case is that we are saying humanity originated from aliens. To the deeply faithful, that must strike them as vulgar. It challenges the contents of the Bible and the other tomes."

"I see your point about aliens, I don't look at them that

way. In any event, I'm enthusiastic about getting started." She gives me a playful smile and says,

"By the way, is the detective that is making the arrest the one you are dating?"

"What the hell. Am I required reading around here?" I can feel myself blushing.

"Ha-ha, we women have quite a network within the Institute."

"I would say so."

"I'm sorry please continue."

"Where was I. Oh, How long will it take you to analyze the three samples?"

"If Vanessa gets me samples by tomorrow morning, I should be able to finish them by the end of the day."

"Now for your costs."

"Don't worry about it. I know you guys are doing this on your own. I can cover it."

"Great, thanks. Of course, we hope to publish in Science,

and you will be a co-author."

"Thank you, that's very generous."

"Hey, I've seen your rates. It's a good deal for us. Alright then, I'm going to head back, thanks."

"I'll walk with you, I'm going to see Vanessa. Seriously, how did you guys make this finding?"

"You know David right?"

"We have never met. I have heard he is a fuckup." That comment starts a wave of growing anger, Luther is spreading rumors. That guy is a prime ass hole.

"David is anything but a fuckup. He is incredibly talented and resourceful. Following his curiosity, he took some of our 'air pollution' samples and looked at them microscopically." I placed the air pollution in air quotes."

"Ooh sensitive. I know you guys are atmospheric scientists. I was just giving you trouble." I can't help but give her a smile.

"Anyway, he found a particle that appeared like it may have broken off a meteorite and started to play with it."

“Amazing. Well, I’m going this way.” She starts to turn down a hall and turns back and says,

“Hey if it doesn’t work out with the detective let me know.”

“Sounds good, I will. Except I have a feeling, you will find out before I do.”

“Ha-ha.”

Chapter 30

Janis received the call that Jake Barnes had arrived in his office. She had obtained an arrest warrant yesterday, and with Tyler made the arrest. Barnes was booked into the Washoe County Sheriff's office. He called an attorney, and the four of them were in an interrogation room. The proceedings are being videotaped. The date, time, and participants are identified, and Janis begins questioning him.

"Mr. Barnes, last Friday night you were involved in a home invasion of Grant Stelzner. You waited for Mr. Stelzner to arrive and then threatened him..." Before she can continue, his lawyer stops her.

"There was an alleged home invasion, it is Stelzner's word against my clients, and frankly, I don't know how you were able to get an arrest warrant."

"Arrived at this case cold did you, counselor?" Janis slides over an iPad and starts a video from Grant's home doorbell camera. Grant assumed he did not ring the bell so, at first, he didn't think of checking the video archive. However, he finally remembered it also records a clip when detecting motion. The video shows Barnes checking the front door and then looking in the living room window.

“So he came to the door realized no one was home and left.” She turns to Barnes and asks,

“Is that your statement Mr. Barnes? That you came to the door, saw no one was home and left, never entering? Barnes looks at his attorney for help but receives none.

Barnes says,

“Yes, that is my statement I never was in the house.”

She starts another video and turns the screen to both men. The motion detector catches him exiting the front door.

“That was fun to watch, you weighing the risk of lying, hoping there was no more video. Not too bright though. If a motion sensor triggers you at the window, it follows that it would catch you exiting. Now I have you for making a false statement.” Both he and his lawyer remain silent.

“Let me tell you a story. The Friday before last, a man stowed away on a research vessel. The person waited until the boat was out on frozen Lake Tahoe and then threw the researcher overboard, drowning him in the frigid water.” Janis studied Barnes carefully. He showed no reaction.

"We think you were the man that committed that murder."

"I'm certain you are not going to produce a video this time because I wasn't on any boat on Lake Tahoe."

"Can you verify your whereabouts on that Friday?" He remains silent while remembering the day.

"Can you give me my phone? It has my calendar on it." Janis gets up and leaves the room. The lawyer asks Tyler.

"Detective Owens, I'm curious, why a Placer County Sheriff Deputy is interested in this minor arrest in Washoe County."

"For now, that curiosity will go unfulfilled." He turns to Blake and says,

"I will tell you this, home invasion is a felony, and you will be spending time in prison. That doesn't seem 'minor' to me." Janis walks back into the room and hands Barnes his smartphone. He enters the password, navigates to the calendar app and studies it. After a few minutes, he says,

"I don't remember, and there is nothing on my calendar, I probably was working at my store."

"If I send a deputy to your store and talk to your employees is it likely someone there will remember if you were in that day?"

"I don't know, my manager runs the day to day operations. I come and go as I need to."

"Shall I send someone to ask around or would you like to admit you don't have an alibi for Friday." The lawyer jumps in before he can comment.

"Mr. Barnes has said he was not at Lake Tahoe, if he cannot account for his time from two weeks ago it does not change that."

"Hey, I'm just trying to rule him out for the murder. Let's try something else."

"Let's," says the attorney.

"We know members of the Rock of the Living Word Church are actively involved in surveillance of Mr. Stelzner, there have been several attempts to kill him, and you broke into his house and threatened to kill him if he did not end his research. I am willing to go to the district attorney to keep you out of jail, if you can establish an alibi for Friday, and if you tell me who in the church you are working for." The attorney grabs his arm, but before he can stop him, Barnes blurts out,

"I'm not working for anyone in the church. I entered his house on my own."

"Again with the lies, Mr. Barnes if you are working by yourself, how did you know what the scientists were working on, how did you know Marcus Kieslar was missing on the Lake. Remember when you threatened Mr. Stelzner..." She pauses to look down at her notes.

"You said, 'Mr. Kieslar has paid for his Godlessness, I would advise you to avoid a similar fate.' Mr. Kieslar's death has not been reported. How would you know of his death?" The attorney interrupts.

"May I have a word with my client?"

"Absolutely." Janis goes to the door and asks for the two to be escorted to a consultation room and for them to be returned when ready. They were escorted to the room, where there are no cameras or audio equipment. They returned after five minutes.

"My client is ready to answer your question." Barnes

begins,

"I am a volunteer at the church. I take minutes at meetings when the secretary is absent. Church leadership learned of scientists studying an alternative theory of genesis based on empirical evidence. There was a concern that their work was going to break in the media and the church wanted to be prepared to deal with it. Dr. Luther, a high ranking scientist in their Institute, is a church member. He was asked about their work. Dr. Luther thought they were incompetent scientists but may have blundered onto something. The Church, concerned with the dissemination of false information, encouraged Dr. Luther to fire the scientists. After all, they were incompetent. He explained that he did not have the authority to terminate their contracts, but would see what he could do. It was Dr. Luther that reported, in the meeting, that Marcus Kieslar was found missing on the Institute's boat on the Lake. He said there was speculation that he was killed because of their origin of life studies."

Barnes takes a sip of water. Janis doesn't ask any questions allowing him to continue.

"As a Christian, I know how life originated on Earth. I don't need some incompetent heathens spreading lies creating more ignorant people in this country. So I paid Stelzner a visit, on my own, the Church knows nothing about it. I never laid a hand on him. I just wanted him to think about what he was doing."

"A man tried to kill Mr. Stelzner and Dr. Piehl in the Sierras last Monday. What can you tell us about it?"

"I can't tell you anything about it. Other than it was not me."

"Who was it?"

"I told you I don't know."

"Do you snow ski, Mr. Barnes?"

"No."

"So if I get a warrant to search your house and office I won't find any skies?"

"No."

"Are you aware of anyone else in the church that may know what the scientists are doing and would want to kill them because of it?"

"No." Janis looks at Tyler to give him the opportunity to ask any questions. He takes it.

"Mr. Barnes, one question. Is there anyone in the Church or your circle of acquaintances that is missing?

"Not that I am aware of, but I don't know every member."

Janis says, "I think we are done for now."

Janis and Tyler get up and leave the room and tell the guard that they were finished. They walk to the parking lot, and Janis asks,

"What do you think?"

"On one hand I believe him, he seems credible. However, I think he is so committed in his faith that if a higher up in the church told him to go silence Grant that he would go beat the crap out of him, skillfully lie to us about it and take the lie to his grave."

"My thoughts exactly. Did you notice that he takes the minutes of meetings 'when' the secretary is absent?"

"Right he takes the minutes when they want the secretary to be absent."

"Exactly."

"What are you going to do about his Friday alibi?"

"I have someone over there right now. He should almost be finished. When are you going to look for the body?"

"I'm not sure. These storms keep rolling in, one right after the other. Beneficial for our snowpack, but not for retrieving a corpse. I hope their coordinates are reliable."

"They are geek scientists, I'm sure they will be spot on."

"Yeah, you're probably right. I'm going to hike in there with a colleague at the first opportunity and evaluate the terrain before I request our search and rescue unit." They reach their cars, and Janis says,

"Alright, take care, keep in touch, I'll let you know about his alibi."

"Good." He gives her a big smile and says,

"Oh and by the way, from what I heard up at Squaw, Grant can't be too big of a geek." Janis laughs, turns bright red, and says,

"Shut up!

Chapter 31

The snowcapped mountains ringing the Reno valley this sunny Friday morning create a beautiful drive to work. Vanessa finished her DNA extractions yesterday and walked them over to Prudence who will start gene sequencing this morning. She was able to increase the magnification of the assumed bacterium LUCA. It is coccus shaped with a visible capsule and flagella. As I pull into the parking lot, Alan, our Division Director is getting out of his car. Seeing me pull in, he waits for me to exit.

"Good morning Grant. How are things going?" We start to walk to our building.

"Things are going well, we have a lead on what may be happing with the Sierra data. Data from the rest of the sites look good, and so far we have 100% data recovery. Our other projects are just humming along." As we enter our building, Alan says,

"Great, I hope you get to the bottom of the Sierra issue. See you later." I'm grateful he doesn't probe into our meteorite work. He knows there is undeclared activity occurring but is being patient, waiting for us to come to him. I get into my office, click my laptop into its docking station and David appears at my door.

"We received an email from Dr. Rod Eastwood. Do you

remember him? He also works for the same energy consortium as Angela. He is an atmospheric modeler at USC."

"I'm drawing a blank."

"We met him in one of the planning meetings. It doesn't matter. His group wants to make background organics measurements in the Tahoe National Forest. They are operating a site in the Yuba River District and want to piggyback on our background site near Cisco. They would provide us with the equipment for the site near Cisco, we would just need to add one of their analyzers. I'm familiar with the unit, we have room for it. They also want us to evaluate and operate a third site near Sierraville. He wants to know if we can evaluate the Sierraville site this Monday. What do you think?"

"Sounds like a nice add-on, I think Monday will work. Did he ask for a budget?"

"Not yet. If we are interested, he will give us instructions to the proposed site and have someone meet us there."

"Fine with me."

"Good, I'll email him back for the directions."

"Janis called me last night. They arrested Barnes for home

invasion. They are checking his alibi for the Friday that Marcus was killed. He claims to have been acting alone, that the church only wanted to keep an eye on us and none of them were involved in the murders."

"Did she believe him?"

"You know I didn't think to ask her. She probably does have an opinion. I guess I just assumed everyone denies it. She said he lied to her stating that he never entered the house. Then she busted him with the doorbell camera video. These kinds of people would lie their asses off to protect the church."

"It will be interesting if he can't come up with an alibi. I'm going to validate some data. Let me know when we hear from Prudence."

David leaves, and we work on our projects until about 3:00 when Prudie calls.

"Hi, Grant. I have some preliminary results. Do you have a conference room over there we can use? Vanessa is going to meet with us."

"Yes, we have one, let me check to see if it is open." The room is open, and the four of us convene there. Once we were settled, Prudie starts.

"Let's start with the easier material. I ran software that transitioned a nucleotide sequence..." She looked at David and said,

"This constructed a protein sequence from the DNA sequence. All three organisms have the same 23 proteins found in cells from the three domains. As you know, the fact that all the domains have the same proteins was a key element supporting the concept for a single common ancestor. Based on this information, life on earth started with three rather than one, and they came from space." She let that statement hang in the air for a while." Finally, David speaks.

"I wish to confirm my understanding of this. When you speak of a DNA sequence, this is the famous double helix structure, correct?"

"Yes, it's the exact order of nucleotides in the DNA molecule. It provides us with the order of the bases adenine, cytosine, guanine and thymine." He asks a follow-up question.

"Based on the structure of these three cells you can say definitively that they do not now exist on earth?"

"Not definitively yet. It has taken Vanessa and me two days just to get to this point. It could take us another year to definitively answer that question. We can generate a strong hypothesis that states these cells did not originate on earth and are the basis for all life on this planet. Then we need to set out to obtain the evidence that supports the theory. The Biological Systematics community has come a long way in developing genome data, but we are not at the point where we can run a search of every organism's DNA and compare it to these data to definitively say they did not originate from earth. The likely next steps would involve obtaining available gene data from the lowest organisms in each domain tree and compare them to our LUCA data."

I add to her answer.

"There are thousands of inquiries that can be pursued from here. For example, if these seeds are continuing to impact earth today, are there new organisms continuing to evolve from them. Or are the conditions of today's earth now unfavorable to sustain them?"

Vanessa adds,

"It was until only recently that scientists discovered some

of the Archaea living in harsh environments. It is assumed that they have lived there for millions of years. Perhaps instead, they are newly developed from these seeds."

Prudie says,

"I believe that in a short period, as the genome of these three cells are studied that we are going to learn that although they are very similar to our earth species that they also have a sequence like no other cells seen on earth. Without a doubt, these findings definitely are going to rock the worlds of evolutionary biology and NASA." This throws a sober blanket of quiet in the room. I am the first to speak.

"David and I have considered, for quite some time now, to hold a press conference announcing this discovery as a way to cease the attempted attacks on our lives. The thinking was that these religious zealots assumed that if they could take out the three of us before anyone else knew what we were doing, that this finding would die with us. We were reluctant to go public until we had solid scientific evidence." I stop there and look at David. He continues my line of reasoning.

"Yes, we are ready. It is time to go to Alan, explain our findings and suggest we hold a press conference." He goes to the conference room phone.

"Hi Alan, I'm glad I caught you. I'm in a meeting with Grant, Vanessa McFadden, and Prudence White. We have arrived at a position that requires your urgent attention. Is there any way you could come down to the conference right now for a few minutes?"

"Excellent thank you. He is coming right down, but has a meeting in 20 minutes."

David provides a summary of our research to Alan. While quietly listening to the information, it is fun to watch his expressions and body language change. First, his pose is one of sure, sure I knew that you were working on something. Then one of 'wait what?' , and finally one of agitation and excitement. He begins a series of excited questions while looking at all three of us in turn and not waiting for answers.

"This is unbelievable. Are you absolutely sure of these results? There is no chance of cross-contamination? Are you sure you are ready to go to the press? Perhaps you need to check on some things, repeat some tests?" I can't take it anymore.

"Relax Alan, we have been diligent. We need to get this out now before someone stops with the accidental death attempts and just puts a bullet in our heads."

Prudie says,

"Of course they may just bomb this place."

Alan walks over to the conference room phone, and while dialing he points to Prudie and says,

"Let's not over-react. Sheriff Deputy Taylor has made an arrest, and I agree that we should get this out..."

"Hi, John. Is it too late to arrange a press conference for this evening's news? We have a major scientific discovery to report." There is silence as he listens to the response of our public relations officer.

"Damn it. I suppose not, no one watches the news on Saturday. Can you make arrangements for Monday sometime around...?" He looks at us to give him a time. Davis says,

"After 1:00." He continues,

"After 1:00? Very well, thanks. He said it was too late. Their news programs start at 5:30."

"Grant and I need to check out a monitoring site Monday morning, it should only take us a couple of hours."

"Fine, I'm going to call our NASA contact and give him a heads up. Hopefully, we can talk him into a large grant. I've got to go. Good luck to all of you and great job!" I say,

"And so it begins, things are going to be crazy around her for a while. David, you better bring a change of clothes on Monday. There is heavy snow up there. Should we consider postponing visiting the site until Tuesday?"

"I think it will be fine, we are meeting him up there at 9. We should get back in time."

"As long as we don't get stuck in the snow."

"Bite your tongue. We are too good for that." Addressing the group, he continues.

"So listen, I don't mind taking the lead at the conference, but I want all four of us up there, we are a team now. Usually, we wait to do these things a couple of days before a paper is published. Hence I don't want to give out too many details. We will tell them that we are preparing a journal article that will contain all the details. If you ladies have any breakthroughs between now and Monday keep us informed. Have a good weekend everyone." David and I walk to our offices. I say,

"I'm going to Janis's place up in Incline tomorrow. Hopefully, I will get more details and an update on the arrest. I will tell her about the press conference."

"Very well, I'll see you Monday, bring your snow gear."

Chapter 32

My doorbell rings as I'm sitting on my back deck with a cup of coffee trying to wake up. Checking my phone, it's Janis's brother, Josh. He texted me last night asking if he could stop by this morning. Opening the door, I say,

"Good morning, come in. Would you like a cup of coffee?

"Yes please." We take our coffees out to the deck and sit down at a small outdoor table. Josh explains the purpose of his visit.

"I wanted to let you know that the church asked me to take another turn at their surveillance of you. From this, I conclude that they are still following you. Have you seen anyone?"

"No, we stopped looking, I had assumed they quit. Did they give you a reason for following me? It makes no sense, did you accept?"

"I asked them. They want to know if you visit the office of Rachel Waters."

"Who the hell is Rachel Waters?"

"I don't know, I hoped you would know. I asked them who she was, but they said just report back to them immediately if you went to her office. They gave me her address. It's in one of those high rise buildings downtown. And yes, I told them I would take the job. It's only for today, and I thought it would afford me the opportunity to learn what this is all about."

"You haven't looked into who she is?"

"No, I haven't had time. They just called me early this morning and asked me to get over here. Periodically, they spot check their investigators to confirm they are actually performing the duties for which they are billed. I picked up a car following me over here from my house. Once I parked up your street, he drove away, and after 10 minutes he hadn't returned, so I thought it safe to knock on your door. Is your computer available?"

"Sure, it's upstairs, I'll go get it. Help yourself to more coffee." With laptop in hand, we sit down at the kitchen table. I ask,

"Shall we Google her?"

"Yes to start, I have some other search engines also." I enter her name into the search box. I say,

"Ok here are several pages of images of Rachel Waters. Unless you have a description of her, I don't see how this is going to help us."

"Well, let's look at Rachel Waters' profiles on Facebook. Yikes, five pages of profiles." It takes us a few minutes to inspect them all. Josh says,

"None from Reno, or Nevada for that matter."

"Here is a Rachel Waters Photography, oh not in Nevada." The next item on the Google list grabs our interest. Here she is! Rachel Waters, Reno NV, Freelance reporter, correspondent, reporter, and investigator. It appears she is in your line of work."

"This is perplexing. The church got wind of you and your colleague working on a scientific breakthrough on the origin of life. They are interested in knowing if you visit this reporter. I don't see the connection, your next step would be to publish the work and at some point make a public announcement."

"Which we are doing Monday by the way."

"This Rachel Waters would have the information at that time, I'm missing something. Also, why only you and not your colleague, David, right? For some reason, they think you might meet with her, but he would not. Any thoughts on that?" I take out my cell phone and hit David's number.

"I have no idea. It's going to voicemail. Hey David, do you know a Rachel Waters? Call me back."

"What are your plans for today?"

"I'm going to Incline this afternoon, to your sister's actually."

"That's perfect. I'm going to go snoop around the address they gave me. You bring Janis up to speed and tell her I will call later this afternoon to tell her what I find. I'll report to the church that it appears you were heading to the lake so I dropped surveillance. Are you taking the Mount Rose highway?"

"Yes. Will do."

Chapter 33

One of the most breathtaking tableau shifts transpires when one crests the Mount Rose highway summit. Suddenly the vista is filled with the expanse of Tahoe's blue water, surrounded by white snowcapped mountains. As the road descends to lake level, the views continue to impress. Following my navigation route to Janis's house, I arrive at a spectacular two-story home overlooking the lake from an elevated position. Very nice on a sheriffs salary. I pull into an open driveway with 6-foot walls of snow on either side and an opening leading to a shoveled walkway. I navigate to her front door and ring the bell. The door opens, and I am again struck by her entire form. She says,

"Hey, right on time it's wonderful to see you."

"Hi, what a superb location." As I step in, she gives me a long warm kiss and says,

"It's picturesque, but the snow removal can get old. I use a service for most of it. Come in, do you have a bag?"

"Yes."

"Good, let's get it later." As we enter, the foyer opens into an expansive living room/great room with floor to ceiling windows with a full view of the lake. The windows cover the entire south wall.

"Oh my God, this is gorgeous!"

"Thanks, just like your view, but of the lake rather than downtown. Come on, I'll give you the tour." Around the corner is a large kitchen with a granite breakfast bar and countertops. Standing in the kitchen one has the same view as the great room. Down the hall, we enter the master bedroom.

"We will be staying in here, additional bedrooms are up the stairs."

"Very nice room, I love your bathroom." The flooring is made of several shades of brown and tan quartzite. There is a large freestanding tub, sink basins on top of walnut counter tops, and a walk-in shower with quartzite walls.

She leads me out a door to an expansive paver patio that wraps around the entire back of the house. There is an outside fire pit built out of stone and a large hot tub. She walks us to the other side of the deck through French doors that open into a large mudroom/laundry.

"Would you like a drink?"

"I could be talked into it."

I follow her into the kitchen where there is a glass cupboard over a built-in wine cooler. Without checking with me, she takes out a bottle of gin and one of scotch. She makes my gin and tonic with a little bit of limeade and half diet, half regular tonic. With a big smile, she hands me my drink.

"Now that's impressive, you remembered the way I make these at home."

"As a trained detective I miss no details."

"Good to know."

"Let's sit outside, it may be warm enough in the sun." We sit at two chairs with a table between us and a great view of Lake Tahoe though numerous pine trees.

"So tell me about the arrest of Barnes."

"It occurred without incident. We got lucky with his lawyer. He was ill-prepared and perhaps not that skilled. He allowed me to walk his client down a path resulting in him lying during interrogation."

"What is your gut feeling about his denial of murdering

Marcus as well as the attempted murders of David and me?”

“I must say that I have trouble reading religious zealots. That said, I think he is telling the truth. However, I suspect that if the church had asked him to kill you, he would do it and never give up the church.”

“Have you talked to Josh yet today?”

“No,” I told her about Rachel Waters that she was a reporter and he was going to try to learn more about her.

“He said he would call you later today with what he finds.”

“Now that is interesting. Even though we still don’t know what the connection is, their pattern of surveillance now is a little more understandable.”

“We are going to hold a press conference on Monday, going public with our discovery that life on earth originated from organisms from space.”

“Oh my! Are you sure?”

“Yes. We need to do much more research to fill in some details. Do you think this will discourage any religious zealots from further action?"

"It will in terms of how they have been going about it, making the deaths look accidental. Of course, it's possible that they might blow up the entire campus."

"That's what a colleague said."

How much detail are you going to provide?

"As little as possible."

"If you don't provide sufficient detail to allow other scientists to follow in your footsteps should you die, it may encourage drastic action. Eliminate the people and equipment, and the ambiguous claim is eliminated. If you can give them just enough information that allows other scientists to repeat your work, they may give up."

"Good point, I'll talk to David about it."

"Let's go inside, and I'll freshen your drink. Are you hungry?"

"I can always eat." Reentering the living room, taking in the splendor of the place again I kid her,

"So how long have you been on-the-take?"

"Ha-ha, I get that a lot. My parents died in a car accident. This was their place."

"Oh hell, I'm sorry."

"No problem, I'm finally over it, as much as I can be. It's interesting, my brother and sister had no interest in the place, and Nicole doesn't even like to visit, where I feel very at home here. It makes me feel like I still have a connection to them. Different reactions to the same experience. There were some other inheritances that Nicole and Josh received to compensate for their share in the house." Janis starts to make me another drink.

"Here let me do that. Are you sticking with Scotch?"

"Yes, please. So true confessions. I have a complete kitchen, but can't cook. I picked up some Chinese food that I will heat up in a little while. I did manage to make us some hors de 'oeuvres." She went to the refrigerator and brought out a platter of vegetables, dip, and cheese. We brought the platter, some crackers, and our drinks to the couch. As we get comfortable her phone rings. She looks at the caller ID it's Josh.

"Hi, how are you doing? Yes, he's here can I put you on speaker?" She clicks on the speaker option, places the phone between us on the table and says,

"Go ahead."

"I went to the address that the church gave me for Rachel Waters. Not all the offices are open because it's Saturday, but the main lobby was open. It has eight floors. I checked the directory, but her name was not on it. None of the businesses listed were related to someone being a reporter. I asked a few receptionists if they knew her, but none did. With so many offices closed, I think I need to come back on Monday so that I can check every office."

"I think that's right bro."

"Based on what Grant told you, do you have any ideas on a possible connection?"

"No, I haven't been able to think of one."

"Alright, I'll let you know what happens on Monday. You too have a good time. But Grant, remember she's my sister."

"I had just taken a gulp from my drink and almost sprayed some out my nose."

"Understood Josh."

"Ha-ha goodbye."

"What did you understand?"

"That's guy talk. He wants me to give it too you hard."

"Liar!" She slaps me on the chest, but then gives me a sly smile and says,

"Can we eat first?"

"If we must." After some delicious Chinese food and a few more drinks, we decide to put on some robes and go into the hot tub. Under a clear sky, naked in the tub, we are in between storms. The moon is almost full, and dots of light fill the night from a bounty of stars. The back of her house is hidden from neighbors. She is sitting on my lap, and we are kissing passionately. She asks,

"How fast can you climax?"

"About 30 seconds after you, why."

"I have the water too hot. We need to jump out, start and finish before freezing to death."

"You really like to live on the edge."

"You have me ready to go. On three, you hop out, and I will follow?"

"Wait a minute, I'm not falling for that again. On three you hop out, and I'll follow you."

"Three." She steps out of the tub. When it comes to these matters, I never allow myself to get faked out or dropped, I'm right behind her. The cool air feels good, but it won't for long. On the deck, I spin her around and push her down, and she puts her hands on the edge of the tub. I slip into her from behind, and we both are facing the moonlit lake. She takes longer than usual, but I am unbothered by the cold air. True to my word I finish just after she and we jump back into the tub. She puts her arms around my neck, sits on my lap sideways, and places her head on my chest. Totally relaxed and motionless. Finally, she says,

"Man you really have excellent control."

"Not really, if you hadn't had gone when you did, I would have been in real trouble."

"Ha-ha, I'm going to remember that. Maybe next time I'll hold on a little longer."

"Like you could. You can't control yourself around me. I'm surprised you lasted as long as you did."

"You are a stud for a nerd."

"Hey." She pets with one hand and slaps with the other.

Chapter 34

It is early Monday morning, and David and I are traveling in Tahoe National Forest to the road that will take us to the site that Rod Eastwood has asked us to evaluate. Based on the location on the map, this site looks ideal. We have the GPS location entered into the NRI SUV and are following the route displayed on the navigation screen which no longer is taken for granted. At least this time we are in a vehicle, but I still brought my personal unit used for backpacking to compare to our SUV's GPS. So far they agree reasonably. I ask,

"So, one of Rod's grad students is meeting us there?"

"Yes, turn left up there."

"Yes. It's weird, I am experiencing a vague feeling of foreboding."

"About the student?"

"No, I think it concerns all of our current projects. Maybe it's being back out in a deep snow covered forest. I can't put my finger on it. I don't think the Living Word Christians killed Marcus. Sure they were provoked by the perception that we were disputing the bible. It's certain we have been the subject of their surveillance and harassment. Janis tends to believe the cowboy that their involvement was limited to manipulating Luther and keeping an eye on us. Just before I left yesterday, you were going to check one more thing regarding the anomalous Sierra background data."

"Yes, I was just going to tell you what I found. I examined the data we downloaded from the final storage values in the datalogger and compared it to our values received via telemetry. The values from the site datalogger did not show any peaks during the same period. It took me a while to confirm this because, as luck would have it, there was a brief power failure which reset the clock. It wasn't reset until Shauna's next visit. So I needed to reprocess the data to be completely certain the values were all zero. All ambient data from the site are below the detection limits."

"So are the telemetry data erroneous?"

"Erroneous is not quite right, altered is more accurate. Someone got to the raw data acquisition computer before your programs processed them into the database. Not only were zero values changed to high numbers the wrong times were corrected. You checked these values and rightly, found nothing wrong. But you didn't notice the gap in the timestamp on the file."

"Huh, I didn't think of that." We arrive at the snow-covered mountain road with snow/ice walls on either side. I come to a stop and say,

"That's the road? Are we sure it's clear all the way to the site?"

"That's what I was told. If we get blocked, we can just reverse out of it." I sigh and say,

"Here we go."

We are on an unimproved road that would consist of trampled grasses and vegetation in the summer. During winter, the drive must be plowed to allow travel by typical SUVs. The sides look to be about 6 feet high. Our GPS has us right on the spot, but it is not really needed as we are really traveling in a tunnel, or half pipe actually. David continues,

"As I was saying, even if you had checked the timestamp of the file it was only off by 20 minutes. You probably would have attributed it to a glitch in the telemetry download."

"These guys are good. And they really know our operation."

"Yes. The timing of the data received by telemetry occurs

at 01:00. Your automated program which grabs the data, reformats it, and inserts the values into the database, launches at 02:00. The time stamp indicated the revision occurred at 01:20."

"Remember when we were in L.A. for meetings, we visited one of Angela's plants. We were in her office, and she was showing how they were obtaining telemetry data from their remote sensors...wait...Shit!"

"What?"

"Shit, Shit, Shit! In Angela's office, there was a picture on the desk of her, her husband and two dogs."

"If you say so, I don't remember."

"I just remembered where I saw the guy in the bar that we thought may have spiked Chang's drink. He is Angela's husband!"

"Shit indeed!"

"Angela had complete access to our labs and is technologically savvy. Based on the video her husband is a big guy, easily capable of tossing Marcus overboard." I bring the SUV to a steady swift stop and throw the gears into reverse." David gets it as I throw him a look before looking behind us.

"I bet it was Angela that directed Eastwood to ask us to come out to this remote location."

I slowly reverse through the snow tube until I'm blocked. An enormous vehicle, a Humvee I think, has appeared from the white curtain that seems to surround us. A man gets out of the passenger side of the car, his door hitting the snow wall. He moves between our vehicles and knocks on my window and indicates he wants me to roll down the glass. I look at David and reluctantly hit the power button. Quickly he puts a gun in my face careful not to allow the weapon to breach the window frame in case I hit the gas. He is wearing sunglasses, but I'm pretty sure it's Angela's husband."

"Put the gear shift in park." I reluctantly do so.

"Unlock the doors." He hears the doors unlock and quickly opens the passage door and repositions his gun behind my head. He brushes notebooks and papers aside, sits down, closes the door and says,

"Keep driving until you hit the shelter, about another half mile." We continue down the white half pipe to a fork in the road. He says,

"Bear left." They have gone through much trouble to

make this road, presumably to kill us. We arrive at an open area that had been plowed earlier in the year but now has been packed down by vehicles performing three-point turns, coming and going to the building.

"Park there." He points to a spot near a set of steps, recently shoveled of snow, leading to the shelter.

"Turn off the engine and hand me the keys."

"Hello, boys." Angela appears at my window, still open. She too is brandishing a handgun. I don't know guns, thus I have no idea what kind it is. The killing kind I suppose. Her husband exits the back, opens my door and says,

"Get out slowly." He looks at David and says,

"You stay where you are." David remains silent. I get out, and he grabs my arms behind me and places a pair of zip ties around my wrists and guides me away from the car near the ramp.

"Stay here." While Angela points her firearm at David, her husband, I still don't know his name, walks over to David's door and they repeat the process.

"Tom, I'm going to unlock the door." There it is. The

outside of the shelter is made of stone with a steep roof, covered with snow. There is an enormous chimney for a fireplace. The snow level is two feet from the roof. The Sierras have many huts and yurts for skiers to use on a first come first served basis while backcountry touring.

"Tom guides us up the ramp while Angela unlocks the door. I ask,

"Tom are you a member of the Rock of the Living Word church?"

"No, why?"

"Never mind."

We stand as she turns on a battery operated lantern. It's one of those designed to look just like the old gas lanterns, but uses a six-volt battery and LED bulb instead of a wick and fuel. As light illuminates the room, it appears to be a primitive hut but private, not available for use by backcountry skiers. It is more substantial than the more primitive yurts but larger than typical skier huts. It has one room, one window, a large stone fireplace rather than the more typical wood stove. There is a primitive catch basin sink, but no running water. Typically snow is melted over the fire for water, but the basin is convenient for rinsing allowing water to drain outside.

Angela takes out a book of matches and lights a gas lantern on a shelf on one wall allowing much more light into the room. There is a desk with miscellaneous junk piled on one side, a desk chair, four metal chairs folded up against one wall and a coat rack near the door. Tom opens two chairs near the desk and guides us over to them. Angela moves the battery lantern over to the desk to spread the light.

I can see a ski pass dangling from a pocket zipper of her ski jacket and say looking at David.

"Hey, Angela how did you do skiing the Saturday before last?" Having set everything where she wanted it, she turns to me.

"I carved it up pretty well, but nothing compared to your run down the chutes. I can't believe you nailed the landing in one piece and then managed to miss that tree." I give her a condescending look and a sullen response.

"The results were in doubt for several seconds. Let me ask you, there were a couple and one other person looking down the gate, appearing to decide whether to enter. Was that Tom and you?"

"Yes, once you bailed, we quietly skied behind you, and when you were near the edge looking down the mountain, Tom slammed your skis sending you over."

"Looking back up the mountain I saw what I now know was Tom, but not you."

"I was behind a tree." As we talk, Tom is behind our chairs using long zip ties to bind our legs to the chair.

"So is Dr. Eastwood part of your evil scheme?"

"No, he thinks this is a possible new site."

David takes the direct approach.

"As you were in my office Friday, I assume Tom here shot Marcus?"

"Yes I was in your office all morning establishing an alibi, but Marcus wasn't shot, Tom just helped him over the side of the boat, frigid Tahoe did the rest." David says,

"I would wager that it was you in my lab, however."

"Yes, you almost caught me, as I was exiting the lab, but you came back too soon, I had to duck behind a filing cabinet. Then I was stuck there. The phone call from your wife saved your life that day. Another few steps and you were done for. Then you found the gas valve on and the tubing, and it was over."

"You must have changed the data on our server to indicate a problem at the Sierra site, but how did you bypass our security? I'm certain we did not give you a user name and password."

"I was with Marcus one day and pretended to have a question on the raw data. He casually keyed in his password with me standing behind him." Now it's my turn to get some more answers.

"When David and I returned from the Sierra site in the whiteout, our GPS lead us to a cliff. That morning when I came in, and you were in the lobby working on your laptop, you had gone in and changed the waypoint to the GPS in the lab, correct?"

"Yes, a while back, I overheard you talking about having the waypoints preset in that unit. I've only been able to piece together what happened that day. You two made it back, but our man did not. Did you kill him?" All this while, both sides have been so caught up in getting answers to our burning questions that I have been ignoring a fit of furious anger inside me and can tell David is fuming, but remaining calm on the outside looking for a way out of this situation. I answer the question.

"Yes, we killed him. We are not the wimps you make us out to be. Who was he?"

"A desperate man that owed Tom a favor. He worked at our L.A. plant. Look, I like both you guys, but we are on the road to ruin based on your measurements." An angry David, who rarely drops the F-bomb says,

"How the fuck are our measurements going to ruin you? We can see the L.A. plume hits the Grand Canyon, but we are ready to report that it is less than 15% of the time and the concentrations are well diluted by the time they arrive."

"What you don't know, is we closed on the purchase of the Laughlin plant last summer. We leveraged all we have to get it. You're right, EPA won't be concerned about the L.A. plume's impact on the canyon. Your work will, however, show them that their models, which predict the air mass will miss the Canyon to the east, are incorrect. They will then conclude that the Laughlin plume will not miss it to the east. Its concentrations will have a significant impact. We will be looking at the need to install scrubbers to reduce the emissions which would be too costly. It would bankrupt us." I say,

"Other researchers would eventually trace the downwind levels to that plant."

"Eventually, but right now EPA modelers have determined that the Laughlin plant impact would be negligible. The meteorology is tricky out there. Don't sell yourself short. Your L.A. signature analyses will carry weight with the scientific community. You two and Marcus were the only ones that know how to make the measurements."

The term 'were' sends a cold chill down my spine. She continues,

"I am an absolute believer. From the data you already have collected, but not yet reported thankfully, I have performed some extrapolations and predict a significant impact on the Canyon from the Laughlin plant. It is critical that we delay anyone from finding out about this. The price of coal is predicted to drop substantially in six months, and we think we can flip the plant and make a tidy profit before the truth comes out, rather than going bankrupt.

We knew we had to shut up Marcus immediately, he was explaining how the technique works during student seminars. Once our attempts on your lives failed, I had hoped that we could avoid further killing. With Luther attacking David, I thought we could work in the background to add to his efforts. Failure of the L.A. Plume project would discredit you both. I don't know what you did to get that wacko church after you, but that really helped to keep us under the radar. However, unlike many others, I know that the two of you are very smart and incredibly resourceful. You would never be terminated or give up, and I can't let my sentiment for you both to dissuade me." I ask,

"Are you going to shoot us?"

"No, I'm still trying to make things look accidental. I'm going to leave you here for a few weeks until you die of dehydration and then move your bodies elsewhere, pump the gas from your tank, and dump you some distance from your car. The only conclusion will be you died of exposure trying to walk out."

She nods to Tom standing behind us and David begins to jerk in his chair violently. I see Tom has a cloth over David's face and he shortly goes limp. I hear footsteps behind me as he walks over to my chair. "Oh fuck."

Chapter 35

I woke with a headache and the sound of David calling my name. We were in total darkness, and I was too groggy to think straight.

"Grant, are you awake?"

"Getting there, my entire body is stiff, not to mention that it's freezing in here."

I tried to stand and could not. I tried to wriggle my hands loose and could not. I was able to push with my feet and lift my weight up to sort of hop off the ground, chair and all, slightly. I'm not sure how that would help. David says,

"I tried the same thing we probably could move around the room some, but that's about it. The metal composition of these chairs do not lend themselves to breaking apart should we attempt to slam them against the wall or floor. I don't think I remember seeing anything sharp at the level of our hands to rub the ties against. Is there any chance you have your pocket knife on you."

"I had it when we arrived." I bend down trying to touch my stomach to the front of my pants pocket. I can't reach all the way, but don't feel anything. I now notice my iPhone is not in my rear pocket. Finally, I say,

"I don't feel it, and my phone is gone. They would have been pretty stupid not to check our pockets."

"Yes I thought so, but hoped they might have missed it."

"I'm sure not looking forward to starving to death in this freezing room."

"We won't starve."

"We won't?"

"No, dehydration will kill us first, and it is incredibly painful."

"Thanks a lot, now I'm thirsty. Your knowledge is endless, how about a way out of here?"

David gives one of his patented contemplative answers.

"According to their plan, they intend on us being found dead after the snow melts. It would look suspicious if both our phones were not on us. Maybe they left them nearby so they could replace them in our pockets upon their return. If so, there might be a chance someone could locate us via our GPS chips."

"Two problems occur to me. They certainly would have powered them off, and there is no service out here. I don't think anyone could locate us." He says,

"Probably true. Do you know how the safety office always preaches to us to tell our supervisor or colleague exactly where we are going in the field and when we are expected to return? And if we are going to return after hours to designate someone to call or text to confirm we are out of the field?"

"Yes, did you do all that?"

"No. However, I don't know what time it is right now, but we either are missing a press conference or have missed it. All those people know we are in the field, but not where."

"Oh, that's right."

After more hours of useless chatter, we hopped around the room checking every potential exit, including the main entrance. Following several hours of fruitless struggling, nearing exhaustion, the room became quiet. Efforts to get comfortable went unsatisfied. Approximately every 2 hours my head would snap up waking me from a light sleep reacquainting myself with the aching hands, feet, neck, cold, and abject conditions. Still, in darkness, I remain quiet not wanting to wake David, in the off chance he is sleeping. His face is indiscernible. I can only make out his outline.

Awake again, I must have dozed for an undermined amount of time as light is now visible under the door. The room is perceptibly lighter. I look over and can barely see David staring at me.

"Good morning," he says. "What would you like to do today?"

"I'm open, nothing like a good night's sleep to get you revved up to start the day." David can't sustain the false cheerfulness.

"I can't feel my fingers. What a terrible night."

"I noticed that they put foam strips around our wrists. When we were knocked out, they must have cut our original tie wraps, wrapped the foam around our wrists and then reset the ties. Last night I thought, well they didn't want the tie wraps to hurt so much, that's nice. Then reality quickly hit, no you dumb ass, they left us to die! They wrapped our wrists to reduce the ligature marks to better fit their plan to make it look like an accident. These are the battles that rage on inside my mind."

"Sometimes they rage on outside your brain as well, it's painful to watch."

"Fuck off."

"Now now, if you aren't nice I won't share my escape plan with you."

"You have a plan? I can be as sweet as pie. By all means, please continue."

"I tried to get a fingernail in the locking tab, but Tom did a good job of placing the box end of the ties out of reach. Is it the same with your ties?" Tie wraps are effective in holding objects in place, but they can be opened by sliding out the open end of the wrap while pushing in the locking tab.

"Yes, last night I fumbled for the box ends, but could not find them."

"Ok, I happened to notice in the pile of junk on the desk there was a spool of thin wire. I'm not sure why they have it here and don't really care."

"Maybe to use it as a snare to catch rabbits or something."

"Maybe. I notice Angela left the lantern sitting on the desk."

"Great it would be nice to let some light in here."

"No. I would like to get the large capacity six-volt battery out of it." Where is he going with this, first the wire now the battery? Then it hits me.

"Hell yes, we wrap the wire around the leads, heat the wire and melt the tie wraps."

"Correct, if we can get the wraps to melt before we drain the battery. Let's hobble over to the desk. As we move, plan to have the back of your chair facing the back of mine so we can have our hands near each other."

By flexing my toes and shifting my weight upward and back, I can move the chair about an inch at a time. I can hear and barely see David doing the same. This process takes us about half an hour to reach the table and get appropriately oriented. Getting there first I quip,

"Now I realize how Lumbricus Terrestris feels."

"I know you like to find ways to use that useless bachelor's in Zoology degree of yours, but I don't know what the hell that is."

"The common earthworm of course. I will have you know that to get that bachelors' I took many more chemistry courses and the same number of math courses as your bachelors' in physics."

"Fine, use those skills to figure a way to get the lantern from the desk into our tied hands. If it drops to the floor the complexity of our task will increase 10 fold."

"So you are saying it will be harder?" He just sighs and refuses to engage in my foolishness. I employ the gyrations necessary to bounce my chair so that I am now facing the lantern. I stretch my body forward and use my toes to tilt the chair, so I can just barely rest my head on the top front edge of the lantern and flip it into my lap. With the lantern in my lap, I return the chair to its level position. Carefully, I push with my toes to slide the chair another 90 degrees, to position myself toward David's back. I can see that his hands are tied together with the wrap. There is another long tie wrap that feeds through the other wrap around his hands and then through a support on the back of the chair, to limit movement. His hands are directly in front of me touching my knees.

“I have it in my lap, how far can your hands reach backward?” He repositions himself and can almost reach my crotch. The extra-long tie allows for some degree of movement, and he manages to touch my inner thigh.

“Hey watch it. Just keep your hands near my knees. I’m going to push it toward you, don’t let it fall.”

“How are you going to push it? With Lumbricus Terrestris?”

“No smart ass with Python reticulatus. So it may be traveling with substantial force, don’t let it roll out of my lap. Here we go.” The lantern rolls into his hands, and he appears to have a good grip.

“I can see the base of this type. Thankfully it is one we can hand screw off rather than embedded screws requiring a screwdriver. Keep a good grip on it I’m going to rotate 180 degrees, to bring my hands next to yours again. I go through the tedious actions of bouncing the chair until my back is against his. I feel for the lantern carefully, so I don’t knock it out his hands.

“I see you have the top in both your hands do you have a good grip so I can start unscrewing the bottom?”

"Yes proceed." I have to think for a second to figure out which way is counterclockwise when my back is to the unit, and then I start. It's turning.

"Be careful when you get to the end that the battery doesn't fall."

"Yes, tilt it down a little, to ensure that it stays in the base half in my hand." The base comes free, and I have the battery in the compartment. I say,

"For the part in your hand, can you think of any use for it? If not you can just let it drop to the floor, so it is out of our way."

"It's mostly plastic, perhaps we could break the LED to cut the wraps if this fails. In any event, it is in our way. If we need it, we will have to find a way to get it off the floor." He lets it drop.

"Hold out your hands, and I'll drop the battery out of the compartment into your hands. Ready?"

"Go ahead."

"I've got it. And we have a bit of luck. Someone placed the battery terminal screw caps inside the battery compartment, and they landed right in my hand. We can use them to enhance the wire connection. I'm secure, go get the wire." I repeat the chair maneuvers until I'm facing the desk again. I can't see it in the dark.

"I don't see it."

"It's on your side between two piles of miscellaneous office supplies."

"I think I see it. But..."

"I know, I thought it might be hard to reach. Is there a bottom piece of paper or cardboard where you could somehow pull everything toward you? Wait, I'm going to move my chair and get next to you." While holding the battery, he takes longer to face the desk. I say,

"Hey, I have an idea. Push that notebook with your head, so it moves that ruler toward me just a few inches. Don't hit this pile of papers in front of me. The spool is just where I want it." He successfully moves the ruler to where I can reach it. Lowering my head down I can just reach the ruler with my chin so that I can move one end until part of it hangs over the edge. I pick it up with my teeth. With the ruler projecting from my mouth, my body fully extended, I direct the end of the ruler through the opening of the spool and flip it back, sliding it down the ruler. It hits my face, and it stings, but not enough to deter from the satisfaction of acquiring the wire. I lower my mouth down on the edge of the desk and drop both ruler and spool of wire. I position my chin behind the spool and push it toward my lap. It hits my left thigh, but instead of resting safely in my lap it bounces off my leg.

"I lost it. I didn't hear it hit the floor."

"It bounced into my lap."

"Thank God!" Of course, the bad news is we need to play more musical chairs, first, to locate my hands in front of his lap and then where both our backs are together. I'm getting sick of this, but it is taking my mind off of dying, so I have that going for me. We do all the repositioning, and now I have the wire, David has the battery, and we are back to back. David walks me through how he wants us to proceed.

"Take the open end of the wire and thread it through the tie wrap and then tightly twist it on one of the leads of the battery. Let me know when you are done, and I will screw on the cap to make a nice tight connection." I thread the wire through the tie and then on to the battery. David successfully screws on the cap.

"Ok, now take the spool and wrap the other lead. Once I screw on the cap, you can drop the spool." The second lead took longer, everything just seems to be in the way, but we finally get it. David says,

"Now we wait. If the battery's capacity is low, it will just run down, and this will all be for naught. It's fortunate we have screw caps because I can pull the battery and put tension on the tie wrap. It was nice of Angela to line our wrist with foam, it will keep my wrists from burning when the wire gets hot."

"Nice, sure, she's a real peach."

"The battery is getting warm." Then I felt David's hand hit my chair.

"I'm free. Damn that feels good. David quickly disconnects one of the leads to save battery current. He runs the wire through the tie in one of his legs and reconnects the terminal. It takes a little longer, but this tie breaks free. With one leg still tied to the chair, he hobbles over to the back of my chair and sets up the apparatus through the tie bounding my hands.

"I think the battery is dying. Hold the battery and keep tension on the tie. I'm going to look around for what else we can use." David picks up the chair while he walks and rifles the desk, but doesn't see anything obvious. I ask,

"Where did Angela put the matches after she lit the lantern?" David went to the lantern but saw none.

"Did your tie break?"

"No, and the battery is no longer very warm."

"Don't worry I'll think of something. He walks over to the metal front door, turns the knob, and it doesn't open. He mutters,

"Outstanding. We'll deal with this later." His foot hits a large rock. Probably there to prop open the door when moving items in or out of the shelter. He goes to the gas lantern brings it over to the flat stone fireplace hearth. Returning to the desk, he fumbles for a pencil in the dark and takes it to the fireplace. Opening the fill tube of the gas reservoir, he pours some gas onto the stone. He dips the pencil into the fuel. Taking the rock, he hits the hearth with glancing blows a few inches from the gas evaporating off the hearth trying to create sparks to ignite the fuel. A spark finally ignites the gas on the hearth. As it burns, David takes the end of the pencil dipped in gasoline and ignites it. He uses the flame to burn the remaining tie from his chair. He walks the pencil over to my hands, manipulating the flame to control the burn rate.

"Don't move even if you feel the heat."

"Whatever it takes." Shortly I felt the sweet release of my hands. David quickly moved to my feet before the burning pencil reached his fingers. I was free! What a feeling. I got up, and David and I gave each other man hugs and firm pats on the back. I looked over at the hearth, and the gas was almost completely burned off the fireplace. I grabbed another pencil from the desk and held it into the dying flame. Once it caught fire, I screwed on the fuel cap to the lantern, pumped up the pressure, turned on the gas valve, and lit the lantern using the pencil. The room filled with light.

"So I couldn't help notice that you tried opening the door a while ago. Is it stuck?"

"Do you remember Angela opening the door when we arrived?" I had to think for a minute.

"Shit."

"That's your favorite word today."

"Well for a good reason don't you agree." I did remember. There was a very large deadbolt welded onto the metal door that slid into a metal housing welded onto the metal siding. A metal cover allowing access to the bolt was secured with a substantial lock.

"What the hell is there to steal in here? You can't vandalize anything it's all rock and metal. What about that window?"

"It appears boarded up. We have that rock, but given the bolt on the front door I'm guessing it's well secured and the rock will not be up to the task."

"So we escaped a small confinement to enter a larger one."

Chapter 36

As we contemplate escape from this disagreeable confinement, David says almost to himself,

"Regarding her plan, I think any medical examiner would be able to detect we died of dehydration and not of exposure."

"Well I'm glad you didn't point it out to her, she might have tie wrapped us to the trees outside, it's cold enough in here."

"I certainly wouldn't have. However, that would have been more convincing."

"I'm thankful she is an inept murderer, but she hasn't failed yet."

To be thorough, David tries the door again by slamming his shoulder into it and gives it a good kick. The door doesn't budge. He says,

"It's certain, we are not exiting that door." He takes the rock over to the window, the window frame and glass actually are missing. He begins to hammer on one side of the plywood. It doesn't budge, but he continues trying to weaken one end.

Meanwhile, I walk over to the fireplace hearth. The fuel has burned off, but I step around that end anyway in case the stone is still hot. Peering up the fireplace flue, I see nothing but darkness. Looking around for a damper lever I find it and try to move it in the opposite direction, but it doesn't budge.

"David, can I borrow your rock?"

"He walks it over to me.

"I'm unfamiliar with these old chimneys. Should we be able to see light up there if the flume is open?"

"We should be able to see light if the spark arrestor isn't covered with soot. The outside chimney looked very large, and it seems like a straight shot. Why, are you thinking of climbing up there?" David has a little claustrophobia, and it shows on his face.

"Maybe. If this lever already is in the open position I didn't want to hammer the crap out of it."

"But if it is already open and you damage it, why would we care."

"Good point." We don't live here stupid. He hands me the rock, and I use it to hammer the lever. It starts to move and then I can push it with my hands all the way over. Black soot drops down into the fireplace. Once fine particles settle, I poke my head in and look up the chute.

"Hello. Bright light."

"So you're thinking of deploying your rock climbing skills?"

"I don't think we have much choice but to try. It has been a while, I'm out of shape."

"It's likely there will be a spark arrestor up there."

"If I do a successful Santa Claus, then what, once on the roof?"

"I remember seeing a small shed on the side, it may have shovels and tools. Either way, you out there is better than us locked in here."

"It's hard to disagree."

"I found this small rock on the hearth, it should fit in your pocket. Take it with you, it might help to remove the screen. Once you get started, I'll move the lantern in the fireplace, for what it's worth." I take the lantern and survey the chimney. Luckily, it's large enough for me to stand in, but not much room to maneuver. In rock climbing parlance this upcoming climb is aptly called a 'chimney climb.' It's too small to be considered a squeeze chimney and not wide enough to be considered a foot-back chimney. A foot-back chimney would allow a lie-backing technique, which I always found to be easier if the distance is not too far. I am in for a strenuous climb and hope I'm up for it. Of course, starving to death, excuse me, dying from dehydration is a motivating factor.

I found a couple of dirty towels that I used to wrap around my knees to protect them from the abuse they are about to endure. I enter the chimney and examine the bricks with my hands as I can't visually make out any features in the dark. They are covered with soot, but not caked. I dig my fingers into the grout between bricks above my head. I test lifting my weight while pushing the toe of my boots into the side walls of the chimney. I can hold myself so decide to ascend. I climb about 9 feet and quickly push my right leg back until my foot makes contact with the opposite wall and move my right knee down forming a bridge between my knee and back. Once secure, I wedge my left knee and rest my fingers.

After a short rest, I resume climbing by moving my lower foot upward while increasing opposing pressure with my hands. I ratchet myself upward by shifting weight between feet, back, knees and hands. I'm covered in black soot, my knees beginning to ache, but I make it to the screen. Reaching into my pocket for the rock, I push out thoughts of legs failing, dropping to the bottom while my face bounces off the walls. I try pushing out the screen, but it doesn't budge, my legs are starting to tremble. Using the rock, I begin hammering the screen in one corner. The corner pops up, and I'm able to reach through the opening and get a firm handhold on the edge of the top brick. Pulling myself up through the opening by pushing my feet against the walls and using my head to push out more the screen, I can get a second hand on a brick. Now I can pull myself up and squeeze through the opening.

As I clear the opening, the cold fresh air is a welcome shock, and I lay on my back on the snow to relax my muscles. It is early afternoon, and the sky is dappled with a few clouds, but mostly sunny, an exquisite sight.

As my back begins to chill, I roll over and holler down to David.

"I made it."

"Excellent, is our car there?"

"Hold on."

The roof has a fairly steep pitch, requiring a careful turn to the front of the building while holding on to the chimney. The car is there. I can't see the front door from here.

"The car is there. I'm going to try and find a way down."

"Don't fall off and bury yourself."

"Nice, good safety tip." I mutter with severe sarcasm. I gingerly walk along the ridge of the roof. Straddling the rooftop, I carefully scan the area. The car is completely covered with snow. It looks like one foot of fresh snow has fallen overnight. I make my way across the roof to one side. I can see the tool shed, it was built right up against the shelter, but it is three feet lower in height. I move down the roof on my butt doing a forward crab crawl until I'm even with the roof of the shed. I swing my legs over the side of the shelter roof above the roof of the shed. Inching my butt and back over the roof, I gently drop to the shed. Repeating my forward crab crawl, I move down the roof of the shed and reach the edge. There is a wooden fascia as part of an overhang that I can grab with my hands as I allow my legs to slide over the edge. Hanging from the roof and looking down I can see that the snow in front of the doors is not very deep due to the overhang. I let go of the fascia and drop softly to the snowy ground. A magnificent feeling to be on snowy, but firm terrain.

They had taken our coats, and it's bitter cold, but the sun and lack of wind keep me from freezing. The window is on this side of the shelter. I can see that plywood is being held by wood screws and two pieces of two by four boards. Given what I know about the metal welded deadbolt I judge the window to be an easier ingress. Thankfully the lock and hasp on the shed door are not very stout. Removing the rock from my pocket, I start hammering on the lock in an effort to pull the hasp off the wood. It is only held there by small screws, and it eventually gives way. I open the door and inspect the contents. A small assortment of tools, a saw, two snow shovels, and a long-handled square shovel. My attention is drawn to a crowbar. I grab the bar, and a shovel to help me get to the window.

Inside the shelter, the window is at head height, but outside standing on the packed snow, it is at my knees. I begin working on one of the two boards. Wedging the crowbar under the board and pushing down to pry one end away from the plywood results in slow separation between the two. Continued action begins to reveal two nails and finally the end of the board is free. I am able to grab the end and pry it entirely off the plywood with my hands. Repeating the process on the other board has equal success.

The crowbar is too thick to get under the plywood, so I return to the shed to retrieve a claw hammer. The claw is able to start a separation, and then the crowbar finishes the job. With the plywood removed, the incoming light reveals a smiling David surrounded by darkness.

"You are a welcome sight. While you were working out there, I checked the entire room for our car keys. They are not in here. I am going to come out there. As he crawls out of the window, I untie the towels from my knees scoop up some fresh snow and use the towel to attempt to scrub away some of the black soot from my arms and hands. David climbs out of the window, he squints as the afternoon sun floods his pupils, but he does not look away allowing the fresh air and sun to envelop him. Seeing what I'm doing, he says,

"It's cold out here. Try that on your face as well."

"Stay in the sun. Let's check out this shed in more detail." When I first entered the shed, I grabbed what I needed and ran out. Perhaps the car keys are hidden in there somewhere. We enter the shed and begin our search.

No sign of any keys." David says,

"They probably took them with them and will bring them back when they come for our bodies. I know you can strip down an older car and put it back together again. Can you hotwire these new cars?"

"If it was sitting in my driveway with all my tools I probably could get it started and drive it. Out here it would be harder. We are better off hiking." I say,

"Well it's noon, we could start hiking, but without our coats, if we run into a problem, we would be exposed. We have had a rough night and I, for one, feel weak and am tired of being cold. We could take those saws in there and gather as much wood as possible to make a roaring fire, make it through the night and then hike out tomorrow at sunrise."

"I don't have a better idea. The other advantage of waiting until tomorrow is we can melt this snow and build up our water supply. There is an old dirty metal bucket in there that we can use to hold melted snow after we wash it with the first batch of water."

"Well, let's get started, we have all afternoon, but most of this wood is wet and hard to access, we may need all afternoon." We start to grab hand saws and an ax when a thought pops into my head.

"I just thought of something."

Chapter 37

Liz had met Angela a few times and even visited her small Reno office once with David when he delivered a report.

"Hello."

"Angela?"

"Yes."

"Hi this is Liz, David Piehl's wife, we've met a few times."

"Oh yes of course, how are you?"

"Worried sick, David did not come home last night. Grant and he were going to evaluate a new monitoring site in the Sierras. Grant did not go to work today, the Institute's vehicle was not checked back in, and I went to his house, he is not there. Do you know where they were headed?"

Angela paused for effect and did some hemming and hawing.

"No, I'm sorry I am unaware of any new sites, and I haven't spoken with them for about a week."

Liz speaking with an agitated voice says,

"This morning I talked to Alan at the Institute, he said they would try to locate them with the SUV's GPS beacon. He just called me and said the service had a bad part and would not have it fixed until tomorrow morning. I'm worried about them spending another night out there."

Angela pauses, for real this time as her heart begins to race,

"GPS beacon?"

"Yes, apparently their new field vehicles have them built in for safety reasons, but they only track them if there is an emergency. They expect to be able to locate them tomorrow morning, but there is another storm progressing and should hit the Sierra's soon."

"I'm so sorry Liz, but listen, those two guys are incredibly resourceful. I'm sure they can weather out one more night."

"I hope you are right, thanks anyway."

Angela frantically makes a call to her husband who is on his way back to California.

"Tom we have a problem, have you left yet."

"Yes, I'm at the State line. What is it?"

"Turn around and meet me at the condo. There is a GPS sending unit in their car. For some reason, they couldn't get a track on it today but will have it tomorrow. We must get to them tonight."

"Bad idea the storm already has arrived."

"You are not getting it if they lock in on their location tomorrow morning we are toast. We need to locate and disable that GPS before morning."

"I get it! I'm turning on to the Floriston exit and will return. Even though I have already geared up with chains to get over the top to Sacramento, we should take the hummer. It does better in the snow, and the road to the cabin is going to be dicey."

"As long as we kill the chip in time, we can camp out there as far as I'm concerned." Tom and Angela meet at their Reno home. Tom says,

"We need complete snow clothes, gloves, hats, goggles. Let's throw in our snowshoes, we need that large flashlight in our bedroom. Let's pack some food and water. Your gun already is in the Humvee, and I just moved mine over from the truck."

"The keys to their vehicle are still in the Hummer." Angela gives Tom an ominous look and says,

"The keys to the cabin, in case we need them, are also in the Hummer." Tom understands her meaning and says,

"I can't wait for all this to be over."

Fully packed with their deadly essentials, Angela and Tom get into the vehicle. Tom drives and using the navigation system, Angela enters the stored location to the road leading to their cabin. As they start their drive. Angela says,

"The route just takes us to the start of the road, I thought you were going to save the actual location of the cabin the last time we were there so we could use it to navigate the primitive road."

Tom says sarcastically,

"Sorry I forgot, I was busy setting up those guys to die!" This earns him a glare from Angela. She says,

"Don't give me that bullshit, you got us into this. I told you I didn't want to buy that fucking plant."

"There just doesn't seem to be an end to this. Let's keep it together and do this one more thing. Besides we don't need the navigator, the road is like a tunnel. There is only one fork in the road, and we bear left."

"Fine"

They reach the plowed road to the shelter. It is snowing heavily. Tom stops at the entrance. He releases his seat belt, puts on his gloves, and exits. He uses his gloves to wipe off excess snow from the headlights, sides of the windshield, and his window. While Tom does this, Angela releases her belt, gets on her knees facing the back seat and reaches for her coat. Tom returns to the vehicle, puts the car in gear and starts down the road. Angela fumbles for the zipper to her jacket.

In the dark, their headlights light the steadily falling snow. The flakes are large, falling silently. Visibility is less than the range of the headlights due to the snow. The road surface is still fairly compact under the new snow, and both sides of the road are a wall of icy snow.

As they continue to drive, all they can see are bright flakes and two beams of light that disappear into boundlessness black space. Tom is not speeding, but maintaining a higher velocity than usual to keep the tires from slipping. Angela asks,

"Shouldn't we have reached the left fork by now?"

She is answered by a bump in the road and a drastic change in their surroundings. The white road turns black as do both sides of the vehicle. Abruptly, Angela falls on the front dashboard, briefly stopping herself with her hands. She had never put back on her seatbelt. Her lower body floats to the roof while her head is forced over her hands, landing in the crack between the windshield and dashboard. Tom, also without his belt, is holding tightly to the steering wheel. His stomach and groin both surround the steering wheel. With his legs jammed against the seat, he is stuck in this position with his head on the roof.

As the front of the vehicle rotates downward in space, finally Angela processes what is happening and screams as a feeling of weightlessness overcome her. The snow is no longer falling perpendicular to the windshield. Instead, they are falling with the snow, racing it downward. Both Angela and Tom are screaming as the SUV accelerates.

The car impacts a rock shelf at terminal velocity. Angela is killed instantly as her head impacts glass and rock. The airbag explodes into her abdomen pushing her partially back into the vehicle. Tom's midsection receives a terrible force as the airbag deploys and forces his legs out from under the seat. The car falls backward over the shelf, tumbles and rotates 180 degrees though space as Tom is pinned to the roof. Angela's body is back inside the vehicle. The upside down car slams into several feet of snow before hitting solid ground at an incredible force. It never catches on fire. Both occupants are dead.

Chapter 38

Twenty minutes earlier. I quip,

"Your wife is an inveterate liar."

David gives me a deadpan look and rejoins with,

"You are a skilled asshole."

"I endeavor to be skilled at everything I undertake."

"Ambition attained."

We are hiding out in the NRI SUV across the street and down the road from the entrance road to the shelter. We just saw the Ward's Humvee stopped in front of the snow covered road to the shelter.

"Well we needed her to be convincing, and it worked." She had never talked to Alan, and there was no GPS tracking unit. I laughed to myself, David was fighting to keep it together, and I was trying to release building nervous tension.

"How long do you think we should wait?"

"They should reach the cliff in about 15 minutes. If they don't go over and don't find the left fork that we blocked with snow, they should be back out in 30 minutes. If they don't go over, but find the fork, dig out our snow barricade, go to the shelter, learn we are not there, they should be back here no longer than an hour, two at the latest."

"Sounds right, keep an eye out for them. I'm going to rest my eyes." I lean back in my nice warm seat and replay the events of this afternoon.

"Well let's get started, we have all afternoon, but most of this wood is wet and hard to access, we may need all afternoon." We start to grab hand saws and an ax when a thought pops into my head.

"I just thought of something."

I grab a shovel and make a path to the car. I yell over to David,

"Is this the car Marcus was driving last month in the Mohave Desert?"

"I'm not sure, the Institute has two of these Jeeps."

I grab the shovel and start digging out snow near the driver side front wheel well. Reaching up above the wheel I move my hand up high and back and forth. My excitement builds finding the metal magnet case. Opening it seeing the key I raise it high in the air and shout,

"Yes. Fuckin a Bubba."

"What is it?" Yelling, I say,

"Marcus locked the keys in the car twice, after the last occurrence he took so much grief he told me he had an extra set made and put it in a magnetic box. When I took the car overnight to Spirit Mountain, he told me it was on the driver side wheel well in case I had trouble."

I pull it out, open it and find a beautiful site. Holding it up to David I make an elaborate show of kissing the key. My mood quickly turns gloomy.

"With our luck, the lock will be frozen, or the battery will be dead." David had walked over to the car.

"Actually we had a lot of luck and made our own when we needed it." He's always the optimist. I insert the key in the car door, and it opens.

"Yes!" joy rushes through my body. As I start to slide into the front seat, David yells,

"Wait." I freeze wondering what's wrong.

"You're pants and shirt are covered in soot let me do it."

"Fine." He inserts the key in the ignition and turns. The SUV turns over, and he lets it idle. Even David can't hide his excitement, but then he is right back to business. He verifies there is sufficient gas and says,

"I'm going to shovel some of the snow away from the tires to help get us started." Always prepared, I loosen the laces on my boots, step out of my filthy jeans, stripping down to my long underwear placing my feet on top of the boots rather than the snow. Out of a gym bag, I had thrown in the back seat, I remove a pair of snow pants and slip one leg on while stepping back into my boot and repeat the process with my second leg. Much of the soot on my boots was scraped off by my maneuvers through the snow. Next is the soot-covered shirt, replaced by a warmer pull over. The dirty clothes are placed on the floor. I slide on to the passenger side seat and open the center console.

"Hey, our phones are in here." I don't think he heard me and all the windows are covered in snow and I can't see him. There is nothing in the back seat save notebooks and papers. I open the door and get out. David is in the back shoveling out the

back tires.

"David, they left the phones in the car."

"Excellent!"

"I bet our coats and gloves are in the back." I open the back hatch.

"Here they are." I hand him his coat and then his gloves. Then put on my coat and gloves and use them to brush the snow off the windows with my hands. David says,

"That should be good. I'm keeping these shovels." He tosses them in the back and starts to get in the driver's side.

"Hey what are you doing? I found the key, I'm driving." He shakes his head, walks around to the other side and says,

"You are such a child."

"Am not."

It feels so beautiful to feel warm. David has two water bottles and hands me one. He can see both excitement and bewilderment on my face and says,

"They were in my backpack."

Once we get up a head of steam in four low, we are able to push through the new snow on the plowed road.

"I'm glad you brought the shovels, I'm going use one on Angela's head."

"As nice as that sounds I think we need to proceed carefully."

We struggle along the snowy road, periodically needing to stop and clear snow from our front end and tires. Sometimes we need to shovel deep areas ahead of us. Riding in silence, beleaguered and somber I break the quietness by more or less thinking aloud.

"We need to hide out until we can determine what to do next. We can go to Janis and tell her our story, but it will be our word against theirs, they left no evidence."

David silently nods his head. More silence until I say.

"We could confront Angela in a safe environment and secretly record her somehow. However, we would only have one shot at it. It would need to be unassailable. If she sensed a problem, she would shut down, walk away and try and figure out a new way to kill us."

Long silence, then me again.

"We could tell everyone we know, go to the papers, go on the nightly news and tell our story. Let's see her try to take us out then, and they would be bankrupt when we report our results."

Looking at David, I can see in his expression that there is a flaw in the plan and then I too see it.

"But they get off for killing Marcus." We reach the fork in the road, and David says,

"Wait, stop here." He is studying the other fork in the road.

"Let's examine this road. Can you make that turn?" Always up for a challenge, I gun it and fishtail in the snow bouncing off the snow wall and start down the road. David says,

"In Eastwood's email, he stressed to go left at the fork. It stated that the guy that was hired to plow the road a few days earlier went off in the wrong direction. He hit a dead end near a deep ravine that arcs around the shelter. They were going to have him back out next week to block the right fork."

"This looks like the end." David says,

"Let's get out." We hike for a while in very thick snow to find an open area and a sharp drop off. David looks at me sternly and says,

"Serious now. Those assholes tried to kill us twice and did kill Marcus. Over money. If that battery weren't there, we would still be bound to chairs on our way to dying of dehydration. I don't want to leave this to the courts."

I snap out of my musing, sit up and say,

"Hey, the snow stopped. How long has it been?"

"30 minutes."

"That is our first milestone."

Earlier this afternoon, As soon as we had cell service, David called Liz who was worried sick and had been making calls to NRI this morning. He told her we were working on something, needed her help, and would call her back. She would stay by the phone. Then David called his cousin who lives 20 minutes from here and has a front end loader on his truck. David told him our story. He nicely summarized a rationalization that I will want to remember in case of later times of guilt feelings. His cousin had responded,

"So we will clear a path that may or may not be used. If used, it will only be by those intending malice of forethought."

David had told him, "Yes precisely."

He agreed to meet us at the road and to give him an hour. We had used the time to drive to a nearby town for food, we were starving, and so I could better wash my hands and face. Later, we showed his cousin what we needed and cautioned him not get too close to the edge.

While David's cousin graded the fork leading to the right, all the way to the flat area of rock, we worked to block the fork to the left. We each climbed opposite ends of the snow wall and are now shoveling snow from above, down onto the road. Eventually, we made an effective looking wall essentially eliminating the fork when viewed from the entrance side of the wall. Once we had everything in place, David called Liz back, gave her Angela's number and the needed script. He told her to wait until 4:30 to make the call to ensure that it was dark before they drove out here.

Now we assume they have driven over the cliff, something they had once planned for us, and need to cover our tracks. We need to make it look like they took a wrong turn.

Investigators may wonder why there was a road leading to a cliff, but we didn't build it, just made it more drivable to the edge. We hope that incoming storms will make the plowing less visible. That it will look like what happened originally, the snow plow went in the wrong direction and remade the road to the shelter. Either way, it should not be traceable to us.

We wait another hour and a half and can't take the tension any longer. David says,

"Let's go." This is the chilling part. We enter the road, and as we progress, I decide it is the creepiest drive ever. It is dark, visibility is 10 yards, snowflakes are large and bright in the headlights, and the SUV is fishtailing in the snow. But the biggest dread is the thought of headlights suddenly shining in our eyes from the opposite direction, or bloody bodies walking in the road. Periodically we can see fresh tire tracks ahead of us. We had reset the truck's trip odometer before we blocked the left fork so that we could easily locate its position, lest we go over the cliff.

We stop at the mile marker and confirm that it's not obvious where our makeshift wall is located in the heavy snow. We get out, find the edges and dig small holes with shovels as markers. I keep looking up the road waiting to see headlights. We return to the car, David backs up, creates some momentum and blasts through the barricade. We back up and drive over the snow several times to pack it into the road. David backs up on to the cliff road to turn around then, now facing the exit to this irksome snow tunnel. He says,

"Let's get the hell out of here."

"A persuasive argument. Hit it."

As we drive down the narrow snow tunnel, I can't shake my unrest and say,

"You know, they might have just gotten stuck out there, and it has taken this long to turn around." David looks over at me but remains silent. I can't wait to reach the end the road hoping not to see headlights behind us. We make it to the end, and I let out a sigh of relief.

Chapter 39

We make it back to the Institute without incident, park the SUV and walk over to our cars. I say to David,

"I don't know about you, but the last 24 hours are going down as the hardest in my life."

"It's about the third for me."

"Vietnam?"

"Yes"

"Well, I'm glad it's over. I'm sleeping in tomorrow, I'll be in late."

"Not too late, we have the termination meeting with the President at 10:00."

"Are you shitting me, that's tomorrow?"

"I couldn't shit a big turd like you."

"Oh no, I'm rubbing off on you. Fine let's both get in at 7:00, we have much to prepare." With that, we get in our cars and head home. I went through a drive-through for a hamburger that will go nicely with a colossal cocktail when I get home. I had noted that Janis left me a message to call her, so I put her on Bluetooth.

"Hi, where have you been?"

"Tied up." You don't get to use that for real very often.

"The weather cleared for half the day this morning so Tyler and a colleague from their rescue division, Rob I think, went out to your location where the guy went over the cliff. Rob repelled down and found your guy. They pulled his phone and wallet to get his ID but had to get out of there before the next storm. Tyler said they will be able to get a chopper in there. Hopefully after this storm.

So get this, he had an employment ID card from 'Ward Energy Solutions.' Didn't you say that you had a client named Alice Ward?"

"Yes, but it's Angela Ward, he worked in their L.A. plant."

"You recognize the name?"

"No. Listen, Janis I know who killed Marcus. You probably are going to want David and me to make an official statement."

"You know who it was? How?"

"I don't know how this works. Should I just tell you over the phone or wait to tell you officially."

"Usually you come into the sheriff's office as soon as possible, but given our relationship, I can do it at your home. I'm at my sister's house can I come over? I have everything I need to take an official statement." I am now in my driveway waiting for our call to end before getting out.

"That's fine if you can make it now. I am dead tired."

"I'm on my way." I turn off the engine, get out of the car and walk to my mailbox. The stress of the day is catching up with me, and I am ready to collapse. I throw the mail on the breakfast bar without looking at it and head right to the liquor cabinet. With drink and hamburger in hand, it's time for a shower. I open the paper wrapper and take a big bite, that's heaven. While alternating from hamburger to gin and back again, I strip off my clothes and turn on the shower to let the water get hot. With the burger gone, I take my glass in the shower with me and rest it in a corner free of the spray. It's incredible how the simple things that you take for granted can become such a treasure. I scrub the soot out of my hair and wash it twice.

Drying off I hear the doorbell ring both downstairs and on

my phone. I navigate to the security app on my phone and view the image. Confirming it's Janis, I press the microphone button and tell her to come in. Then hit the unlock button to the front door. I hear her enter and her relocking the deadbolt. While pulling on my sweat pants, I holler,

"I'll be right down. Make yourself a drink." A tee shirt goes over my head, and my empty glass and I go barefoot down the stairs. She is pouring a diet coke, holds up the bottle and says,

"I'm on duty right now. You do look beat."

"Do I have a story for you."

"Give me a quick summary, and then I can record the details for the record."

"Angela's husband, Tom killed Marcus, he knocked me over the cliff on my skis while Angela watched. Angela tried to kill David in his lab. I finally identified Tom as the guy who spiked Chang's drink in the brewpub, albeit a little late." Janis is just watching me wide-eyed. I continue,

"As you know the dead guy on the rock worked for Angela and Tom. So we were way off with the church members, they were just watching us. Angela was trying to stop us from reporting our results that the L.A. plume can make it to the Grand Canyon because that would mean their newly purchased Laughlin power plant's emissions could make it to the canyon. That plant is much closer, but EPA models have predicted there would be no impact. Our results dispute that. I think that's it." Janis is speechless. She finally says,

"How in the hell did you find all this out since the last time we talked?"

"Ah, that was the hard part. Angela lured us to a shelter out in the remote Sierra's, tied us to metal chairs at gunpoint, and dead-bolted us in a dark, cold cabin. Before leaving, she answered our questions about Marcus and the attempted murders."

"And you escaped?"

"Yes, today. Last night we were tied up and freezing."

"This is unbelievable. I know you are tired, but let's do this for the record with full detail."

"Ugh, I'm going to need another drink." I started with the email from Eastwood that Angela instigated, luring us to a remote primitive cabin and took her through our escape, finding the keys, and driving out. I fudged on the time a little, having us drive out just after dark so that I would not have to account for our time from noon to when I returned her call. David and I had agreed not to tell her that we set up those assholes to drive off a bluff to their demise. I probably will tell her later, but want to wait to see what happens. If she learns what we did, I don't know if she would be pissed or would understand our predicament. Her life in law enforcement presumably would bias her toward us getting out of there and calling her or 911.

"May I assume they believe that you are still locked up in the cabin?"

"We sure as hell have not contacted them since escaping." This was the truth.

"I need to work on an arrest warrant and start gathering evidence to support your statement and must get David's statement tonight. I will call him in a few minutes I know he won't be happy about it. Can you locate the road to the shelter on a map, I need to bring a team out there tomorrow morning." I fire up my laptop and start Google Earth while she calls David. Navigating to the road location, I can see the deep ravine, and a wave of nausea sweeps through my body.

"I woke him up, but he understands I need to get his

statement now." I drop a pin at the road entrance and print the map to my wireless printer.

"Here is the location. The road is basically a half-pipe of snow. There only is one turn to make, at a fork turn left. Bring a good 4-wheel drive and something stout if you want to get past the deadbolt."

"I have one thing for you. Josh spoke with Rachel Waters."

"Oh, tell me."

"She is writing a scathing report on the Rock of the Living Word Church, covering both national churches and the local Temple in Reno. Someone leaked to her that you, and only named you, as getting ready to break a major discovery that was going to shake up what we know about the origin of life. She said she intended to contact you, but hasn't had a chance as yet. Josh thinks the church only wants to know what information is going public so they can better brainwash their members. It's getting late. I've got to get to David's. I don't care what they say about you guys being feeble nerds, you guys are badass."

"Thanks. Wait, who says that."

"Got to go." David and I had discussed the need to call Janis and, for now, agreed to leave out our involvement in the road diverting work. I'm going to bed.

Chapter 40

David and I run into each other in the parking lot and swing by Alan's office to see if he is in yet. He is at his desk, we knock and enter just a few feet to signify we don't have time to sit.

"What happened?" I say,

"It's a long story, we will fill you in later, we need to get ready for the meeting." David asks,

"How was the press conference?"

"It went well. The ladies did a good job. They generated a lot of excitement without giving away too much detail. You two were briefly mentioned." We back out of his office, and I utter a sarcastic comment.

"How nice of them."

In my office, David and I start working feverishly on data and paperwork from old projects as well as our Sierra background study issue.

"So did everything go well with Janis last night?"

"As far as I know, I just told her everything from my

perspective and modified the time we left, per our agreement."

"Good." We work for several hours up until the time of the meeting. We run into our nemesis, Dr. Charles Luther, in the hallway on route to the conference room. He gives us a smirk and enters the room ahead of us. David says,

"Charles thinks my termination is a fait accompli." We enter the room and see that all the other participants are present. The original three committee members, Alan Demyan, Melissa Wagner, and Richard Blake, with the addition of the director of Human Resources, Kate Wilson and our President Dr. Ron Freeman.

We sit across a large table from the three committee members and Luther. Alan is standing at a counter pouring a cup of coffee and sits on our side. I like to think he is on our side figuratively as well. The President sits at the head of the table. Alan remains the committee chair and will run the meeting, but the President alone will decide David's fate.

Alan begins the meeting in a similar fashion as the first meeting. Luther will bring forth only four complaints this time as the committee agreed to drop the Denver smog project. Alan added an additional point for this meeting.

"These complaints were leveled against David in the first meeting. He was aware of some issues, but not all. The time between these two meetings has allowed David, should he wish, to go back and review the details of these older projects to support arguments on his behalf."

Upon completing the introduction, he hands out Luther's packets of information to each person, Alan then turns the meeting over to Luther.

"Good morning everyone. As Alan stated, I will present 4 projects involving tasks performed by Dr. Piehl that were complete failures and wastes of project funds. Originally there were 5 tasks, but for some reason, the committee chose to exclude one." Alan is irritated and says,

"We excluded it, for lack of credulity and it is not up for discussion today. Please move on to the next item."

Way to go Alan. I give David a smile, he remains passive. I lean over to him and whisper,

"Now in front of the President, it's Dr. Piehl rather than just Piehl." David gives me a small head nod and smirk. Luther continues,

"Very well. In chronological order, the first project was the San Joaquin Valley Air Quality Study. David developed three specialized instruments. We deployed them, they appeared to work properly in the field, but when we made intercomparisons with our other data, they made no sense, completely erroneous. It cost our sponsor $20,000 for zero usable data, and they had been very interested in those parameters." For effect, he turns to the president and says,

"It reflected poorly on the Institute." Alan says,

"David?"

"It's true I fabricated these instruments in my lab, they were based upon proven principles used in commercial units, but I was able to get lower detection limits with my instruments."

I start handing out copies of photographs of the instruments to each person while David continues,

"In the photo, note the original design had one temperature gauge. I was not involved in the field work, but prepared a detailed set of SOPs to aid the field people."

While I hand out a folder containing several documents, He turns to Kate and says,

"Standard Operation Procedures." As a non-scientist, she may be unfamiliar with the term.

"In your folder please find a copy of an Email from Charles to me. Note that Charles requested that a Fahrenheit temperature gauge be added along with the Celsius gauge. It says he was going to have engineering students operate the instruments and it was more common for them to use Fahrenheit. Further note in my response thread that I told him it was an unnecessary addition, and I was disinclined to make the change. He called on the phone and ordered me to 'just do it.' He was paying the bill, accordingly I agreed."

"So what?" yells Luther.

Ignoring him, David says,

"I draw your attention to the SOPs which describe the operation of the instrument. Note the highlighted paragraph on page 3. It states that the oven temperature should be set to 50C/122F. The third set of bound papers contains the completed field forms for the instruments. Note that under the column reading for oven temperature, the values range from approximately 49 to 51 degrees. However, the units on the form, in every case, shows the F is circled rather than C. Operating the oven at 50 F was only 10 C and would explain why the instruments did not work properly."

Luther violently snags one of the field forms and studies it with a scowl. David continues,

"The next page shows calibration data that are nowhere near the target values. Had this been brought to my attention after the first failed calibration, I could have set the engineering students straight. I never was informed of a problem. Alan steps in and says,

"Thank you, David, for this new information, Well Charles, I am not pleased that it appears that you have attempted to blame David for your failures on this portion of the project."

Luther starts to speak, and Alan holds up his hand and continues.

"I must say the addition of a second temperature gauge was not only unnecessary but in this case resulted in confusion and the reason for your lost data. If engineers want to work with scientists, they need to be familiar with the metric system. It also appears that you should have been aware of the failed calibrations and brought David in to fix the problem." Luther sighs and puts his head in his hands. Alan says,

"Let's move on to the next complaint." Luther has lost his cockiness but presses on with determination.

"David was given a task to perform for the Mohave study. This time he set up commercial ozone monitors, calibrated them, and trained our own technician how to use them. They seem to work fine in the field, but when we compared his data to our other parameters, the expected relationship between the values indicated his data were biased high. We did some post calibrations on our own and found his calibration was wrong. Thankfully we were able to rescale the data using our correct calibration values and include the data in my report. "

He turns to the President and says, a little more tentatively this time,

"This seems like a minor problem, but when taken into context with the next two projects shows a pattern of incompetence." This time I remain silent. Alan says,

"David?"

"The calibration data provided to you by Charles was an attachment to an email from me to his grad student who was coordinating the field measurements. He has since graduated and moved to Boston as I understand it. What Charles did not provide you, is the email that went with the data."

I recognize David's unspoken beckon for paperwork. Again I stand up and hand out a copy of the data that had been attached to the email to everyone. It is just so much more dramatic this way compared to giving them all the information in one packet. I can see Luther furrowing his brow.

Luther leans over to read the email which states, 'Charles, attached are preliminary calibration data for the ozone analyzers that you insisted I send you. However, as I told you, these data overestimate the conversion to engineering units. I am making some changes and will repeat the calibration. I will send you the new calibration data when they are finished.'

David waits, for effect, until all heads lift up before continuing.

"Charles also failed to provide the follow-up email and revised data."

I slide over a second email and printed attachment of the revised calibration data.

Charles grabs the new material, looks at it and an irate expression dominates his face as anger spills from his voice as he faces David.

"I have never seen any of these Emails, this is some kind of cover your ass trick."

David calmly asks, "This is your correct email address is it not?"

Luther slams his hand down on the paper and brings it to his face. After a few seconds, he slams it back down and says,

"Yes, but that doesn't mean I read it, I was leaving the field task to Ron."

"Well, I had wanted to send the calibration data directly to Ron and cc you the data on the email. You insisted I just send it to you and that you would pass it on to Ron. You managed to send him the bad data. Had you also given him the final calibrations there would have been no issue" Alan breaks in and says,

"Charles, based on this new information from David, it appears that again you have attempted to blame David for your failures on the project. I suppose we should continue, but perhaps I can try to summarize what you told us in the last meeting." Again Luther has his head in his hands. Alan turns to the President and says.

"Charles was considering submitting a proposal to EPA on a Modeling evaluation study. A contact of his there warned him that a proposal from our Institute might not be viewed favorably because his contact had heard the data that was collected at the Nevada Test site was not agreeing with a model being developed by someone in one of the petroleum companies. The test site data were collected by David, but the project was managed by Grant."

Alan turns to me and says,

"Grant will you address this issue?"

"Yes. This project was considered an enormous success, my EPA sponsor was happy with the results then and remains so now. I spoke with him a few days ago. He said there has been widespread use of the data by modelers who have been very satisfied. When I asked him about one of the oil company guys having a complaint, he said that the person has abandoned development of his model. It wasn't working with any of the archived data."

"Good, this also is not an issue. Let's move to the next supposed problem. Charles, and frankly many of us, have been concerned with David's highly publicized L.A. air mass signature technique producing impossibly high values at the background site in the Sierras. Have you gotten anywhere with this problem?"

"Yes, there is no problem. There was an issue when the Sierra telemetry data was processed into our database. It has been corrected. The instrument at the background site never saw any elevated values." Alan says,

"That's excellent news and a big relief." Alan turns and looks at President Freeman. He, in turn, looks at Kate and says,

"We are not going to terminate David. I don't want any of this in his file. Can we just end this without any further paperwork?"

"If Dr. Luther is willing to dismiss his complaint, then we can just end the process, and nothing will be placed in his file. If not, then we need to write it all up and place in the official record." All eyes point to Luther. He just says,

"Fine." Alan says,

"Good let's all get back to work." We all stand up and head to the door. President Freeman calls to Luther.

"Charles, may I have a word." Luther sits back down in his

chair. Out in the hall, I say to David,

"We vanquished that son of a bitch."

"Just so."

"Here's what's beautiful. We have Luther off our ass. We found Marcus's murderer, and we survived three murder attempts. Janis has cleared the church. I still can't believe we got that so wrong. No one is left to try and kill us. We have confirmed that your L.A. air mass signature technique works. And saving the best for last, we made the discovery of our careers, life on earth began from seeds from space. We will be published in Science." My litany of 'beautiful things' is halted when we see Janis walking to my office. David says,

"You may have spoken too soon," I call down the hall,

"Janis!" She turns, sees us, and then waits.

"If you have time I can fill you in on what I have learned today."

"Absolutely, let's go into my office." I sit behind my desk, and they take my two guest chairs.

"I led a forensic team to the shelter. We took

photographs of the cabin, of the window that you broke out of, the wood on the floor, and the broken lock on the front door. Inside we found the battery you two described, burnt tie wraps, foot and hand prints in the chimney and found at least 4 different sets of prints in the building. Which reminds me, you two need to go down the street to the Sheriffs' office and get printed. Basically, we found ample evidence to support both your stories."

"That's a relief." I say

"Yes, we left the site to go into Reno to obtain a warrant to search Angela's home. I was driving my own car. When I reached that fork in the road, something made me stop. In this job, like yours, one must have a sense of curiosity. I turn down this right fork, now on my left, to see what's down there. With all the new snow it was tough going, and I eventually had to stop. I decided to hike it for a while."

She looks at David and then me.

"Do you know what I found?" David can be completely inscrutable, but I'm afraid my face is doing a jig. David says,

"Tell us." Janis looks from him to me and stares at me for what seems like minutes.

"The road dead ends to a precipice that drops sharply to a steep canyon." David looks at me and says,

"Oh right. In Eastwood's email, he stated that the guy that plowed the road went off in the wrong direction to the shelter and he backtracked and made the road to the left."

"Interesting, please forward me that email. Well, I found a safe place to peer over and could just make out a vehicle pancaked down there. I was able to get our search and rescue boys to the SUV, and they found two mangled bodies inside. We ran the plates, and the car was registered to Angela. I got an unofficial identification of Angela and her husband." She looks at me and asks what do you make of that?

"I'd say they were on their way to the shelter, maybe just to shoot us this time, and missed the turn in the heavy snow." She stares at me again for an insufferable length of time and says,

"Well, that's what I'm going to put in my report. Still, I have a feeling I'm missing something." She gets up, walks to my door and stops giving me one last stare. Then she leaves without another word. David says,

"She suspects us."

"Yes, that was eerie. But she can't put it together. We are on a roll partner."

Immediately after I said it, a feeling of dread and regret washed over my body.

Epilog

It's been six months since our decision to send two human beings over a cliff. Out of nowhere, I get twinges of guilt and unformulated feelings of anguish. My actions resulted in the death of two human beings. I occasionally wake up in a sweat, remembering a subconscious visage of the man on a rock in a pool of blood or an out-of-focus cinematic of Angela and Tom smashing to the ground far below our plowed road. However, I had been correct about the 'malice of forethought' rationalization easing my conscience. I did not run them over with my car while they innocently crossed the street. They went over that cliff attempting to ensure that David and I would die. This was their third attempt to kill us. Thinking of Marcus's body floating in Lake Tahoe also is helpful to expunge my guilt. Thus far, David seems at peace with himself.

Recently we have learned that there was a second murder by Angela and Tom, again this time by Tom's hand. Apparently, an elderly woman walking the shoreline saw Tom throw Marcus over the side. She had called 911 stating she had seen someone thrown over a boat with our markings on it, but her cell call was dropped. The operator continued to return the call, but the lack of service resulted in reaching her voice mail.

Due to a massive call volume that day and a glitch in the system, the call wasn't reported to an investigator. She was later found dead in her car, and her death was preliminarily ruled a heart attack. Two weeks later an autopsy found she was suffocated. They checked her phone, saw she had called 911, and then retrieved the lost call. Janis was called in, and she pieced the whole thing together. The number of known successful murders now totaled two.

Speaking of Janis, she has been aloof lately. We talk, but she only returns a fraction of my calls. We have gone to lunch once. Attempts at asking her 'what is wrong' results in a single response, 'nothing.' I have asked her out several times, but she seems always to have a conflict. I surmise that in my office that day, her looks were pleading with me to tell her the truth. My failure to do so may have cost me our relationship. She can't know for sure what we did, but detectives are incredibly intuitive. I suspect female detectives are doubly so. I have lied by omission, and somehow she knows it. It may be too late, but I must risk her condemnation as a police officer for taking the law into our own hands to remedy a latent falsehood between two lovers.

Charles Luther left the Institute after being pressured from Alan who had the full support of the President. Before he departed, I resolved a nagging question concerning how he knew that it was Marcus taking the clarity run that day. At the lake, we were told he had learned it from the Sheriff which was inconsistent with what we were told by Alan. Luther temporarily forgot that he had received an email from Jackson the night before, stating Marcus was going to substitute for him. Apparently, Jackson reconsidered not clearing the change with Luther. I didn't press Luther for proof but rather, later confirmed with Jackson that he had indeed sent the email. We had suspected that Luther had turned on the gas in David's lab because the card key print out showed him there on Sunday. We wrongly assumed that Barry Franks' hourly student had used the guest card key. Evidently, Angela was still in possession of the guest card and used it to gain entry that Sunday.

David, Vanesa, Prudence, Marcus and I published an article in Science generating substantial interest along with much skepticism. This is not uncommon. In the article, we acknowledged that not all meteoroids are expected to be from the big bang, but could have been from other planets or moons that had exploded. Unfortunately, several investigators have repeated our techniques on their own meteorites and have not been able to replicate our findings. We may have been lucky to find two in a row. We are confident that it's just a matter of time before someone repeats our work and we receive full acclaim for our discovery.

An article was published in the New York Times by free-lance writer Rachel Waters. It had an anti-religious slant with a focus on the Living Word Church. She cited our recent Science article stating that although we still don't know how the Universe started, all accounts of the Origin of life on Earth, described in the Bible, are fallacies. She writes that given all we now know about the universe, that any enlightened reader of the Bible will conclude that it is a collection of fables rather than doctrine on which one should guide their lives. It was learned that Marcus leaked our Genesis experiment information to Waters, Luther learned of it and reported it to the Church. She and I finally met and discussed the results of our experiments. Josh cleared up the odd pattern of surveillance. Sometimes they would stake out Waters rather than me, explaining why sometimes they would not be following us. The day that Barnes came to my office to question the follower, no one was there because the church knew she was out of town.

Since Prudence and Vanessa held the first press conference in our absence, they have been the face of our team, attending TV talk shows and the like. They are both smart and presentable making them media darlings. This is fine with us. As David and I are not astrobiologists or even cell biologists for that matter, we prefer to allow Vanessa, Prudence, and others to pursue this research. We are more satisfied studying the particle aspect of the project while laboring in the world of atmospheric sciences. David's tracer technique has proven to be accurate. We have just signed two large contracts using the method. One studying Denver's brown cloud and the other from EPA to calibrate a long-range transport model. These two projects should keep us out of trouble for a while.

Made in the USA
Columbia, SC
16 June 2020

11217847R00245